The Lion
in the Lei Shop

The Lion in the Lei Shop

KAYE STARBIRD

Harcourt Brace Jovanovich, Inc.
New York

81354
St 2 L
71582
October, 1970

For Irene and Mary

with love

"I was a stranger,
and ye took me in . . ."

Acknowledgments

With special acknowledgments to others whose hospitality made the writing of this book possible:

Dorothy Westervelt and Bertha Kolk of Burlington, Vermont.

Elizabeth and Luther Bridgman of Charlotte, Vermont.

The staff of the MacDowell Colony at Peterborough, New Hampshire: George Kendall, Louise and Lloyd Crockett, Al Worcester, John and Lester, Jane, Perry, and the Marlows.

Henry Sauerwein, Jr., and Burton Phillips of the Wurlitzer Foundation at Taos, New Mexico.

Also, all Starbirds and Jennisons.

The characters in this book are my own invention, and any resemblance to people living or dead is purely coincidental. The plot and story line are also mine, but the peripheral circumstances and situations both during and after the air raid, however subjectively viewed, are history.

Contents

One

THE DAY

1

MARTY

"I don't want to hear about my father!" I said. "I don't want to hear about him! I DON'T WANT TO HEAR ABOUT HIM!"

I was shouting at my mother. We were sitting by the swimming pool in the spring sunset, and everything about the evening had been relaxed and pleasant until my mother mentioned my father.

"You're getting to look like him," she said as I pulled up my skirt to keep it from getting wet. "Your hair is turning dark and so are your eyes." She watched me splashing my feet in the pool.

"You sit like him, too," she added.

That's when I did the shouting. It surprised both of us.

Mother stubbed out her cigarette in the ashtray on her chair arm. She twisted it round and round and round, long after the red coal blackened and fell apart.

"What's wrong with you, Marty?" She was shocked, but she was also puzzled. "What's come over you all of a sudden? Why don't you want to hear about your father?" Her fingers were soiled from the cigarette ash, and she wiped them on the grass.

"Shut *up* about my father!" I said. I knew I was being heartless as well as rude, but I said it anyhow. "I hate my father! I'll always hate him!"

My mother killed a mosquito on her knee.

"It isn't your father you'll always hate," she told me as she brushed the mosquito away. "It's the war."

"It's my father." It troubled me to see I was hurting her, so I became defensive. "I guess I ought to know," I said.

Mother gazed at the sun slipping like a shined penny into a slot between the mountains.

"Try to be fair," she said to me or the sun. "Think back. Can't you remember your father when you were a little girl? Can't you remember his Spring Song? Can't you remember how he used to build you castles in the sand?"

"No, I can't remember," I said.

The sun was gone, so Mother stopped looking at the sky. She lowered her gaze to watch a robin moving across the lawn. Hop, hop, hop; stop. Hop, hop, hop; stop. She had no great interest in birds, but she concentrated on the robin.

"I didn't think you'd ever forget," she said, and her old sorrow began making its wall between us.

"Never mind," I said, because I'd had enough of the sorrow and I'd had enough of walls.

Mother opened her mouth to say something else.

"Never mind!" I repeated.

I must have been nine years old then. Or ten. I don't know. All I know is I dreamed again that night.

Mother was standing by the bed when I opened my eyes.

"What are you doing here?" I asked.

"You were screaming," she answered. "Would you like a glass of warm milk?"

"No," I said. "I'm sorry I woke you up."

"I was awake anyway." Mother flipped her hair out from under her bathrobe collar. "What were you screaming about?"

4

"I had that dream again," I said.

"What dream?" The night air was chilly, and she pulled her robe closer around her.

"I told you about the dream," I said.

"I suppose you did." Her tone was vague. "Or did you?"

"I did," I answered, though for a minute I wasn't sure I had.

"Well, it doesn't matter." She pretended to yawn. "Dreams don't mean anything. Not even the bad ones. Don't worry. Everything's going to be all right."

"That's what Father used to say." I wished I hadn't spoken, but I couldn't take back the words.

Mother was silent a minute. I hoped she hadn't forgotten our conversation by the pool.

She hadn't forgotten.

"We won't discuss your father," she said. "We won't ever discuss your father after this unless you say so. I fixed your purple jumper so you could wear it to school tomorrow. How do you like your new school?"

"I like it," I said, "and I like our new house. So does Jill."

"I'm glad." She bent and kissed me. "Try to go back to sleep now."

So I went back to sleep, and I wore my purple jumper to school the next day, and we never discussed my father again until a number of years had gone by.

My mother loved me, but she couldn't help me. I had to sort out the past and present and future, I had to sort out my relationship with my father, in my own time, in my own way.

I seldom dream about the war any more; but when I was a child I used to dream about it at least once or twice a year. The dreams varied at first, then became distilled into one recurring nightmare, in which I was standing with my mother on the deck of a ship, a railed and rocking platform that seemed higher than smokestacks, higher than planes or birds, yet still on a level with the flat and blue and endless ocean.

I was dressed in a yellow pinafore with white forget-me-nots embroidered on the hem of the skirt, and I was crying. Far below the deck, at the bottom of some steps that slanted downward and outward from where I was standing, a man was smiling up at me, and I knew he was my father—the way you do in dreams—although I couldn't see his face. My mother was waving and calling, and Aunt Liz and all the rest of the women were waving and calling, too, crowded together in a thicket at the rail, where the other children and I were as dwarfed among them as lantana under the mango trees, existing hardy but hidden below their branchlike arms, unable to see either over or out. Yet I saw my father and I saw the steps. I kept pulling and pulling at my mother's dress, trying and trying to tell her about the steps, but she wouldn't listen. She just stood there, smaller and prettier than most of the women but equally tired-looking, with her copper hair falling straight to her shoulders and shining in the sunlight, while she called and called and waved and waved and didn't notice what I said at all. She didn't notice the steps moving away.

Then the dream changed, and I found myself running, running, running, toward a blue emptiness that might have been ocean and might have been sky. As I ran, the deck swayed under me, and I stopped and reached for the handrail. But, when I tried to steady myself, the rail turned into a strand of barbed wire, and I clamped my lips together so I wouldn't scream. Because I knew where I was. Even before I looked, I knew where I was. I was outside the little locked house where the lion lived.

"No, no!" I cried in the dream. "No-no-no-no-no!" And often I was still crying the word aloud when I woke up sobbing.

It's hard to know what you remember from early childhood and what you only think you remember. I suppose if you stay in the same place doing the same things day after day and year after year, the world and its happenings are apt to run together into one fading unaccented panorama . . . with maybe a day when a picnic was called off because of rain or a moment when you were sitting under a tree in a striped sweater watching a spotted dog run by remaining forever in your mind for no accountable reason. But even if you don't stay in the same place doing the same things day after day and year after year, the details tend to shift around and get blurred. I was five years old the morning the Japanese planes roared improbably out of nowhere into the safe everyday skies over our rooftop in Hawaii, with the goggled, helmeted men sitting in the cockpits and the round red suns painted on the backs of the planes. And as the months and decades passed, I heard that morning (and the mornings and afternoons and nights that followed) described so often and variously that it was easy to confuse the legend with the reality and my own memories with the memories of others. And, of course, there were some things I remembered for a long time that never happened, that never were true. Like the lion living in the lei shop.

Now, if I care to, I can picture the lei shop the way it really was, the way it used to be before the lion moved in, before the air raid. Later, people called the air raid Pearl Harbor, but Pearl Harbor was different. Pearl Harbor was the sudden place beyond the black cane fields, the sudden daylight that couldn't be daylight over the sudden silver-and-orange sea. Somebody else's business. When any of us spoke of December seventh, we spoke of the air raid. It was the name we had for the thunder that wasn't thunder and the planes and the men in the planes. It was when everything stopped being usual and right, when everything changed.

Before the air raid, I could look through the back window of my bedroom to the road that led away from Schofield Barracks and see the two big happy Hawaiian women sitting on their wooden benches in front of the lei shop, stringing blossoms into necklaces all day long in the sun. The lei shop wasn't a real house, not a real store, just sort of a playhouse-size shack where I guess the extra flowers were kept. I don't

7

know for sure, because I never went behind the awninged area where the brown and smiling women sat forever threading their flowers. I liked the women. I liked seeing them and knowing they were there, as I liked the colored butterflies patterned over and over again on my bedroom wallpaper or the poinsettia trees outside my second-story window sill. The women used to laugh together, and sometimes they called to soldiers passing in the road.

A week after the planes came, the flower shop was closed and barbed wire was twined around it in thorny metal coils. And when I asked Willard Seymour, the twelve-year-old boy who lived next door to me, what had become of the brown and smiling women who threaded the carnation and pikaki and ginger blossoms all day long in the sun, Willard said they were gone and wouldn't ever be back. The fact was, said Willard (Willard always said "the fact was"; he picked it up from his father); the fact was, he said, watching me carefully as he spoke, a lion had eaten the women . . . biting their heads off first, then crunching the rest of them slowly and quietly, arm by arm and leg by leg, until there was nothing left but the women's shoes. The lion didn't care much for shoes, said Willard; shoes didn't have any juice to them. What he really liked was eating people, little girls mostly but women in case he couldn't find any little girls. According to Willard, the lion was living in the lei shop and could see through a crack in the wall as he held up his heavy maned head in the windowless darkness, restlessly twitching his tufted, slashing tail. He knew how to open the door with his teeth and was waiting there with his eye to the crack, ready to spring through the door and over the wire to catch anyone else who happened to wander by. Well, not so much men and boys, said Willard. The fact was, the lion usually let men and boys alone; they were too tough to chew. What he was mainly hoping to catch was a little girl, so he could crunch her even more slowly than he had crunched the unsuspecting flower women, not only arm by arm and leg by leg, but

8

eyeball by eyeball and ear by ear and finger by finger and toe by toe, until there was nothing left but a pair of sad little sandals and maybe a sock.

"He likes girls about your size," said Willard, and the only expression on his face was a growing glint in his marble eyes.

"Girls with curly red hair," he added thoughtfully. "Like yours."

I never went near the lei shop again, but even as far away as my house I felt threatened. I didn't like to look out the window any more, but there the window was. You can't hide a window except by pulling the shade, and then the shade reminds you of why you pulled it. I'm not sure why I'm going into all this, because my window didn't have a shade. It was a many-paned French window that opened inward on hinges, and the only way I could avoid seeing it was to stay out of my room.

As for the lion, I know now he was a figment of Willard's imagination, his personal contribution to the terrible inner and outer devastation of that dark December. But I didn't know it then. When I think back to those days, I can still see the small locked shop with the tangled swirls of wire around it and the cruel and menacing face of the lion I never saw. He was a green lion.

Once, several years later, when we were living on the mainland—waiting for the war to end, waiting for the waiting to end, waiting waiting waiting for my father to come home —Aunt Liz paid us a visit, traveling from her apartment in New York to our new-old farmhouse in New Hampshire, as she occasionally did, to share and assess and try to forget her hopes and doubts with Mother. I still believed in the lion then, and I decided to ask Mother and Aunt Liz about him, sort of casually, even though Willard Seymour—who never left any loose ends when he was weaving a web of terror— had sworn me to secrecy. (The fact was, said Willard, the lion liked best of all to eat little girls who were tattletales.)

Mother and Aunt Liz listened to me in the mannerly, non-

9

listening fashion that grownups frequently use with small children, and I could tell they didn't have any idea what I was talking about, so I stopped talking, which was just as well. That's when I first learned that memory, right or wrong, is a subjective thing. The lion hadn't been part of their private war, any more than had the bald-headed sailor with the black teeth, or the square-toed shoes that hurt my feet, or the cigarette burn in my yellow pinafore. My mother saw the sailor because he sat at our table for a while, and she bought the shoes, and I showed her the cigarette burn. But those weren't the things she remembered.

The steps were something else again.

When I mentioned the steps that led downward and outward from the ship to my father, the steps that always moved away in the dream I kept having, my mother looked puzzled a minute. Then she said: "Oh, you mean the gangplank. Those weren't steps," and she quickly switched the conversation to familiar inconsequentials. I didn't say anything more about the steps, because I knew what she and Aunt Liz were about to do, and they did. They began talking the way they always talk when they get together, in that different tone of voice they started using the night of the air raid; and pretty soon they were discussing how to be beautifully pregnant during a bombing and what the well-dressed woman wears to a war and the sea gull that wanted to see San Francisco, and the pleats coming back into my mother's red plaid skirt. Also the Filipino steward they called Art with the big heart and Mrs. Daly's Daly Dozen and the rest of it. In other words, the sea trip back from Hawaii. Not the terrible time before or the terrible time afterward. The sea trip was a terrible time, too, but Mother and Aunt Liz preferred not to remember that it was. Over the years they have settled on that particular period in the past as an interim oasis. Not a safe oasis. Not a happy oasis. Just an oasis where, in retrospect, they can rest long enough to forget how they got there and where they would be going when they left. I guess a lot of people have these oases.

There is always a beginning to a story, though seldom a recognizable beginning to anything else, so I'll try to start at the beginning.

It was December seventh, nineteen forty-one. No, that's history, not the beginning of a story. In the story, it was a rainy Sunday, and when I woke, the mynah birds were quarreling in the avocado trees on the lawn, and the rain was splashing and dripping from the great red poinsettia blooms outside my window. Not the back window that faced the lei shop; the side one that faced Willard Seymour's house. I listened to find out whether or not anyone else was awake and stirring, but the rooms were quiet. I lay in bed and looked across at Willard's rain-dark rooftop, where a flock of little gray doves was huddled together, mourning to one another. The day was grayer than the doves, but I wasn't worried about the weather. My parents and I were going to the beach later, and I knew the day would be golden and warm at Wianae on the other side of the island, at the picnic place, the Sunday place where we always went on winter weekends. We usually packed a lunch after church was over, left home a little before noon, and stayed at Wianae until suppertime. I looked forward to Sunday all week, every week.

My big, black-haired father used to swoop me up in my orange life jacket and carry me into the breakers and afterward help me build castles in the sand, the kind with little moats around them to let the water in. I used to laugh a lot, partly because of the moats but mostly because I loved my father. My mother was always nearby, lying on a piece of straw matting with her hair tied back from her face and her dark glasses on and her bathing suit beginning to get tighter across her stomach because of the baby. She usually had her eyes closed as she lay there on her side, as relaxed and decorative as a sleeping kitten. Only she hardly ever was

11

sleeping. We could tell because every now and then she sifted some sand through the small neat fingers of one hand or smiled at something my father said or reminded me to put my sunbonnet back on. There were men and women body-surfing and children throwing balls or digging tunnels and mothers pouring lemonade out of Thermoses and teen-agers burying each other's legs and lovers strolling off toward the point looking for shells. They were all Army people, and I knew most of them by sight. Sometimes they stopped to speak or sit down to oversee the castle building or stretch out for a while beside us, gazing into the distance where the gulls wheeled and the waves rolled, and sometimes a young officer known as Sharkbait swam beyond the other swimmers out toward the far horizon line where the clouds were massed white and unmoving above the blue water. I was used to all of it and happy because of it, although I didn't know the meaning of the word then. The beach, the sea, and the untroubled sky, like my parents, had existed forever and would continue to exist until the end of time; and I took them for granted, as most children take love for granted, or their hands or eyes. I say that children take these things for granted. Actually, my mother took them for granted, too. She doesn't now, but she did then. She had grown up—I later learned —in an old and well-to-do Boston family, where life had been both pleasing and protected; and, though her marriage had changed the surface pattern of her world, it had done nothing to alter the basic structure.

My father was different. He once told me how he'd lived in a Chicago orphan asylum until he was sixteen, never knowing who or where his parents were; and when I asked him what an orphan asylum was, he explained about the bleak rooms and the tired people who cooked the food and mended the worn blankets and broke up the fights in the halls. There wasn't much to see there, he said, and there wasn't much to love. He went on to say maybe it was a good thing, though: it took a long night of darkness to appreciate a day of sun.

"You understand that, Marty?" he asked.

"No," I answered, "but I believe you, Father."

To my father, every day was like an undeserved gift, and he could watch a man laying bricks, a bird riding the air currents, a papaya tree growing faster than a tree should grow, or the water seeping into the sand-castle moats with a delight that almost amounted to awe. As young as I was, I sensed this, just as I sensed that he considered my mother and me the greatest gifts a man could have.

I keep trying to get away from the morning when everything changed. I'll get back to it. I was lying in bed watching the doves, and after a while I went to the dresser and took out a box of shells I kept in the bottom drawer. I carried them back to bed with me, along with a couple of green glass fishing floats that my father had found for me in a rocky cove one afternoon. I looked at the shells for a few minutes, then turned on the bed lamp and held one of the transparent floats up so the light could shine through. It was pretty, but I wished eight o'clock would come, so my parents would wake up and get breakfast, busying themselves with the waffle-cooking and letting me do things like pour the fruit juice or fill the brown pitcher with syrup. Sunday was the maid's day off, when Iyaga went home to visit her children and grandchildren on the pineapple plantation. I didn't miss her on Sunday because it was a special day, but the rest of the week I liked having her around. There was a serenity and agelessness about Iyaga that I found pleasing. She seldom talked, so I didn't know much of her history except that she had been born in Japan and hoped to go back there someday. I didn't want her to go, because she was part of the framework of my world like the wallpaper butterflies and the lei-shop women and the green-gray mountains that ringed the post and hid the sea.

Willard Seymour came to his window, and I slipped out of bed to go wave at him. At first Willard just stood there with his pale spiky hair bristling up around his head the way it always did. Finally he saw me waving and put his hand over his eyes in an "Oh, no, not you again" gesture and stuck out his tongue at me. Sticking out his tongue didn't mean anything except that Willard was what he was: a rude and disagreeable child, according to Mother. I wasn't used to judging people then, so to me he was simply the boy next door who knew more than I did because he was older.

Anyhow, as he was sticking out his tongue there was a distant booming like the firing of the alert gun, and I could hear planes flying and more booming. I didn't pay much attention. There were air maneuvers going on most of the time, and I was accustomed to seeing and hearing planes. The alert gun used to scare me at first, going off without warning in the middle of a still night, so that I woke to the sound of front doors slamming and men's feet running outside on the dark pavements where the streets lamps no longer shone. Mother sometimes fumbled her way to my room after putting out whatever indoor lights were burning, and once or twice she got into bed with me. There was an eeriness to it all, but she said it wasn't anything to get nervous about.

"It's just practice," she told me.

"What kind of practice?" I asked.

"The kind the Army has to do when the world's the way it is today," she answered.

Once, during an alert, she and Father were having a dinner party, and she carried me downstairs after the gun was fired because I cried when she turned off the night light. There in the dark living room where she and the other women sat waiting for the men to return, I heard them telling each other in whispery voices not to smoke because passing planes were able to see the tiniest glow inside a house, and I wondered whether planes had eyes. There was other talk—something about losing the Japanese fleet—but I was too sleepy to listen.

I'm getting away from the booming and the planes flying and Willard Seymour standing at his window. To me, the only immediate problem was Willard sticking out his tongue instead of waving at me when I was anxious to communicate with something or someone besides sea shells and fishing floats. I was just winding my window open to call across and ask him whether or not he was planning to go to the beach, when there was a wild whining roar high up in the sky that moved swiftly and awesomely down toward the rooftops and dimmed my voice.

Willard took his hands from his eyes and looked interested. I don't know why I remember that but I do, perhaps because I tended to rely on Willard's superior appraisal of most situations. Even now I can see—or think I see—his face at the window during that short unlikely interval before the sound of the diving bombers turned into a series of deafening blasts that were like nothing I had ever heard. The doves rose from the opposite rooftop in a sudden gray and scattery cloud, and as the floor lurched under me and two panes of glass shattered at my feet, I ran screaming for my father.

I didn't have to run far. My father was already at the door of my room. He picked me up quickly, without seeming to hurry, and told me to block my ears if the noise was too loud. He didn't tell me not to be afraid. My father never bothered to say anything meaningless. He held me as safe as he could and kissed the top of my head several times as he carried me down the shuddering hallway into the linen closet, where my mother was crouched on the floor in her rust-colored bathrobe with her eyes big and her fingers twining in and out of one another. She seemed to have trouble untwining her fingers, but she finally managed to do it and when she did, she drew me down onto the floor beside her.

"Sit down, Marty." Her voice had no inflection. When she saw I was crying she said something else, but I couldn't catch what it was.

My father spoke, bending over and shouting to make himself heard.

"They're bombing Wheeler," he said. "It's not as close as it sounds." Wheeler was a nearby airfield where I went to playground nursery school. "There's nothing here at Schofield but a little artillery and a lot of grounded men, so maybe we'll be okay. We can hope for that. Stay in the closet. It's the best place there is for now." He kissed the top of my head, as he'd done in the hallway, and then he kissed the top of my mother's head, almost as though we were both his children and equally in need of reassurance. When he kissed us, I stopped crying and my mother started. As she crouched there silently, letting the tears run down her face and slide off her chin, my father put his finger against her cheek for a second and gave her a smile that wasn't quite a smile. Then he touched my cheek.

"My April and my Spring Song," he said.

April was my mother's name, and by Spring Song he meant me. He called me that sometimes.

"You'll be all right," he said. "Everything will be all right."

His voice was easy and sensible and made me feel looked-after, the way it did at the beach when a wave was coming and he'd tell me, "Here comes a big one," and we'd ride it together. So long as my father was with me, there was never anything to fear.

"I have to leave you," my father said, and went out of the closet, shutting the door behind him.

"Oh, no, Lang! Not now!" My mother stopped crying as the door closed. At least, I think she stopped crying. There was no light, so I'm not positive.

"Where are you going?" she asked on a rising note.

"Out," was all my father answered.

Louder explosions rocked the closet. A roll of toilet paper tumbled off the shelf, and I jumped and hunched as though a boulder had landed in my lap. The door swung open, and in a momentary flash of half-hope I thought perhaps my father was coming back, but he didn't. I could see him headed for the stairway with his khaki uniform still unbuttoned and his shoes untied over his twisted socks.

"Father," I called, but I don't think he heard me because

16

my mother was calling him, too, in a voice I didn't recognize, pleading with him not to go out until the bombs stopped falling.

"The planes aren't at Wheeler now," she said. "They're at Schofield. They're here!"

"I know." My father told my mother to close the door, and his words were an order, not a request. Mother obeyed without arguing, and in a brief interlude of quiet I could hear my father's footsteps clacking down the stairs and away.

I wasn't sure whose planes were flying or whose bombs were falling. I wasn't even sure what bombs were, except that they caused the noise and fear and were therefore bad. They had ruined my beautiful Sunday and drained the charm and gaiety from my mother—my lovely mother who embroidered my dresses and read me bedtime stories and played with me—shutting her into herself when I needed her most, so that I was left isolated with my own terror. Even when I couldn't see or hear her, I could sense her desperation filling the small lightless space the two of us occupied but did not share. I longed for my father.

"Where's Father gone?" I asked.

"To the company." I couldn't understand how Mother knew, because Father hadn't said he was going anywhere but out.

"For how long?"

"I can't tell you."

"Why is he going to the company?" I realized the day was all wrong, but I needed help with the details. "He never goes to the company on Sunday."

"We're having a war." Mother seemed to be trying as hard as I to sort out her thoughts. "Although we weren't having a war." She bumped into me as she slid from a crouch into a sitting position. She didn't raise her voice enough for me to hear the rest of what she said.

"This is how a war *is*," I think she said.

I didn't bother to ask her anything else. I blocked my ears, as Father had suggested, and it's possible I shrieked from time to time. I know I wanted to shriek, and when I relive that morning I can still remember the shrieks welling inside me. I no longer remember how they felt, but I can remember feeling them.

The linen closet smelled of sheets and towels and sun and soap and lavender. My mother's shoulder trembled against mine as we sat there in the dark. After a while there were no more thundering crashes, just planes humming back and forth overhead like huge angry hornets, and bullets clattering against the walls and roofs of the houses. I unblocked my ears. Every now and then I could hear Mother moan a little, then carefully stop, the way she did one time at the beach when she sprained her ankle. Once, in a passing effort to comfort me, she said we were playing hide-and-seek, and I suppose that was as good a name for it as anything. It meant more to me than the word "war," and it probably did to her, too. In the strange new world of the morning, she was struggling to clarify things by grasping for some plausible fragment out of the familiar past, because nothing about the present was familiar to either of us. Even the smell of sun and soap and lavender had a strangeness about it, because it had no meaning any longer, although it remained the same.

Time wasn't like time that day, so I don't know how long we stayed in the closet. But at some point I became aware of a great stillness, and I knew that a while before the stillness I had heard the planes drone off.

Mother opened the door and ran down the hall to the bathroom where I could hear her being sick. Probably because of the baby. I didn't know whether to go after her or stay in the closet, but I remembered Father had said to stay, so I stayed. I might have stayed anyway. Without the noise, without my mother's fear to magnify my own, there was a peacefulness to the closet that gave me a chance, not to assess the recent storm, but to be relieved it was over. I was grateful to see daylight again, even the rainy gray daylight, and I glanced at the corner across from me where the broom and mop and cleaning bucket were. There was a brown salamander on the handle of the toilet brush. I took a green towel from the shelf over my head and put the salamander on it upside down, and he turned a pale green. Usually salamanders scooted or dropped suddenly from the ceiling, but this one seemed happy and unhurried. I was getting a yellow washcloth, so I could put him on it and see if he'd turn yellow, when my mother reappeared. She had combed her hair, and she must have washed her face, because her bangs were wet. I showed her the salamander, and she said he was nice, but she didn't say it very convincingly. She told me to go get into my shoes and coat.

"But Father said to stay in the closet." I checked to see if the salamander was all right before I looked at her.

"Did you think he meant *forever?*" My mother was very white under her tan.

"Well, maybe not." Hearing it put that way, I stood up. "When is he coming back? Father, I mean."

Mother didn't answer.

"Go get into your shoes and coat," she repeated and started toward her bedroom at the front of the house. She didn't tell me whether I was supposed to wear my coat over my night-gown or whether she wanted me to change into my daytime clothes first.

"Hurry, Marty," she said.

I took the yellow washcloth and the salamander and went down the hall to my room. I put the washcloth into my empty goldfish bowl that used to have the guppies in it and laid the salamander on top of the washcloth. I debated about getting dressed and finally decided to take off my nightgown and wear a sunsuit. I knew I couldn't snap the back snaps, so I didn't try. I found some socks and put them on and sat on the bed to get into my toe-peeper sandals. While I was buckling the straps, the salamander in the goldfish bowl turned kind of a brownish-yellow.

I looked to see if Willard was anywhere in sight, but he

19

wasn't. The rain was still dripping from the red poinsettia blooms outside my window, and the little gray doves were fluttering back onto Willard's rooftop. There was no sound from the mynah birds in the avocado trees, but I could hear a couple of ripe avocados thud to the ground.

I put on my navy-blue coat with the gold buttons, the one I'd gotten for my birthday two days before, when I had six friends to my party and Iyaga baked a chocolate cake and we all went to the circus and saw the monkeys and lions and clowns and got cones of spun sugar and colored balloons. My orange balloon was still in the corner of my ceiling, bobbing a little as the air blew through the empty panels of my window frame. I thought about getting it down, but I didn't do it. There was a thread hanging from the hem of my new coat, and I took my snub-nosed scissors and cut it off. Then I began to button my coat buttons, and as I buttoned them I started to shiver, which surprised me, because until then I hadn't known I was cold.

A voice sounded from downstairs, cutting into the peculiar stillness that wouldn't have seemed like stillness on another day.

"It's me . . . Sanderson," the voice said. "Can I come up, Mrs. Langsmith? We're going to battle stations, and the captain wants I should get his things pronto."

Sanderson was Father's orderly. He came around to the house a lot, and sometimes he baby-sat with me on Iyaga's night off. He was young and easygoing, and he always chewed gum, adding a new piece to the old every hour or so to sweeten the taste, and usually giving me a stick if I asked for one.

Mother told Sanderson to come up, and he took the stairs two at a time. I met him on the landing.

"Hi, Sanderson," I said. "Can I have some gum?"

"No gum today, Marty. Musta went and forgot it." He brushed past me. There was sweat on his forehead, and he was wearing a flat round metal hat I'd never seen him wear before.

I was disappointed about the gum, but I didn't say so.

Mother wanted to know about Father.

"He's okay, ma'am." Sanderson joined her in the bedroom. "But a coupla the dogfaces ain't. We got a bomb in the quadrangle and all the company was standing around looking at the sky when the captain showed. We thought the planes was camouflaged and maneuvering out of Hickam. I better not talk. The captain told me to get his bag and pack his underwear and a clean uniform and like that. Where's his suitcase at?"

"I'll get it." Mother went to the closet. "You go collect his razor and things."

I followed Sanderson into the bathroom and sat on the edge of the tub.

"What are battle stations?" I asked.

"Places at the beach." He opened the medicine cabinet.

"Can I go with you?"

"Not this time, Marty." His hands shook as he took out a razor and lather stick and a brush and comb. "It ain't the same beach you go to, and besides this ain't a good beach day."

I thought of the Sunday picnic place at Wianae that was always sunny. The place where the sand was white and the blue breakers rolled in and out forever.

"I know what," I said. "Let's all go to Wianae." As I spoke I could see the skies over the beach wide and still and peaceful in my mind.

"They never have any *rain* at Wianae," I pointed out logically. "So why should they have any war there?"

Sanderson wiped off a piece of wet soap instead of getting a fresh one.

"Which toothbrush belongs to your pa?" He didn't pay any attention to what I said about Wianae.

"The red one. Are you going to wear that hat to the beach?"

"Yes," said Sanderson.

"How long will you be gone?"

"A while." He hit a can of tooth powder with his wrist, and

it clinked into the basin and some of it spilled. He reached for the can without bothering to slide the top closed, and rolled it in a bath towel with the other toilet things.

"Like an hour?"

"An hour?" His mind seemed to be on something else. He folded the ends of the towel, but he didn't do it very well.

"What *about* an hour?" he said.

"Is that how long you'll be gone?"

"Who knows?" He swung around. "Come on now, Marty. Be a good girl and don't cry, and I'll bring you a whole pack of gum when I get back. Black Jack." He flicked some sweat off his forehead with the hand that wasn't holding the towel.

I wasn't crying. I don't know why he said that.

"I'm not crying." I trailed him to the door of the front bedroom where Mother was stooped over with her back to us putting things into Father's suitcase. She lifted her head when Sanderson handed her the towel.

"You look scared, Sanderson," she said.

"That's because I am, ma'am." He took some handkerchiefs out of Father's dresser. "I only come into this man's Army to eat three squares a day, not get trapped out on this here rock with a bunch of yellow slant-eyes taking pot shots at me."

I remembered the salamander.

"I found a salamander," I said. "He's yellow. Or anyhow, he was. I better go see."

"Watch his tail don't come off." Sanderson snapped Father's suitcase shut as I started for my room.

The salamander's tail was all right. He was still lying on the washcloth, and I wrapped him lightly in it, so he wouldn't smother or escape, and took him to show Sanderson.

I was too late. Sanderson was already on his way to the stairs with the suitcase. His hat must have made his head hot, because there was more sweat on his forehead where he'd flicked it off.

"Take care of Captain Langsmith." Mother stood at the

door of her room, watching him go. "And take care of yourself, Sanderson."

"I'll try, ma'am. And you take good care of yourself and Marty."

Mother pulled at her bangs.

"How?" She seemed to be seeking a set of directions. Any set.

I'm not sure if Sanderson didn't hear her or if he just didn't know what to answer.

"I always did say the best view of these here islands would be Diamond Head off the back end of a transport headed for Frisco." His words got mixed up with the clack of his footsteps, going down the stairs and away as my father's had done.

I put the wrapped salamander in my coat pocket and waited for what came next. I hoped my mother could figure out a program of some kind.

Mother must have read my thoughts, because she stopped pulling at her hair.

I noticed for the first time that she looked sort of funny. She was wearing her nightgown tucked into a black wool skirt that she hadn't finished zipping up, and she had on pink high-heeled evening slippers and my father's old West Point sweater with the big A on it. She had lipstick on her upper lip but none on her lower one. She said to come along, hurry, we were going out. I took her hand, and we went down the stairway and through the living room and across the lanai and out the screen door that always banged, into the misty rain.

We went to Aunt Liz's. There was no one on the sidewalk but us. As we passed a patch of clover between our double house and the next, I dropped my mother's hand to squat down and look for four-leafers, because I always looked for four-leafers there. Only I didn't have time to find any. The thing I found was something like a short silver pencil but blunter. It was warm when I reached for it.

"What's this?" I opened my fist.

"A bullet." Mother pulled me upright and took my hand

again. She didn't do it roughly, but I knew I'd better not look for any more four-leafers. Her pink heels clicked faster and faster on the flagstone pavement, and I put the bullet into one of my coat pockets, the pocket without the salamander, while I skipped once or twice to catch up.

As we hurried along I could see trucks stopping in the rear road of Mason Loop, where we lived. A group of soldiers with hats like Sanderson's jumped down from the trucks and started climbing onto the low roofs of the maids' quarters, yelling to each other and hauling something with them.

"What are all the men doing?" I asked.

"Setting up machine guns." Mother kept walking.

Halfway around the Loop, Mrs. Workman came out of her side of the two-family house where she lived. She had a raincoat over her pajamas, and her hair—which she usually wore in a fancy updo—was hanging loose outside her raincoat. She was carrying a blue china vase, a loaf of bread, a pistol, her jewelry box, and an oil painting of her father. I knew about the painting and the jewelry box because I saw them when I went to play with her daughter, Elaine. Mrs. Workman had the bread and the box tucked to her left side with her arm, and she held the vase in her left hand with the pistol sticking out of it upside down like a wilted flower. With her right hand she was half-holding, half-dragging the painting.

Elaine, who was freckle-faced and fat and never moved fast if she could help it, was ambling after her mother with only one pigtail braided. She was wearing a white sock and a brown sock and her dress was on backward under her open coat, but she was as unaware of her hodge-podge clothes as she was of the rain. Elaine wasn't ever dressed right unless Raico, the maid, saw to it. Raico, who wasn't much taller than Elaine although she was going on twenty, was trim and pretty with a mind as happy and uncomplicated as mine was then. Whenever Elaine showed up downstairs with her clothes on every which way, Raico always put the palm of her hand

24

over her mouth and giggled uncontrollably before she re-dressed her. Elaine didn't care how her clothes looked, but she enjoyed the attention, and she and I both liked to hear Raico giggle. I don't know how Raico happened to slip up on her job that morning or, rather, I didn't know at the time. She moved silently after Mrs. Workman, wearing her red-flowered Sunday kimono with the white hibiscus flowers on it, and there was no sign of laughter on her face. She didn't even giggle at the way Elaine was playing with the blue balloon she'd gotten at my party . . . holding the string with one hand and reefing it and unreefing it with the other, so the balloon kept bobbling raggedly down and then swiftly shoot-ing skyward again.

Mother stopped to speak to Mrs. Workman.

"Going somewhere, Jean?" she asked.

Mrs. Workman reached the curb where her car was parked and opened the rear door. She put the pistol and vase and jewelry box in the front seat and tossed the bread into the back one.

"What does it look like?" Mrs. Workman spoke in a clipped, harsh tone I wasn't used to. "Naturally I'm going somewhere or I wouldn't be carting all these valuables."

Maybe the china vase and the jewelry box were valuable, but I couldn't see what was so special about the pistol or the loaf of bread. Or the painting either, for that matter. To me, it was just a dark ugly picture of an old man with a white mustache and a beard.

"Where do you plan to go?" Mother didn't make any com-ment about the valuables.

"Kole Kole Pass." Mrs. Workman acted more and more irritated. The painting was about four feet high and she was having a hard time getting it into the back of the car. "You certainly don't think I intend to stay around here and get murdered, do you? Where in the name of God was that great invincible Navy we're supposed to have? I thought this island

25

was meant to be the safest place in the world." She began to sound really mad. "Hurry *up*, Elaine! Did you *hear* me? *Get a move on!*"

"Kole Kole's closed," Mother said. "It's been closed for months, and you can't get over the mountains. I wouldn't go there if I were you."

Mrs. Workman ordinarily spoke politely.

"You mind your business, April, and I'll mind mine." Her voice was pitched high, and her tan hair was like raveled rope in the falling rain. She didn't look or sound like Mrs. Workman.

Elaine was rereefing her balloon string.

"Hi, Elaine," I said. "Hi, Raico."

"Hi, Marty." Elaine didn't seem perturbed by anything that had happened or was happening. "See, I still got my blue balloon."

"Stop talking, Elaine, and *move*." Mrs. Workman's voice went higher and harsher. "Get in front. *Hurry!*"

Elaine shambled into the car, and Raico moved the balloon so it wouldn't get caught. Then she closed the door and started toward the back seat.

"Not *you*, Raico!" I couldn't understand what was wrong with Mrs. Workman. As she turned and shook her fist, her face was blotchy and contorted. "Go-away-I-said-go-away-you-heard-me-you-rotten-Jap-you-and-don't-ever-come-anywhere-near-me-again!"

Raico, who had her fingers on the door handle, pulled them back the way she did once when she had been making popcorn for Elaine and me and touched the hot popper by mistake. She didn't say anything, but tears came to her eyes. I didn't like Mrs. Workman being so mean to Raico.

"You damn two-faced Japs trying to kill us all!" Mrs. Workman gunned her motor.

Mother and I began walking again. Mother looked surer about things after hearing and talking to Mrs. Workman.

Elaine waved.

"Bye, Marty," she said. "See you."

Mother quickened her steps as we moved parallel to the moving automobile.

"Don't go to Kole Kole, Jean." As she spoke there was a new droning of planes in the distance, coming closer. "There's nowhere to hide up there and it's open road all the way."

"I'll-go-where-I-please-you-get-killed-if-you-want-to-sweet-Jesus-here-they-come-again." Mrs. Workman's words dwindled off as she stepped on the gas and hurtled away.

"Are the Japs trying to kill us all?" I asked.

Mother tightened her hand around mine.

"Yes," she said. "Run, Marty."

I wanted to turn and see what happened to Raico, but I was too busy trying to keep up with Mother as we ran.

We reached Aunt Liz's house at the end of the Loop and pushed open the front door just after the planes reappeared above us, diving so low that I could see the men inside them, the men who threw back their heads and laughed as they came down even with the chimney tops to fire their bullets at whatever was underneath. The strafing began again, and I could hear answering gunfire from the roofs of the maids' quarters.

Aunt Liz, who was Mother's sister although she didn't look it, was sitting in her living room. Her short dark hair was carefully arranged, and she had on a neat white maternity sun dress and white shoes. She was putting red nail polish on her fingernails. My Uncle Bert was slumped on the couch reading a newspaper, and my cousin Joey, who was a month or two younger than I, was lying on the floor in his bathing suit and a feather Indian headdress, throwing a ball for Duff, his police dog. I don't know what the Indian headdress signified except that Joey had a fetish about hats and never went anywhere without something on his head, preferably something to fit the occasion. He even wore a hat to bed.

"The electricity's off." Aunt Liz made the remark in her drawly way, crossing her long legs and putting one hand on her knee so she could study her nails and see if she'd gotten the polish on straight. My aunt used to work for a magazine called *Lovely Lady*—she was always telling Mother about it —and she paid a lot of attention to her appearance.

"Good Lord, April." She raised her eyes to stare at Mother. "Where did you dredge up that outfit? And there's another question I'd like to ask. Is it always this noisy around here?" She and Uncle Bert and Joey had been at Schofield only a month, but—even so—I don't know why they didn't question the sound the bullets made hammering against the house and pinging into the back-yard ash cans.

Mother didn't answer either of Aunt Liz's questions.

"Get-in-the-telephone-closet," she said, running her words together like Mrs. Workman. "The-one-under-the-stairs. Bring-Joey." She waited for my aunt to move.

"Are you out of your mind, April?" Aunt Liz put the brush back into the nail-polish bottle and screwed the cap on tight. "First, you come in dripping wet, looking like something left over from a rummage sale, and then you want everyone to get in the telephone closet. Is this some kind of a game?"

"When can I have breakfast?" Joey took the ball out of Duff's mouth and threw it into the dining room. "I want a poached egg."

"As soon as we get some electricity." Aunt Liz blew on her nails, touched her ear lobes with her finger tips to make sure she'd put her pearl earrings on, and made a face.

"So much *noise*," she said, meaning the planes and bullets.

Uncle Bert laid aside his newspaper and stretched. He was dressed, except for his uniform blouse.

"Not much news," he said.

Mother was pulling me toward the lower hall, when my uncle added: "Well, breakfast or no breakfast, I'd better get on up to the hospital. Maybe I can grab a fast cup of coffee at the cafeteria before I start treating the hangnail-headache-and-sore-toe set."

"Poor love." Aunt Liz's voice drifted toward the doorless

closet as we entered it. "But then you *would* insist on being a doctor."

Uncle Bert scratched his gray crew cut and eyed us in a wondering way as he meandered past and up the stairs.

I sat down on the telephone stool.

"What in the name of all that's holy is the matter with you *both?*" Mother, who was standing, kicked the wall below where I sat. "Especially you, Bert. I always thought you were so solid and sensible."

"*Us*, dear?" It was Aunt Liz commenting from the living room. "What gave you the idea there was something the matter with *us?*" Aunt Liz prided herself on being wiser and more in command of things than Mother. I guess because she was thirty-two and Mother was only twenty-five. Also, she didn't look as much like a young girl.

"Stop it!" Mother was very angry. "You talk like a war was a garden party!"

Uncle Bert's feet halted abruptly on the slanted ceiling above us where the stairs were.

"War!" He spoke the word like an accusation. "You don't mean this is *real?*"

"Of course, it's real." Mother's patience, what was left of it, had run out. "Look through the window if you don't believe me. American planes don't have rising suns painted on them."

Men kept clacking on stairways that morning . . . first my father, then Sanderson, then Uncle Bert. While Mother was still speaking I heard him rapidly returning down the stairs. He didn't stop long enough to look through any windows, which was lucky, because a spatter of bullets broke the one on the stair landing about the time he reached the ground floor.

Uncle Bert was suddenly giving orders.

"Liz"—he was pulling on his blouse as he passed us— "bring Joey and get in the closet with April and Marty *this minute!*"

29

Aunt Liz minded Uncle Bert better than she minded Mother. She and Joey crowded in with us, moving toward the back of the closet where Aunt Liz had to stand bent forward from the hips because of the slanted ceiling. Joey sat on the floor, and his Indian headdress tickled my knees and got shoved down over his eyes.

"Watch out for my Indian hat," he told me crossly as he shoved it back in place.

Uncle Bert was thinner and rangier than Sanderson or Father, but his footsteps sounded the same as theirs as he clacked across the lahalla rug in the living room and through the step-down doorway to the lanai and onto the lanai and over it.

Aunt Liz called to him. Her voice made a lot of noise in the closet.

"Bert!" she called. "Come back!" But the screen door slammed, and there was no answer.

The planes were still moving back and forth through the skies, now and then humming away toward the mountains or the cane fields before they returned to batter the areas nearby.

"Oh, God, oh, God." Aunt Liz held her knees. "This can't be true. It just can't."

But she knew it was true, so she gripped the telephone shelf and got herself back in control. It wasn't so much a matter of choices as a lack of them.

"This closet was meant to hold one person, not four," she said. "I don't know why they didn't make cellars in these damn houses so we'd have some kind of decent bomb shelter. If I stand like this much longer I'll turn into a hunchback—a six-months-pregnant, stiff-necked hunchback."

"Your stomach's bumping my head," said Joey. "Where's Duff? Hey, Duff."

"That's all we need in here." Aunt Liz tried to shift position and couldn't. "A dog and maybe a horse or two."

Duff stuck his head through the doorway and lay down half inside the closet and half out of it.

"Good dog," said Joey.

"Air. I've got to have air." Aunt Liz pressed her thumbnail to her lips. "I think I'm going to throw up."

"Mother already did," I told her. "Back home in the bathroom."

"I'll never make the bathroom." My aunt choked, and Joey jerked sidewise on the floor below me.

"Don't throw up on me and Duff," he said.

The planes were moving off in the direction of Wheeler Field.

"Oh, hell, Liz." Mother didn't swear very often. "This is hopeless. Let's get out of here and stand in the hall. We can always come back if we have to. Marty, stay where you are. You, too, Joey." She and my aunt left the closet.

"Why do *I* have to stay?" Joey always thought he was a special case.

Mother didn't answer him, and Aunt Liz couldn't because she was throwing up.

"It's babies that do it." I wasn't talking to my aunt; I was talking to Joey. "I guess we're going to name our baby Vernon after Father. What are you going to name yours?"

"I don't know. Maybe Duff. Duff's a good name."

"Are you crazy? People don't name babies after *dogs*." I tried to set Joey right on the proprieties, but he didn't pay any attention.

"I don't like this place." He hooched around a little to make more room for Duff.

"Who does?" I remembered what Father had said about the linen closet when he left Mother and me there.

"It's the best place there is for now." I put my hand over my nose as Duff moved farther in. "Duff smells."

"I'm going to wash him at Wianae," said Joey. "He got into some garbage."

"You can't go to Wianae." I sat up straighter on the stool, trying to unkink my back. "Nobody's going to Wianae."

"How come?"

31

"Because we're having a war." I blotted out a quick mental picture of the untroubled Wianae sky just as a phantom plane droned into one corner of it.

"Who cares?" Joey patted Duff. "I bet we go anyhow. We always go as soon as Dad gets back from the hospital."

"I bet you don't."

"Why not?"

"People just don't go to Wianae when there's a war, that's all."

"You mean we're having a war *now?*" Joey, who'd seen a bunch of Western movies, looked pleased instead of worried. "Boy, it's a good thing I wore my Indian hat."

"It won't do any good. It's not a cowboy-and-Indian war. It's the Japs." Mrs. Workman's words echoed back to me. "The damn Japs are trying to kill us all," I said.

"I didn't see any Japs." Joey hooched around some more.

"They were in the planes." I pushed Duff with my foot because he was slobbering on my sandals. "At least, most of them were in the planes. All except Raico. She was in Elaine's yard. She didn't have a gun, though."

"What makes you think she didn't?"

"Because I saw her. She was wearing her red Sunday kimono. The one with the white hibiscus flowers on it."

"She might have been *hiding* a gun. Cowboys don't hide guns, but sometimes the bad guys do."

"Raico isn't a guy. She's a girl. *And she didn't have a gun.*" I was sick of Joey. I wanted to ask Mother if I could leave the closet, but she and Aunt Liz had disappeared somewhere. "It was Mrs. Workman that had the gun. And the men in the planes. I saw the men when Mother and I were running. The men had goggles. Goggles and guns."

"Did they kill anybody?"

"They *may* have," I answered. "Like I said, they were trying to."

Mother came to tell us we could get out of the closet. As

Joey stood up, his headdress hit against the wall phone and got knocked crooked again.

"Darn it. This Indian hat's too big." He pulled his ears outside the headdress to anchor it better.

"Then why don't you take it off?" Mother's interest was a token one.

"And go around *naked?*" Joey was indignant. "With the Japs flying all over everywhere shooting the place up?"

"They seem to be gone now." Mother finished pushing a rag around the hall floor where Aunt Liz had been sick.

"Gone where?" said Joey.

"Probably back where they came from." Mother started to leave the hall. "Wherever that was." She suddenly stopped and lowered her voice. "Carriers," she said. "It must have been carriers." She lowered her voice even more. "Oh, God," she said. "Troopships."

I got off the stool and rubbed my rear as I stepped over Duff.

"Joey says Raico had a gun," I said. "She didn't have a gun, did she?"

"Of course not." Mother started walking again. "Why on earth would Raico have a gun?"

"See, Joey." I tried to lose him by following Mother to the kitchen, but he and Duff were right behind me.

"I still bet she did." Joey began riding Duff horseback. "Bad guys *always* have guns."

He anticipated my next words before I spoke them.

"*Even* if they're girls," he said.

Two bullets had gone through the lower part of the back door, leaving a couple of round jagged holes. I don't know where the bullets were. Maybe behind the stove.

"Hey, for crying out loud, what happened to our door?" Joey got off Duff and went over and put his eye to one of the holes.

"I can see the trash can," he announced in a disappointed tone, "and two of the leaves on the trumpet vine. But that's all."

Aunt Liz had scrubbed the front of her dress, or possibly Mother had. Anyhow, it was wet. She was sitting on a metal chair at the kitchen counter, with her head down on the red-and-white checkered oilcloth. Her hair was mussed and there were yellow stains on her white shoes. One of her earrings was on the floor under the counter. I picked it up, because I knew it was a real pearl-and-gold earring and she thought a lot of it. She thanked me, but she didn't reach to take it, so I laid it beside her on the oilcloth, choosing a red square where she could find it better when she got around to putting it on.

"I must look a mess." Aunt Liz didn't sound as if she cared much, and she wasn't talking to anyone in particular.

Mother opened the refrigerator.

"You're not working for *Lovely Lady* any more," she reminded Aunt Liz.

"I might say more's the pity, dear." My aunt slid a hand under her cheek to cushion it. "Not that I don't love Bert. God knows I do. That's the trouble with love."

"What's the trouble with love?" Mother left the refrigerator to go and peer in the breadbox.

"Let's put it this way. There I was earning five thousand a year, whirling around New York dressed to the teeth and minding my own business, when who messes it all up? You, that's who. Coming through town with Lang and dragging me off to dinner with your medical bachelor friend." She made an inconclusive motion with the hand that wasn't under her cheek. "So here we all are five years later. Plus two down and two to carry."

"Oh, be quiet, Liz." Mother closed the breadbox. "You're not doing any good rambling on like this. What were you planning to live on all day? Two eggs and half a can of papaya juice?"

"Manuela's off." Aunt Liz might have been addressing the

34

tabletop. "We always buy lunch at the beach on Sunday and have supper brought in from Lu Chai's. Joey has a poached egg for breakfast—Bert fixes it—and Bert and I just have coffee, which Manuela makes before she leaves." She gazed absently at the cold percolator on the stove.

"I probably ought to learn to cook sometime," she said.

I started to say Mother was learning from Iyaga—she could even make waffles—but I knew Aunt Liz disliked being outdone by anyone, especially Mother.

Mother studied the ceiling as though it were the sky.

"I think the planes are really gone," she said, "so why don't I run home and pick up what we need for breakfast?" She began making an oral list and when I added jam, she said there must be a jar or two in my aunt's reserve cupboard.

"*What* reserve cupboard?" Aunt Liz acted peevish. "I don't have any reserve cupboard."

"You don't? General Short ordered each of us to keep one."

"He probably issued the order before I arrived." My aunt sat up. "Anyhow, who gives a damn now? Me, I couldn't gag down a mouthful of hummingbirds' eggs on the half shell."

"That's you. Maybe the kids could."

"Ick." My aunt pushed her elbows tight against her sides and swayed sidewise in her chair. "I'm sure having a bad case of bomb stomach or strafing stomach or whatever the hell it's called."

I never heard Aunt Liz swear so much.

"A big stomach," said Joey, and Mother held up her hand at him, like an M.P., before she said: "I'm going now. Marty, do you want to come along or stay?"

"I guess I'll come," I said.

"I can't see why anyone's going anywhere." It was my aunt again. "You seem to forget there's no electricity."

"Oh, damn. That's right." Mother was starting to swear quite a bit, too. "Do you know how to build a fire in the fireplace?"

"Are you serious, April? That's servants' work and I wasn't raised to be a pioneer woman any more than you were. Besides, I doubt if I could lift myself at this point, let alone a piece of kindling."

"Try," said Mother.

My aunt stayed in her chair.

"Come on, Liz. I'll be right back with the food, and we could at least heat the coffee and make the kids some cocoa."

Joey was excited over the idea of a fire.

"Maybe we could toast marshmallows," he said. "How's about it, Duff? I'll give you some of my marshmallows. Only don't vomit like you did before. Remember how Duff vomited all over the rug the last time we had marshmallows, Mom?"

Aunt Liz must have remembered because she ran to the sink and began to retch.

"Boy, a fire," said Joey. "I'd better go get my fireman's hat." And he raced upstairs and returned in his red fire-chief helmet.

Mother held a wet dishtowel to Aunt Liz's forehead.

"Why don't you lie down?" She eased my aunt's hands off the drainboard. "Go in on the couch and I'll do the fire when I get back. I'll only be gone a few minutes. Coming, Marty? Joey, you stay here and watch out for your mother."

"Sure. Me and Duff will." Joey threw an arm around Duff.

"I don't know why I keep doing this." Aunt Liz moved in slow motion as she straightened up. "I haven't been sick in months. Oh, well"—she brightened a little—"only twelve weeks to go." She turned. "I can hardly wait."

As she turned, her glance fell on the door where the bullet holes were, and she squinted at it as if she'd never seen a door before.

"That is," she said, and the brightness went out of her as she dragged herself toward the living room and the rest of us followed, "I *thought* I could hardly wait. . . ."

Her voice trailed off.

"Though I don't suppose *now* . . ." she said as she dropped down lengthwise on the couch without bothering to put a pillow under her head.

There was a short silence while she lay staring into space as if she saw something printed or drawn in the empty air.

Then she closed her eyes, apparently trying to shut out whatever it was she saw, and cried my mother's name.

"Oh, April," she said, and her voice had a scary sound to it. "What's going to happen? What's going to happen to us all?" And as Mother bent to give her a pillow, Aunt Liz broke into great tearing sobs and turned her face to the wall.

Joey started crying right after Aunt Liz did. I didn't blame him. It wasn't so much the crying as the way she did it. I didn't like seeing her myself.

I felt sorry for Joey, so I made a passing attempt to divert him before I left.

"Why don't you play with Duff?" I said. "Throw his ball. Teach him some new tricks or something."

"Duff's just a *dog*. What the heck good is a *dog?*" To my surprise, Joey crossed the room and gripped my hands in his. "Stay with me, Marty. Stay with me till somebody's father gets back."

"My father wouldn't come here." As I spoke, I had a feeling that maybe the war was over, that maybe Father was already on his way to Mother and me, and the more I considered the idea, the realer it became.

"The planes are gone, so probably Father's home right now," I said.

Mother put an afghan over Aunt Liz and told me to come along if I was coming, but Joey was still holding me.

"Turn me loose, Joey," I said, but he didn't. If anything, he gripped me tighter. He didn't care if I saw Father or not.

Father was home. I knew he was. In my mind I could hear him whistling as he came up our front walk. I could see him shutting the screen door softly so it wouldn't bang. I could see him smiling as he walked through the living room toward the lower hall.

"Let *go*. I mean it, Joey Snyder!" I tried to free my hands and couldn't. I never knew Joey was so strong.

Father reached the stairway and sprinted up it. From eight houses away I watched him. I watched him through walls and lampposts and bushes and fences and trees.

"I've got to see Father!" I kicked at Joey's shins and he dropped down onto his knees. I dragged him along with me trying to join Mother as she moved onto the porch.

"Where's my April and my Spring Song?" Father strode straight and tall down the upper hall toward the linen closet.

"I could kill you, Joey," I said and meant it.

Father was still whistling, whistling and smiling when he reached the closet. He took hold of the knob and opened the door, and as he opened it, his whistling stopped, his smile vanished, and while I drew in my breath and watched him from another room in another house, a queer thing happened. Instead of being myself fighting with Joey, I suddenly became my father and gazed at the closet floor in disbelief, seeing it through his eyes.

No one was in the closet. No April. No Marty. Nothing. Not even the salamander on the toilet-brush handle.

"Don't go, Father; I'm coming!" I'd forgotten the salamander.

"Look, Joey." I spoke calmly, not because I was calm, but because my anger wasn't getting me anywhere. "Be good and I'll give you my pet salamander. He's in one of my pockets."

"Let's see." Joey knew I never lied so he let go. And though he didn't deserve anything better than a good punch in the eye, I reminded myself a promise was a promise. I reached my left hand into my left pocket and my right hand into my right pocket, trying to find the salamander. Then I pulled both my pockets inside out before I turned and ran from the house.

The yellow washcloth fell noiselessly to the floor, and the silver bullet fell with a little echoing "clunk."

But that was all.

I don't know how or when or where he went, but the salamander was gone.

2

APRIL

When Marty was around eleven—no, I guess she was younger than that—we were out on the terrace one afternoon discussing what color to paint the swimming-pool ladder, when I noticed how much she was getting to look like Lang. I told her so.

"It isn't so much your looks," I said, "as your expression."

What happened next took me completely by surprise.

Marty jerked herself out of the wrought-iron chair where she was sitting and replied with a fury that appalled me.

"Don't talk about my father!" she said. "I don't want to hear about him! I don't want to hear about him. I DON'T WANT TO HEAR ABOUT HIM!"

I was distressed but I was also startled and mystified.

"What's wrong with you, Marty?" I said. "I thought you loved your father."

She walked to the swimming pool a few yards away, and there was antagonism in the way she held herself, the way she moved, the way she spoke.

"I hate my father," she said, and sat down on the rim of the pool with her back to me.

I took a deep breath.

"Why?" The question was inadequate, but I had to begin somewhere.

"That's my business." Her voice was sullen.

I wasn't surprised at the sullenness; it had been going on for several weeks. In fact, if she had said she hated me instead of Lang, I'd have accepted that. I wouldn't have understood it, but I'd have accepted it, just as I accepted her hostility, although I didn't understand that, either.

I appealed to the Marty-that-used-to-be, the helpful and responsible Little Old Lady Marty who had recently changed back into a child.

"Look," I said, "we're both sensible people. Give me one reason why you hate your father, and then we won't talk about it any more."

Marty ripped a blade of grass lengthwise down the middle and threw the pieces aside.

"Come now," I persisted. "Surely you can give me one reason. That's only fair."

It didn't occur to me that Marty was tired of being fair.

She tore a second blade of grass in half before she replied.

"All right," she said at last, and she said it reluctantly. "I'll give you one reason, but you won't like it."

I saw her back go rigid.

"I hate my father," she said evenly, "because all he's ever caused is trouble."

"Trouble?" I was outraged. "Trouble! You can't possibly sit there and say . . ."

Marty cut me off.

"You said *one reason* and after that we wouldn't talk about it any more." She splashed her feet in the pool—good shoes and all—perhaps to show defiance, perhaps as a diversionary tactic, perhaps both. Whatever purpose she had in mind doesn't matter now and didn't matter then. What mattered, what really mattered, was that the taut and frayed lines of communication between us were about to snap.

41

I couldn't afford that, and neither could she.

I forced the next words out.

"I'm sorry, Marty," I said.

I took my sunglasses from my lap and polished them on my sleeve. They didn't need polishing, but I polished them.

"We won't discuss your father ever again," I promised.

Marty went on splashing her feet in the pool, testing me.

It was a cloudy day, but I put my glasses on. I lit a cigarette. I blew on the match and broke it.

Marty the child turned sidewise, jackknifing her legs onto the grass, and I saw her watching me out of the corner of her eye.

"I got my shoes wet," she announced in a pleased, retaliatory way.

I exhaled a mouthful of smoke.

"So I see," I said.

I wanted to say: All right, you can wear your wet shoes to school tomorrow. I wanted to say: Marty, I've had enough of your inexcusable behavior. I wanted to say: Go up to your room until suppertime and think things over.

"We never decided what color to paint the swimming-pool ladder," I said. "How does black strike you?"

Marty gave a shrug that was just short of insolent.

"Why ask me?" she said. "It's your ladder."

"Or green." I was afraid if I lost my temper I'd lose Marty. "Green would go with the water and lawn and trees." I put out my cigarette. "What do you think about green?"

She shrugged again, but the shrug was a less elaborate one. There was a balanced moment when I could sense her trying to make up her mind, not about the ladder but about me.

She untied the laces of her shoes.

"Green's okay," she ventured at last.

"Or blue. What about blue?" I found I was grinding the dead cigarette round and round in the ashtray on my chair arm, so I moved my hand down onto my knee.

"I'll leave the color up to you," I said.

42

I wasn't stupid enough to believe I was fooling Marty with my contrived generosity and pseudo-patience. I was simply giving her time to consider how long a way we had come together and how long a way we still had to go.

She turned her shoes upside down to dump the water out. Then she spoke as if she wasn't ready to speak and didn't have faith enough in me to speak but didn't care to cope with the alternatives.

"Blue would be good." She made a calculated decision as she took off her socks and squeezed them. When all the water was out of the socks, she squeezed them again.

"I kind of like blue," she said.

"Fine." I stood up. "As soon as Jill's finished her nap, I'll go to the store and buy the paint. You can come and help me pick it out, if you want to."

"Can I go barefoot?" Marty was still testing me. I didn't usually let her go barefoot in town.

"I don't know why not," I answered.

Marty the child reached for a ladybug that was moving by and caught it.

" 'Ladybug, ladybug, fly away home,' " she intoned. " 'Your house is on fire; your children will burn.' "

She kept looking into the distance instead of at me, as though she were still talking to the vanished ladybug.

"Hey, you know what?" she said. "While we're in town, why don't we get one of those orange life jackets for Jill, so she can swim in the pool with the rest of us this summer?"

"Why an orange one?" I spoke before I thought.

Marty gave me a level, last-chance glance.

"That's the kind all the little kids have, isn't it?" she asked.

My mind was somewhere else.

"*Isn't* it?" she repeated.

I took off my sunglasses.

"Why yes," I answered. "I guess it is."

I got Jill up, and the three of us went to the store and

bought some blue paint and an orange life jacket, and Marty seemed happier than I'd seen her in years. Later, she helped clear the dinner table before she read *Peter Rabbit* to Jill. She even cleaned up her room. I complimented her on the way it looked when I kissed her good night.

"Sleep well," I said.

"I will," she answered. But she didn't.

An hour or so later she had one of her nightmares, and I heard her screaming. I went to her room and found her drying her eyes on the edge of the pillowcase.

"Everything's going to be all right," I told her. "What were you dreaming about?"

"The war," she answered, "and the lion. It doesn't matter. I'm better now."

"Would you like some warm milk?"

"Yes," she said.

So I got her some warm milk and straightened her covers, and after about twenty minutes she fell asleep again.

It took me longer than that to settle down, and when I slept I dreamed about the war, too. It was the old stepping-stone dream in which I was struggling to get across a vast rushing river by hopping cautiously from stone to stone, and each stone had a name: Oahu, Guadalcanal, Bougainville, New Georgia, Truk, Rabaul, Japan. I used to have a good many bad dreams, just as Marty and everyone did (Liz kept having one about Fifth Avenue changing into a jungle path), but lately the dreams are vaguer and occur less frequently. And when I have them I try to forget them, the way I try to forget the past and the war and the air raid.

Especially the air raid. Because that's where all the bad dreams started.

One of the scary things about the air raid was the fact that there was no war at the time. Oh, Europe, of course, but America wasn't having a war. The Army had been on alert for about a week, which was mildly disturbing, because an alert had never lasted that long before. And what with all the rainy, chilly weather we'd been having, everything seemed a little dreary and out of kilter, but certainly not ominous. The men couldn't leave the post, so we missed a couple of dinner parties downtown: one at Pearl City and one at the Finebergs' up on Tantalus. But we weren't alarmed, just slightly uneasy, the way we were the time nobody knew where the Jap fleet was for a few days. There was occasional talk of how Hawaii couldn't exist more than a month in a state of siege, because the Big Five owned the islands and wouldn't let anybody grow anything there but pineapples and sugar cane; everything else had to be shipped in, which pleased the Big Five because they also owned the ships and the docks and the banks. But even though we kept a cupboard of reserve supplies in *case* of a siege, we never honestly expected one, and I kept forgetting to rotate the food in the cupboard, stuff like cereal and raisins and flour that got weevils in them if they were kept too long. The reserve cupboard was just a precautionary measure and more of a nuisance than anything else. We had the biggest Navy in the world at our doorstep and plenty of fighter planes scattered around at Wheeler and Hickam and other places, and there were new bunkers to protect the planes at Wheeler—although, as things turned out, all the planes were lined up for Saturday inspection *outside* the bunkers on December seventh, with the men in tents beside them, so the Japs just went up and down the lines of planes and tents, killing the men and destroying the aircraft. They got the planes at Hickam and the planes on the beach as well, and that took care of the fighters. Also, although half the Navy was meant to be constantly cruising, it wasn't that morning, as we later learned. But nobody could foresee any of this. We simply knew that, along with the ships and fighters, we had bombers that could fly thousands of miles out to sea, we had coast artillery along the beaches, and—if worst came to worst

45

—the infantry. And, besides, why should any foreign power want the islands in the first place? They were too close to the United States for an enemy to protect and hold.

I got a few concerned letters from friends and relatives during the fall, people in the States who thought they knew more than we did, but I didn't worry. None of us worried. An attack of any kind seemed ridiculous.

That's why I've never been sure how Lang knew there were Japs in the dive bombers, but he knew. He sat up in bed beside me when the first bomber started diving, plummeting down like a plane out of control; and he was on his feet almost as soon as he sat up. I was already awake, because I'd been having a bad time with morning sickness—I always do the early months of a pregnancy, and my third month wasn't quite up—and I'd just gotten back under the covers after a second trip to the bathroom when the trouble began. Marty was still sleeping.

Lang looked upward, narrowing his eyes and listening, listening. Then he said for me to get in the linen closet.

It seemed an odd remark for him to make.

"Why?" I asked.

That's when he told me the Japanese were in the planes.

As I grabbed my robe and hurried past the hall window, I glanced out.

"What's all the smoke off toward Honolulu?"

"I don't know." Lang glanced out the window, too, while he was running to get Marty. "It may be Hickam. It sounds like they're bombing hell out of Wheeler now, and unless we're a whole lot luckier than I think . . ."

I missed the rest of what he said, because he disappeared into Marty's room, and besides, there was too much racket. He brought Marty back to the closet and then he left us. I didn't think he'd leave, but he did. I should have realized, I suppose, that he was a soldier as well as a husband, but I'd really never thought about it till then. He wore a uniform as a banker might wear a business suit, and—though I'd known all along that war was his business—knowing a fact and believing it are two different things.

We were in the closet quite a long time; at least it seemed long, and Marty kept shrieking. She was as horrified as I was by the noise (most women and children are sensitive to inordinately loud noises) and it upset us almost as much as what it stood for, the way the sound of a dentist's drill is nearly as nerve-racking as the dental work itself. And after the bombs stopped falling, we kept expecting them to fall, which was just as harrowing in its fashion. The strafing wasn't as bad. I don't know how many minutes it lasted—everyone's version of the morning is a little different, and nobody can prove whose clock was right or who really looked at a clock—but the planes finally went away. And after I'd recovered from the paralysis of panic, the paralysis where any actions are either detached or reflex ones, I decided to take Marty and go to Liz's. I didn't think it would be any safer there; it was just something to do and somewhere to go. At first I started to leave in my bathrobe, but then I remembered it was raining and figured I might as well get dressed. I told Marty to put on her clothes, but all she did was get into her shoes and coat. She says now that she got dressed, but she didn't. She also says Sanderson came in before we left the house, but he couldn't have, because there wasn't enough time between waves of planes. We barely made it to Liz's.

There was a big hassle when we arrived. Liz and Bert didn't believe there was a war going on. They thought it was some kind of show, the way a good many people did, which I found pretty maddening and frustrating. They were mainly annoyed because the electricity was off. Joey, my nephew, was lying on the floor in his fireman's hat, complaining because there was no breakfast, and Bert was toying with the idea of building a fire in the fireplace so he could heat the coffee. Liz had mislaid one of her pearl earrings and was trying to find it. (Marty discovered it later in the kitchen.) I had a hard time getting my sister and brother-in-law to come to their senses, but when I finally managed to get through to them, Bert went rushing off to the hospital . . . and none too soon, either, with the planes zooming overhead again and the ambulances and trucks screeching by the end of the Loop, carrying the wounded from Wheeler.

The rest of us crowded into the telephone closet, but Liz and I didn't stay; there wasn't enough room. We watched the second covey of planes out the lower hall window. They weren't bombing, just strafing and dumping leftover ammunition, and we decided the closet wasn't any real protection except maybe from shrapnel—a fast conclusion that turned out to be wrong. We could see the Japs in the planes throwing back their heads and laughing, as if they were enjoying some monstrous celebration, and out on the roof of Manuela's house a few enterprising and foolhardy enlisted men were firing a machine gun they'd hurriedly set up. One of the men kept waving his arms and shouting, "Get 'em, dammit. Get the bastards!" I don't know why he wasn't killed. Liz and I moved into the living room when a spate of bullets broke the stair-landing window above us. And then she got sick, which worried me, because she'd had a second miscarriage the spring before and wasn't meant to have any excitement.

She didn't keep much food in the house, so when things quieted down, Marty and I went home to collect some. I had Marty put on a sweater and sunsuit, and just as we were leaving, Sanderson came to get Lang's clothes. I recall that clearly, because he and I forgot to pack Lang's razor and toothbrush, although we remembered his toothpaste and razor blades. Sanderson gave Marty some gum, the way he usually did, and when we returned to Liz's, hurrying because it was raining harder, Marty kept fussing at me as we walked along. Something about a salamander she'd left behind in her gold-fish bowl.

The only people we saw on the way were Jean and Elaine Workman and Raico, their maid. Jean was carting a number of so-called valuables to her car; I can't remember just what, except a silver teapot and a gun and a portrait of her mother. She had two paintings in her living room, one of her father and one of her mother—some famous artist had supposedly painted them—and she was always pointing at them as though they were great works of art, like everything else in her house. Although all the double-family houses were similar on each side of the horseshoe-shaped road, Jean was a major's wife and could afford honest-to-gosh wool carpets and modern furniture and red velvet drapes in her quarters, whereas the rest of us—even Liz and I, who could have gotten money from home and didn't—had to make do with lahalla rugs and rattan furniture and target-cloth curtains. Jean was about thirty-five and what my family would have called possession proud. I never understood why she wanted to save the portrait of her mother. The portrait of her father was equally good or bad, depending on how you judged the situation. In spite of her preoccupation with household effects, Jean was a kind of lazy-voiced, friendly enough person before the air raid, but she changed for the worse that morning. Among other things, she said Raico was dangerous, which frightened Marty so much she made me run all the way from the Workmans' to Liz's because Raico was standing there in the yard. There were a number of Japanese on the island, and no one knew or knows yet how they'd have behaved if the foreign Japs had landed, although most of the young ones like Raico seemed to prefer our freer way of life and most likely would have remained loyal to us, like the Nisei. Still, they could have swung one way or another under pressure. The older ones like Iyaga, our maid, had mixed loyalties and were therefore greater risks. I don't mean Iyaga herself; I'm not certain about her. She never came back after that morning, and a week later I noticed all her clothes were gone, but I never found out whether they were stolen or if she took them or what. Liz's maid, Manuela, also left, and when I told Jean Workman, she said what did I expect; you couldn't trust a damn one of the Japs or the damn "gooks," either, for that matter, because most of the gooks had Jap blood. By gooks she meant everyone who wasn't Caucasian. Jean kept going off at tangents that day and in fact every day from then on. For example, while I was talking with her beside the car she thought she heard planes again and went barreling up to Kole Kole, though there was nothing to protect her in the shadowed lantana and lava mountains, not even any trees except the scrub mangoes, and she had to turn around and come back as soon as she went up. I can't recall whether she was the person who insisted there were parachutists in the hills, but somebody spread the rumor, and it sounds like Jean. She also said the Panama Canal had been bombed, and Wake and Midway. I have no idea where she got her information, but we all believed her in the beginning. We believed anyone in the beginning.

When she arrived home from Kole Kole, she took a shovel and tried to dig a bomb shelter under her house, which may have been a good plan in theory but didn't work out very well in practice; the mud kept sliding into it, and after that the stubborn volcanic soil, all of which she took as a personal affront.

"Goddamn it to hell," she'd say. "Get out of there! *Get out of there!*" And she'd bat her shovel at the inconsiderate earth, trying to teach it a lesson in manners.

Jean wasn't going to be caught unprepared in any future emergencies: she carried a pistol around with her everywhere, even before the rest of us did, except for when she was digging, and then she was afraid it would get wet in her pocket, so she propped her screen door open with a chair and put the pistol on top of the chair, loaded and maybe even cocked for all I know. And later she acquired a couple of gas masks somewhere (a gas attack was one of the things we feared most); a mask for herself and another for Elaine. I can't imagine what good she thought Elaine's mask would do, because it didn't fit (those Mickey Mouse masks for children hadn't yet been invented) and none of us could understand how she was going to feel happy about saving herself if she couldn't save Elaine.

Liz and I never did eat breakfast, and neither did Joey and Marty. We didn't even bother to heat the coffee after the electricity went back on. Jean Workman or someone said the water supply was poisoned, and even though Manuela had made the coffee several hours before the air raid, we decided not to take a chance on it. As for the rest of the meal, nobody was hungry enough to want it. I'm usually starved when I'm pregnant, but I wasn't that morning. All of us had what we called "bomb stomach," even Joey, who kept asking for food and then feeding it to Duff, his dog.

I don't know when we made up our minds to pack and leave Liz's; possibly after the sentry began coming around with the hourly printed bulletins telling us what to do and what not to do. I wish I'd saved the bulletins, because I can't remember what many of them said, at least not in any sort of entirety or sequence, and I never learned who composed them; it was as if God or the elves were sending directives. I only know that at one point we were told to go in for communal living—two but not three families to a house, the bulletin writer said—and we chose my house because I had a well-stocked refrigerator and reserve cupboard. According to the bulletin writer's reasoning, two adults under the same roof meant mutual company and support, whereas three might easily make for gossip, dissension, and group hysteria. I guess he wasn't thinking of Jean Workman when he wrote the order. Boots Daly moved in with her and would have given her soul, such as it was, for a third adult around the house to help *combat* the gossip, hysteria, and dissension.

I believe it was the bulletin writer who told us to move our mattresses down to the first floor, so we'd be safer from later strafing—not from a direct bomb hit; no one was safe from that—and also where we could get out of the house more quickly, if the necessity arose at night. I wouldn't let Liz haul the mattresses; Joey and Marty and I did it, and I can't say it was an easy task. We let Liz carry the bedding. I doubt if it was the bulletin writer (though it may have been) who said in case the Japanese landed we'd better shoot our children first and ourselves next, rather than submit to rape, torture, starvation, or worse, whatever worse was. I just remember that someone told us and it was before the men came to dig the trenches, though we weren't issued pistols until the following week.

The idea couldn't have been the chaplain's, although the chaplain visited everyone on the Loop, going from house to house to tell us our husbands were safe and urging us to trust in God's infinite wisdom and mercy. We needed something more specific to trust in, but of course there wasn't anything, and we knew it as well as the chaplain did.

Liz and I met him when she and the kids and I were moving from her house to mine. He was standing on the wet sidewalk outside the Workmans', looking older than his fifty-odd years. His body drooped, and there were lines around his mouth that I'd never noticed before.

Jean kept her back to him and went on shoveling until he began telling her to trust in God's mercy. Then she flared out at him.

"Go peddle your holy propaganda somewhere else," she said, and whacked the ground with her shovel.

The chaplain walked with us as far as the next house.

"See if you can get her to stop digging," he said.

"Maybe later," I replied. "It wouldn't do any good now."

I asked him where the Japanese had come from, how much damage they'd done, and when and if they'd be back.

"I doubt if they'll be back." He touched one of the metal crosses on his shoulder, and I wondered if he was lying to me out of kindness.

"So many dying boys," he said, and his words sounded like a speech from an old World War I movie, not like anything related to life as we knew it.

"So many dead boys," he remarked quietly, and I could feel his grief. "So many and so young." He wiped his spectacles on a crumpled khaki handkerchief. "And I can't help them now," he said.

He couldn't help us, either, but he was a good man.

Many things about that day are hazy in my memory and may have occurred in the morning or afternoon or evening. I can't remember at what hour or moment we were ordered to park our cars on the grass in the back yards to free the roads for military purposes, or when we were told the laundry whistle would serve as a danger signal. I can't even remember how many toots were meant to be sounded for an air attack, how many for a land attack, and how many for an all clear. But I can still remember the sound the whistle made, because I've never liked hearing laundry whistles since, or factory whistles, or any whistles for that matter, any more than I can stand hearing dive bombers. Not now, I don't mean. There aren't any dive bombers now, just prop planes and jets. However, for years after the war ended, if a plane dived in the sky while I was sleeping, I dived under the bed; I didn't even have to wake up to do it. My husband used to laugh at me, saying there was no longer a war going on, but that didn't alter my reaction. To me, it wasn't much of an argument because, as I've said before, the day the Japs came there wasn't any war going on, either.

To get back to the morning: Liz and the kids and I turned the living room into quite a passable dormitory. We made up the beds on the floor and even put a flashlight and a box of crackers and a tin bucket within reaching distance, looking ahead to the hours of darkness. Marty practiced going to the bathroom in the bucket, but it kept tipping, and Liz couldn't squat down, so Joey and I were the only ones who had any success trying it out, and my success was only moderate. As for the flashlight, we forgot it wouldn't be any good in a blackout; we kept forgetting things like that at first. We thought of the radio, but it was in the repair shop. Liz said why not get hers, and later I went after it. "Let's not forget the key to your house when we go," I said to Liz, but she told me she hadn't bothered to lock the door.

"What's there to steal, dear?" she asked, and that's when I looked around my own house with the six-year-old silver gleaming from the dining room and the flower arrangements everywhere in silver and crystal bowls and the Chinese candlesticks on the mantel under the good water color Lang and I had saved our pennies to invest in, and it came to me there wasn't anything in the place that wasn't expendable, except perhaps the photograph album. I haven't had much respect for possessions since that Sunday (if people want anything more than I do, they can have it) because, in the end, it's just as Liz said: "What's there to steal?"

Marty and Joey entertained themselves jumping up and down on the beds, so the bed-making wasn't much of a success, either. I could have stopped them, but the jumping kept them occupied. Duff wasn't too happy over his new location; he kept prowling around the outer edges of the mattresses, now and then putting a paw on one, then drawing it back and whining. He broke into loud barks when the men came to dig the slit trenches in the front yards, and we had to shut him in the kitchen.

The diggers came around noon. There were eight of them —all native draftees, as I recall—and a young bachelor lieutenant from the Nineteenth Infantry named Dawson was in charge of them. I didn't know him well, but I knew he'd been a football hero and an Olympic swimmer at West Point though he didn't look or act like a star athlete. He graduated three years after Lang did. He was sandy-haired and medium tall with a slow smile and a slow way of talking. Everyone liked him.

When he arrived with the diggers, we all went out on the lanai to speak to him. All of us but Liz. As soon as the kids stopped jumping on the mattresses, she decided to lie down and rest.

"This is a fair-looking ceiling," she said and pulled a blanket over her stomach.

"As ceilings go," she added, and fell asleep.

Marty waved to Lieutenant Dawson.

"Hi, Sharkbait," she said.

"That's Lieutenant Dawson," I corrected her. "Don't be impolite, Marty."

"I'm *not* being impolite. That's what everyone calls him at the beach."

"Don't fret, Mrs. Langsmith." Lieutenant Dawson smiled his slow smile. "I've been called a heck of a sight worse and by bigger people." He winked at Marty. "You think you could get me a glass of water, pretty little lady, if the trip wouldn't put you out too much?" He turned to me as if it were an ordinary hour of an ordinary Sunday.

"Guess I wrapped myself around too much ham at the mess last night," he said. "I've been dryer than a dust storm ever since. *In*side, that is. Outside, as you can see, I'm wetter than a Saturday night in Houston." He had no overcoat on, so his field uniform was soaking, and rain trickled from the brim of his combat helmet.

The other men were wearing fatigue hats and raincoats. They stood watching as Lieutenant Dawson paced off the trench measurements and drove four stakes into the earth with his foot.

"Guess that'll do it," he said, and the men began digging. They worked silently, their faces impassive as they bent over their shovels. Many of them were part Japanese, and I found myself mistrusting their silence. It was one of my first experiences with the latent mechanics of suspicion, and I had to remind myself that if the men had been boisterous or even cheerful, I would have been equally mistrustful.

"Aren't you scared of catching cold out there?" Marty said

to Lieutenant Dawson. "I got frozen walking back and forth to Aunt Liz's."

"It hadn't come to mind. There's a chance I might shrink if I stay out too long. Or I might melt like a lump of sugar does, but that's not likely. I've never been sweet enough." To amuse her and Joey, he crossed his eyes and blew a drop of rain off the end of his nose.

"Thought it was a fly at first," he said.

Marty laughed while Joey explained about the water.

"Mom says nobody can drink out of the spigot," he told Lieutenant Dawson. "Why don't you stick out your tongue and catch some rain off your hat? That's a good hat."

"So is yours." Lieutenant Dawson regarded the feather headdress that Joey had exchanged for his fire helmet somewhere along the line. "Yes, I'd call that a mighty fine war bonnet, chief." He raised his arm in an Indian salute. "Paleface say 'How' to Chief Wild Buffalo, last of the mighty Blackfeet."

Joey looked down.

"My feet aren't black," he said.

"I got a feeling mine are." Lieutenant Dawson's shoes squished as he moved onto the sidewalk. "But getting back to the subject of drinking, what's wrong with the water?"

"We heard it was poisoned." I was about to offer him some ginger ale or fruit juice when Marty interrupted.

"How come they call you Sharkbait if your name's really Lieutenant Dawson?" she asked.

"That's just my swimming name." He ordered one of the diggers to cut the roots of a poinsettia tree that was near the trench. "Why don't you bring me my glass of water, pretty little lady, and I'll see if I can find out what's what with the drinking situation?"

When Marty brought the water, he reached in the door and took the glass.

"Gee, aren't you scared of being poisoned?" asked Joey.

"Sharkbait's never scared." Marty caught my eye. "*Are* you, Lieutenant Dawson?" she added quickly.

"I don't figure there's anything to be scared *of*." He smiled another of his reassuring smiles. "Well, try it out on the slaves is what I always say." He drained the glass.

"Tastes like pure, unsullied, A-number-one water to me." He wiped his mouth on the back of his hand.

"See, I knew he wasn't scared." Marty was anxious to have us notice and admire her judgment. "He's like Father. He isn't scared of anything."

"I bet he's scared of the Japs," said Joey. "*Aren't* you scared of the Japs, Lieutenant Sharkbait?"

"That I don't rightly know." Lieutenant Dawson gave another Indian salute.

"Take a gander down the street in half an hour, Chief Wild Buffalo," he said, "and if I'm still watching over the digging, have yourself a big swig of water." He measured the depth of the trench with a long pole he'd left lying on the ground.

"You can move on now," he said to his diggers.

I didn't want to talk in front of the children, but I was desperate for information, so I walked out and joined him in the rain.

"Do you know what's happening anywhere?" I asked. "I mean, how bad the situation is?"

Lieutenant Dawson postponed his reply. He tapped his little finger against the pole he was holding.

"It's bad," he said.

"How bad?"

He hesitated.

"All our fighter planes are gone." He furrowed his forehead and carefully unfurrowed it. "And most of the fleet."

"Someone said there were enemy parachutists in the hills. Is that true?"

"Not that I know of. And I'm pretty sure I'd know if there were. We'd all know." He hit the pole against the side of his shoe.

"You'd better go inside," he said. "There's no point getting wet."

No enemy parachutists in the hills, I thought. No Navy, no Air Force, but thank God no enemy parachutists in the hills.

No enemy parachutists *yet*.

No bombers returning to destroy the vulnerable Maginot lines along the beaches, no troopships gritting onto the quiet sands, no ruthless yellow men leaping out of the troopships into the shallow water at the edge of the sands.

None of these things *yet*.

Despair gripped me as I returned to the lanai, and I felt a deep and unreasoning hatred for the rain.

Back when everything was as it should be, back when weather was only weather, a rainy day was just a rainy day. I could either go out and walk through it singing, or I could stay inside and light the fires and lamps against it, keeping it beyond me. But with nothing right any more, nothing as it should be, the rain became an omen, an evil omen that pervaded my senses and threatened my rationality.

And the rain kept coming down—down and down and down—falling from a sky that had no sign of lurking brightness in it, no clouds in it, just the hushed and everywhere grayness of fear. Once upon a time there had been women and children passing in butterfly clothes, and men in rainbow Aloha shirts, and maids in blossom-brilliant kimonos. Once upon a time there had been the yellow of sunshine, the blue of skies and the green and mauve and crimson of moving cars where laughter floated. But that was once upon a time. Even the foliage of the trees and vines and bushes, even the grass, seemed to have turned gray that morning, like the once-white stucco houses changed to cobweb color by the rain; and the only brightness in the world came from the bright and oblivious poinsettias, Christmas-red a day ago and blood-red now.

The diggers waited next door, leaning on their shovels.

58

Joey, always aware of rights and privileges, addressed me accusingly.

"How come *I* can't go outdoors?" he demanded. "*You* went."

It was all I could do not to slap him.

"Shut your busy little mouth!" I was startled at the words I uttered, startled at the vehemence in my voice.

"Steady there." Lieutenant Dawson spoke gently to ease the reprimand.

Joey looked hurt a minute, then forgot about going outdoors and gazed past me.

"Boy, Sharkbait, your diggers sure made a mess of Aunt April's lawn." He scowled at the mounds of tamped earth walling the three-by-ten gash in the yard, scowled as the rootless poinsettia, cut by the silent men, began to tilt slowly over the open trench. A few petals drifted down from the wide flat flowers and disappeared from sight.

Lieutenant Dawson reached for the trunk and caught it.

"Make a pleasant little house plant for Christmas." He leaned the eight-foot tree against the screen beside the steps. "Cheerful up the place for Santa Claus when the old gentleman comes around with his fine reindeer and his big duffle bag full of extra-special presents for extra-pretty little ladies and extra-brave Indian chiefs." He moved over in front of the other section of the building, the section where Captain and Mrs. Bendel lived, and began pacing a right angle in the grass. Then he pounded his four stakes into the earth again.

"Knock a little of that dirt off your spade," he advised one of the diggers.

There was the sound of a door opening on the neighboring lanai, and he grinned a grin like the sun coming out.

"Hello, Sharon, O thou most beautiful," he said. He took off his hat and bowed.

Sharon was a house guest of the Bendels'. She was Dora Bendel's nineteen-year-old sister. I couldn't see her because of the partition between the porches, but I knew what she looked like: golden and fragile and lovely.

"Hi, Adam," I could hear her saying to Lieutenant Dawson. "Seems as if I went and missed the boat again."

Sharon was always missing boats. She kept putting off leaving for another week and another week and another week, ostensibly because she loved the islands, but really because she loved Lieutenant Dawson. Often when he came to pick her up in his open car, I used to watch the two of them drive off together, looking as if the world contained no twilit spots, no flaws, no ugly secrets; laughing as if the universe had been designed and burnished especially for them.

"I was going to leave this morning," Sharon went on. "I honestly was. But the ship didn't sail. Anyhow, I don't suppose it sailed."

"Never mind." The tenderness in Lieutenant Dawson's voice made me ache for Lang. "If you hadn't missed the boat, I'd have missed you. Maybe it'll all work out."

I wanted to weep, but I didn't, I wanted to run to my car and get in it and drive wherever Lang was, calling "Lang, Lang . . ." until I found him. I didn't do that, either. What I did was pick a dead leaf from the coleus plant in the corner and put the leaf tidily in my skirt pocket. Then I straightened the cushions on the wicker chairs where no one was sitting and no one was about to sit.

"It's all so awful." Sharon's voice was full of wonder and fear. Mostly fear. The fear that was everyone's warped yardstick for measuring hope. "They say if the Japanese land and capture the women, we'll all . . ." She didn't finish.

"Oh, Adam, aren't you *scared?*" she said.

"Sharkbait's not scared of anything." Joey opened the door and put his hand out to test the rain.

"That's not purely true, chief." Lieutenant Dawson's words had a faraway sound, and as I glanced through the screen, I noticed he had stopped smiling.

"No, sir, chief, that's not true at all," he said.

And kind Lieutenant Dawson, controlled Lieutenant Dawson, bent over and took a loose clod of earth from the new trench and hurled it at a lamppost as hard as he could hurl it.

There was a long moment of silence interrupted only by the grating of the shovels. Even Joey was quiet. I watched three mourning doves flutter past the propped and perishing poinsettia and disappear onto the roof overhead. I wanted to go inside the house, but the act of going seemed wrong, just as staying seemed wrong, as the silence seemed wrong, as Sharon's finally breaking the silence seemed wrong.

I tried not to feel anything about anyone as she spoke.

"Oh, Adam," she said. "Say you won't leave me. Say you won't ever leave me."

Her pleading both saddened and irked me. Without seeing Sharon, I could see the look of fright, the longing for protection, in her gentian eyes. I could see her beautiful unused hands reaching out for what had been hers a day ago. I could see the woman who wasn't yet a woman struggling to stay cocooned in a yesterday world.

Adam Dawson rubbed his dirty palm on his pantleg.

Doesn't she know any better? I thought. And I began mentally to criticize, then defend her, knowing that though she was only one semiadult among us, she was all of us.

Why should she know better? I argued. Does a girl like Sharon grow up overnight? Remember, she's young.

But I'm young, too. What right has she to stay young and pleading?"

What makes me do this? I wondered. I've always liked Sharon. I've never resented her dependency before.

She doesn't have a corner on dependency. I was dependent until this morning.

I thought of how Lang used to cherish me back when I didn't need cherishing.

And where is he now that I *do* need cherishing? I asked myself.

Somewhere else. Going about his own affairs.

With an effort I got myself back in hand.

I can't afford this, I thought. My inner questions don't listen for inner answers. They merely protest and reply with more protesting, till the intellect can't pick its way through the thornbush of emotions back to the open meadows of reason.

The rain, I told myself. It's all the fault of the rain.

Lieutenant Dawson lifted his head and lowered it as though his neck hurt. Then he half turned toward the Bendels' side of the house and disciplined whatever dreads and yearnings were in his mind out of his face and voice.

"I'm going now," he said to Sharon. "You'll be fine with Dora."

"That'll be all here," he said to his men.

And without looking back, he walked ahead of his diggers into the next yard.

I read somewhere that time doesn't pass; it stands still and people pass through it. It's a concept I never understood until the Sunday of December seventh, when the day didn't go by; I traversed the day. I can still remember how time became space that Sunday and changed from a moving process arbitrarily measured by clocks and calendars into a bleak, unhorizoned territory through which I myself moved. Since there was no plan of action to follow, no purpose in devising a plan, I tried not to long for the vanished sanctuary of the past or to look ahead into the wide uncharted wasteland of the future.

Liz slept on. I closed the sliding glass doors between the living room and the rest of the lower floor so she wouldn't be disturbed and threw together a lunch of sorts for the children and me. Again, no one was hungry but Duff, who swallowed down the half-eaten sandwiches and barely touched milk, while Joey patted him and said, "Good dog," as if eating and drinking were rare and laudable canine accomplishments.

"*Now* what'll we do?" asked Joey.

"I haven't decided." Because the duties of a normal day

had suddenly become frivolous and dated—things like putting fresh flowers in the silver bowl on the dining-room table or hemming the new bathroom curtains or going over the menu for next month's dinner party—I didn't bother to rinse the plates and glasses or throw away the banana peels and eggshells and lettuce in the kitchen sink. Instead, like an uncertain sailor returning to his lookout, I gravitated back to the lanai to see if anything was happening in the sky or on the street.

The rain had stopped. Jean Workman was no longer digging. Two women, Boots Daly and someone else, were talking together over toward where the Loop curved from view; and across the street a yellow cat went scudding between two of the houses. Out on the front lawn, that atrocious child from next door, Willard Seymour, was tramping around under the avocado trees, squashing ripe avocados under his heels.

"You can go outside and play now if you'd like," I said to Marty and Joey, who had joined me. "Only be sure and stay on the sidewalk and don't go any farther away than Workmans'."

"Play what, for gosh sakes?" It was a characteristic Joey remark.

"I'll pull you in my wagon," Marty offered.

While I was taking the wagon down the steps, Willard Seymour picked up an avocado pit and heaved it at the curb. The pit bounced a foot or so and dropped into the gutter.

Joey eyed Willard.

"Who's that guy?" he asked.

"It's Willard Seymour, of course." Marty looked glad. "Hi, Willard."

Willard didn't answer.

"The reason we didn't go to the beach is we had a war," she went on conversationally. "That's what all those planes were."

Willard reached for another avocado pit and bounced it.

"I *think*," said Marty, "we'll all go next week, though. We'll all go to Wianae. As soon as the war's finished and Father's back."

I tried to connect the war with Lang. I tried to picture him walking around on some near but unknown beachhead, giving orders and assessing the terrain. I tried to picture him tall and confident and invincible, standing with his hands on his hips gazing out over the water. But a mist rolled in from the sea, and all I saw were troopships moving shoreward through the mist.

"Quit that!" I spoke the words aloud, and although I spoke them to myself, Willard Seymour gave me one of his granite stares and stopped bouncing avocado pits.

I went over to where the slit trench lay like a great dark wound in the earth, and studied its soggy, uninviting interior.

"That's a big hole." Joey came up next to me. "How come Lieutenant Sharkbait got his men to dig it?"

"It's not a hole; it's a trench." I tried not to say too much. "We're meant to get into it if the planes come back, and stay there till they go away again."

"Not me." Joey wrinkled his face. "There's too much mud. You ought to cover the bottom with something. A rug maybe."

Not a rug, I thought. Something high or solid enough to keep the watery soil from seeping through. Boards or stones, perhaps? No, there were no boards or stones around.

The quartermaster had been reflooring the pantry, and I remembered there was still a roll of linoleum leaning against a column on the rear porch. Grateful for the fortuitous forgetfulness of the workmen, I hurried after it and dragged it into the kitchen. Duff backed under the stove and lay watching me as I spread the roll on the floor and began hacking at it with a pair of garden shears.

The shears were blunt, and the linoleum kept buckling and trying to reroll itself, so that by the time I'd finished cutting, my patience was frayed and my fingers had ugly red grooves in them. To make matters worse, while I was holding my hands under the cold-water tap to relieve the soreness, Joey —consistent in his ill-timed aggravations—began hollering in the front yard.

"You *knew* I couldn't do it," he wailed at the top of his lungs. "Darn you! You *knew* I couldn't do it!"

I found I was swearing as I lifted the strip of linoleum and carried it clumsily out through the house.

"Can't you ever *ever* be quiet? You heard me say not to wake your mother!" I looked around for Joey, but I didn't see him. Then the limp filthy feathers of his Indian headdress appeared over the inside edge of the trench, followed by his grimy face and neck.

"I don't care!" He lowered his voice but not much. "Willard said to jump over the trench, and he *knew* I couldn't do it. Not only that but he hurt my ear."

Dora Bendel came out onto her steps.

"Anything wrong?" she wanted to know.

Dora wasn't much older than I was, but she already had a matronly appearance, so I always thought of her as older. It was hard to believe a person so plain could have a younger sister as lovely as Sharon. I know sisters aren't necessarily similar; Liz and I aren't alike in build or coloring, and our viewpoints often differ—though not so widely now—but there are resemblances. There were none between Dora and Sharon.

"No, there's nothing wrong." I felt better at seeing Dora. Maybe, as Liz said, she wore the wrong clothes and weighed a little too much for a small woman ("dowdy" was the word Liz used for her), but there was a kind of glow about her, and she was a good neighbor and friend.

"Why don't you come over for tea in an hour or so?" A strand of Dora's brown hair straggled down from the bun at the back of her neck, and I noticed her slip was showing, but her manner was unself-conscious and reassuring. "Sharon and I made a cake, and I've asked one or two people to come by. Bring Liz and the children."

"Liz is asleep. But you can count on the rest of us."

Dora disappeared, and I turned my attention to Joey, who was clambering up onto the grass, helped by Marty.

"Willard didn't hurt your ear," she was saying as she made a halfhearted attempt to brush some of the mud from his ruined clothes. "He only knocked a bug off you. And he *thought* you could jump the trench. *He* jumped it, so he thought *you* could."

"He's bigger than I am." Joey glared at Willard, who was slouched against the trunk of an avocado tree tearing the petals from a poinsettia blossom.

"What do you have to say for yourself?" For all my admonitions about silence, I heard my voice growing louder as I questioned Willard.

"Why me?" He flung the stripped flower aside, and there was neither concern nor apology in his tone. "The fact is, the stupid kid fell in the trench." He wiped his hands—sticky from the white milk of the poinsettia stem—on his shirt.

"Well, see that he doesn't fall again!" My anger was about as effective as if I'd been talking to one of the lampposts or trees. Willard's face registered no emotion . . . no shame, no apprehension, no displeasure, no delight; and it occurred to me he was not only disagreeable; he was also soulless. As soulless as a statue.

I turned from him in exasperation and addressed Joey.

"Come get cleaned up. I'll find you some dry clothes and bring them down to the kitchen."

Joey followed me inside, where Liz, surprisingly enough, still lay dead to the world, and when he and I went out again, Willard was gone.

"Where'd that mean Willard go?" Joey peered into the trench and behind the trees.

"He didn't say." Marty was holding the wagon handle and rolling the wagon absentmindedly back and forth. "He just went. Willard does that sometimes."

"He better not pinch my ear again." Joey touched a spot below the band of his bedraggled Indian headdress. "Before he told me to jump the trench, he pinched my ear. He said there was a bug on it, but I didn't feel any bug."

"There must have been a bug if Willard said so." Marty, affectionate and innocent by nature, was indiscriminate in her loyalties. "Willard's pretty smart."

"Smart, my eye. He's just mean." Joey would have gone on talking forever if Marty hadn't stopped him.

"Oh, who *cares*, Joey." She centered the wagon on the walk. "Get in, and I'll ride you down to the Workmans' and back."

The strip of linoleum was too long, and I had to get the shears and trim it before I dropped it into the trench and slid in after it. In sliding, I took a pile of earth from the bank along with me, which got spread around as I stamped up and down trying to get the linoleum to lie flat. The strip still buckled and, while I was walking, its edges teetered and scraped against the trench sides, dislodging more of the wet soil. I was in no mood for criticism when Joey, back from his ride, felt called upon to observe and comment.

"Good gosh, Aunt April. What in heck are you doing? Like I say, you need a rug. Where's that piece of linoleum you brought out?"

"In *here*, if you'll just look." It was all I could do to keep from screaming as I hoisted myself onto the upper ground.

"I don't see it. Oh, yeah. Now I do. Not much of it, though." He shook his head. "How come you got mud all over it?"

"How come you don't mind your own business? You're supposed to be riding in the wagon." I whisked my hands ineffectually over my muddied pink skirt and scuffed the soles of my shoes—a white suède pair I'd slipped into during the air raid—on the grass to clean them.

"I'm sick of riding," said Joey.

"You only rode once." Marty picked a crinkled leaf from one of the wagon wheels.

"Just the same, I'm sick of it. Besides, I've got to go to the bathroom. I guess I'll go use that pail by the mattresses."

I almost let him do it. I almost said: Go clomp your noisy little feet into the living room and wake your mother. Shout if you want to. Kick the pail over. Just do something, anything, so someone else will have to cope with you before I go completely berserk.

Dora Bendel kept me from putting my thoughts into words and deeds.

"Do you have an extra lemon I could borrow, April?" she called from her porch. "Two if you can spare that many."

"I can if Iyaga hasn't used them." I stopped Joey before he went to the pail. "Can Joey borrow your bathroom? I don't want him to go through the house and wake Liz."

"Sure." She opened the door for Joey.

I got the lemons and left them with Dora, and then I got Joey, whom I'd have happily left with Dora (or with anyone, for that matter), and he and Marty and I walked to Liz's.

"I want to get the radio before it starts raining again." I glanced at the leaden sky and moved more rapidly.

When we arrived, Marty squatted down on the side lawn to look for four-leaf clovers and Joey hurdled the low wooden sign that read CAPTAIN BERTRAM SNYDER, M.D.

Captain Bertram Snyder, M.D. isn't home, I thought. He doesn't live here any more. He lived here yesterday—just as Lang lived in a house like this and other men lived in other houses like this, but Captain Snyder doesn't live here now. No one lives here now.

My morbidity persisted while Marty stayed in the clover patch and Joey (figuring he'd have more control over Willard by donning a more suitable hat) found his policeman's cap and rejoined her. As I unplugged the radio and wrote a note telling Bert where his family was, I tried to subdue my imagination; I tried to look upon the temporary emptiness of the rooms as temporary. But I couldn't shake the illusion that the house no longer belonged to anyone, that it had changed since morning into a haunted museum of a house where no one would ever live again. The shattered hall window seemed

68

the work of passing vandals, and I felt like a trespasser as I tiptoed into the kitchen to see whether or not the bullet holes were really in the door.

They were. While I traced their edges with my finger, I found myself quoting some lines of verse I had learned long ago in school, back in an impossibly serene country, in an impossibly serene time.

> "They are all gone away,
> There is nothing more to say."

Although I wasn't frightened by the stillness and the solitude, not really (I knew the whispering and tiptoeing were caused by the improbability of the day), I was glad to leave the house.

Honey Lopez (she actually used Honey as a nickname) was going past, exercising her toy poodle. I didn't know her very well, partly because she was a new arrival and partly because I disapproved of her in spite of myself. She walked with her usual hip-rolling gait, wearing an open black sateen coat and a too-tight, too-short orange dress that showed off her incredible, six-foot figure.

"Not my idea of a jazzy afternoon, but join me." Honey, who used to be a walker in a circus before she married ("All you have to be is statuesque, stacked, and stupid," she once told me), slackened the leash she was holding. "I don't know why Lopez bought me this bat-eared caterpillar on stilts for a pet." Honey always referred to her husband by his last name. "I feel like an ass every time I take the stinking beast out to unplug his plumbing. A Russian wolfhound would have been more my style. Been to see Liz?"

"No, I just went after the radio. Liz and Joey are living with me." I called the children and fell into step beside her. "Who are you living with? Or vice versa?"

"Myself, so far." Honey, who'd grown more or less accustomed to the snubs of her neighbors, sounded more philosophical than self-pitying. "No other offers. What happened to your shoes? You look like you've been slogging through a swamp."

"I kind of have." My explanation seemed ridiculous, so I kept it short. "I was putting a linoleum rug in the slit trench to make the bottom drier, but the idea didn't work out."

"You never know till you try." She stopped while her poodle investigated a hibiscus bush. "Me, I've been wandering from house to house, looking for a roommate, and I find the so-called ladies are ganging together in nervous, talky little groups. You know. The social types at JayJay Murphy's saying, 'My goodness, who would have thought at yesterday's sherry hour we'd all be having an honest-to-gosh war today?' The Army brats over at the Wilsons' saying what their parents told them about the last war, and deciding how this one should be run." She watched the adjutant's wife going into Mrs. Hunter's.

"And I suppose the senior officers' wives gathering in lonely splendor at Mrs. Hunter's, though I could be wrong about that. Needless to say, I skipped that stop. Mrs. Hunter always makes me feel like I should of stood with the circus." She nudged her poodle with one of her stilt-heeled patent-leather pumps. "Well, let the old girl look down her nose, I say. God knows with a beak like that she ought to get a good look."

"Oh, Mrs. Hunter isn't all that bad. She's just older and more conservative." I didn't care much for the commanding officer's wife myself (she always went around looking regal and acting as if she had as much rank as her husband), but Lang didn't like me to gossip.

"What you mean is she isn't that bad to you." Honey scratched her left ankle under the rhinestone anklet she always wore. "Life is different if you're one of the 'in' kids. Anyhow, I guess it's different. I wouldn't know from experience."

70

"I'm going to Dora Bendel's for tea." I decided to change the subject. "Why don't you come along?"

"That seems a pleasant program. At least it beats the hell out of slinking from door to door like a stray cat." Honey smoothed her swinging platinum hair as the sentry went by. "Looks like the town crier's handing out another batch of announcements. We'd better not let him get too far away. He's the only man around except for the chaplain, and it may be a long, cold, lonely war." She kicked the air behind the poodle as it stopped again.

"Sorry," she said. "I guess I shock you with my candid comments, don't I?"

I wanted to tell Honey that Army wives were conservative, that none of them—even in fun—hinted at consorting with men other than their husbands, especially with enlisted men. I wanted to tell her to tone down her looks: her unseemly dress, her dyed hair, her rhinestone anklet. I wanted to say: You're too overblown, too brash, too blowzy.

"No, you don't shock me," I said. "Why should you?"

"Because I'm a freak in this tight little military setup, that's why. Although I must admit you and Liz and Dora don't go out of your way to rub it in, like some of the other females I could mention."

The rain started again.

"This Christ-awful rain." Honey buttoned the glittering top button of her transparent dress. "I sometimes think it's a secret weapon the Japs are using to bitch up whatever's left of our morale. I hear the bastards are going to rape us all if they land. I'll be interested to see the happy little fellow who takes on old lady Hunter. Or me either, for that matter. Though, like my poor long-suffering mother used to say, there's always a bright side. At least no runty yellow son of a bitch can plant any seeds in *my* garden. I'm already six weeks gone."

"Congratulations." I found Honey's language as disturbing

as her appearance. "I'd like to unload this talk-box." I let the radio, which was heavy, slide down onto my hip. "I hope Liz can work it, because I can't. Would you shoo the kids into Bendels' for me, please?"

"Sure, if you think I'll be welcome."

"*Anyone's* welcome at Dora's." I didn't mean the remark to come out as it did. "That is," I amended hastily, "the more the merrier."

"Don't explain." Honey signaled Marty and Joey. "If the rest of you aren't proud, I'm not." Although the sentry was going from house to house across from us, she pulled up her dress and hitched at her slip as if she were in her bedroom instead of on the street.

"I'll be along as soon as I wake Liz." I was unnerved by Honey's immodesty and found myself chattering compulsively. "She ought to be ready to get up about now."

"What's there to get up for?" Honey asked, and Liz asked the same thing when I went in and shook her.

"Go away, dear," she murmured. "I'm right in the middle of a great dream." She rolled onto her other side and tucked the blanket closer around her soiled and rumpled sun dress. "I'm wearing a red velvet cocktail gown with tinselly stuff at the bottom, and the boss is giving a Christmas party. You should see the house decorations and tree ornaments. All blue and silver. How do you like my new snowflake earrings? I got them at Tiffany's." She gave a contradictory moan, as though something in the dream pained her, and was asleep again before I could reshut the sliding doors.

There was a small group of people at the Bendels'. Not exactly the cream of the crop: Dora had a tendency to mother the lonely and rejected. Jean Workman, a little less frenetic for the moment, was there with Elaine. And, of course, Honey, the flamboyant social misfit. And Willard's mother, AnnaLee Seymour, a steady-drinking ex-Atlanta belle who was doing her best to be a social dropout. And Boots Daly, who was pretty enough with her neat page-boy haircut and neat body and features, and presentable enough with her well-pressed pastel clothes and careful boarding-school manners, but boring . . . boring.

I was surprised to see Boots until I remembered that her erstwhile sidekick, a Gladys somebody, had sailed on the last transport to the mainland. Liz had dubbed Boots and Gladys the Westchester Bobbsey Twins, not because they looked alike but because they thought alike and dressed alike and were inseparable. They both wore bright eager expressions, cultured pearls, McMullen daytime dresses, Bermuda sweaters, and brown-and-white spectator pumps. They both were correct but not showy, both had what they referred to as small modest trust funds, and both were unimaginative and humorless. They entertained together, took up shell collecting or needlepoint together, and shopped together. (They were always searching the Honolulu stores for vital items like white fur bathroom rugs, sensible brocade slipcovers, antique finger bowls, or watercress, none of which they could find.) They'd even managed to get pregnant at the same time; it was their latest bond and project, and they were giving it their mutual undivided attention (exercising, dieting, consulting pregnancy books together) when Gladys' husband was ordered to Benning and Gladys had to leave. Her departure was a betrayal of sorts: Boots had to muddle her way toward motherhood alone. And she was really alone, because she hadn't bothered to make any other friends. ("I mean, how many people can you find around here who like white fur rugs and watercress and brocade slipcovers?" asked Liz.)

It might have been any afternoon at Bendels', except for the mattresses on the dining-room floor. Dora had a fire going, and Sharon—a little stricken around the eyes—was passing sandwiches. Jean Workman was pouring tea, Boots was practicing a new knitting stitch Dora had taught her, and Honey was poking up the logs in the fireplace. AnnaLee Seymour, cutting cake, was humming "Lovely Hula Hands" quietly to herself as she worked at keeping the knife on course.

73

Good old dependable Dora, I thought. She's got everyone occupied. Temporarily, anyhow.

"It takes someone with a steadier hand than mine to handle this teapot." Dora nodded at me as she refilled it. "Hi, April. Is Liz still sleeping?"

"Yes." I dusted some rain from my hair.

Marty and Elaine Workman were sitting on one of the mattresses. They had Honey's poodle between them.

"How come your mother stopped digging?" asked Marty.

"I don't know. She just did." Elaine, whose braided pigtail had come unbraided, scooped some frosting from the cake on her plate. "She quit when the men came around and dug up the yard."

"Your dress is still on backward." Marty scratched the poodle's chin and gave it a cookie. "Where's Raico?"

"Gone," said Elaine.

"Gone where?"

"Just gone."

"Where's your mother's gun?" Joey sat down with them. "The one she had on the porch chair."

"In her pocketbook." As Elaine inclined her head toward the oversized black purse in her mother's lap, I hoped Jean knew more about guns than I did.

"It's got real bullets in it"—Elaine scooped another fingerful of frosting into her mouth—"so I'm not supposed to touch it." She blinked her eyes fast several times, and I thought she was afraid of the gun, but that wasn't what was troubling her.

"My balloon popped, Marty." She kept blinking. "I caught it in the car door when I got out."

Jean, pouring tea in a disinterested fashion, was fretfully expounding on the tribulations of her most recent vain endeavor: trying to get a couple of clipper reservations back to the coast.

"There must be *some* way to reach the clipper office." She was talking to AnnaLee Seymour, who sat near her, frowning or smiling when she thought the occasion demanded it, but

74

not saying much. AnnaLee (whom Liz described as a Southern magnolia with the blight) was wearing faded red shorts although the weather was too cold for shorts, and a cigarette hung, as always, from her lower lip. She looped her vari-colored hair, which could have used a good washing, behind her ears.

"Maybe the clipper office is busy." She winked the rising smoke out of her eyes and spoke fuzzily, either because of her Georgia accent or the alcohol; I never could tell which.

"Or maybe the phone's off the hook." It was Boots Daly from Westchester. "Do you think the clipper's safer than a ship? If so, I'd better get a reservation. Not for myself. I wouldn't mind the ship. But there's the baby to consider." Boots was only a few months pregnant (two and a half, according to her own belabored and exhaustive estimate), but I noticed she had already discarded her McMullen uniform for maternity clothes.

Predictably, she started holding forth on prenatal care. Prenatal wartime care was something she hadn't covered, but she was working at it. She went into the possible relative effects of plane and boat travel on an unborn child, then said she hoped the air raid hadn't influenced her future baby's future emotions too much.

The way she expressed it was: "I'm trying to keep my mind cheerful and uncluttered so the baby won't *realize* about the war." She found herself frowning over her knitting and changed to her bright look.

"This is his second sweater," she announced. "I'm planning on making six. I could buy them, but anyone can do that. I want him to come into the world feeling loved."

"Loved because of a *sweater?*" Honey yawned. "How's he going to know you made it? By osmosis?"

"Something like that." Boots took a sip of tea and asked if a teacup held the same amount of fluid as a glass because, war or no war, she had to keep drinking her eight glasses a day. The book said so.

75

"That's why Dora gave me this pitcher of water." She pointed a knitting needle toward the table. "To catch up. I forgot to drink my usual quota this morning because of all the trouble."

AnnaLee Seymour, who didn't look as if she'd forgotten to drink *her* usual quota that morning because of all the trouble, left her cake-cutting and floated across the room to add some rum to her tea.

"Just another teensy dollop," she said.

Jean Workman went to try the clipper people again and returned berating them.

"They *still* don't answer." She banged back into her chair. "There's no excuse for it. Absolutely no excuse."

Boots said she hadn't taken her regular postbreakfast walk to Wheeler, what with the bombing and all, but she'd gone around the Loop six times, which ought to add up to a mile.

"The pregnancy book says daily exercise is essential. It keeps the muscles toned." She downed a tumbler of water, proudly pronouncing it her seventh glass, and turned to Honey Lopez.

"There's so much to think about when you're pregnant." Boots may not have intended to sound patronizing, but that's how she sounded.

"So I'm beginning to find out." Honey gave another yawn. "However, like the man says, that's the price you pay for getting yourself knocked up."

Boots gasped.

"I beg your pardon." She fought for composure. (Expectant mothers should stay calm for the child's sake.) "This was a *planned* baby. I don't believe you'd make a remark like that if *you* were pregnant."

"I *am* pregnant." Honey shoved her legs out in front of her and yawned a third time.

Boots looked as if the admissions committee had slipped up and let one of the wrong members into her private club. She rose in search of a new audience and went over to bore Sharon.

Dora sat down in her empty chair.

"I'm so happy to hear you're going to have a baby." Dora's pleasure for Honey was heartfelt and heartwarming. "I envy you. I've never been able to have children."

"We're all your children." Honey's reply, like everything about her, was spontaneous and uncontrived, and I began to like her—or at least to like her honesty.

"Even though we're too old for it," she said to Dora, "we're all your children."

"What about children?" AnnaLee floated over to the rum again. "Me, I find one little monster enough." As she bent over the bottle, her hair fell forward and she relooped it behind her ears. "I just can't do a thing with that boy," she added inexplicitly, referring, I suppose, to Willard.

The doorbell rang, and the sentry handed in the latest missive from the bulletin writer. Jean Workman snatched it.

Joey, complaining that the house was too hot, scuttled out in the wake of the sentry.

"I have to go exercise Duff," he said.

Jean read the bulletin and exploded.

"They never know *what* they want us to do." She rustled the sheet furiously. "First, they tell us to bring our mattresses downstairs where it's safer and get in the trenches if the planes come back, and now *this*."

"Now *what?*" Sharon, who was passing more sandwiches, clattered the plate down on the coffee table and widened her eyes apprehensively, while Boots sat up straighter, either from interest or because the book said it was the proper way for expectant mothers to sit.

Jean moved impatiently and her purse slid out of her lap. I half expected the gun to go off, but it didn't.

"THERE WILL BE A COMPLETE AND TOTAL BLACKOUT BEGINNING AT NIGHTFALL." Jean clamped a foot on each

77

side of her pocketbook as if she expected one of us to run over and steal it while she was reading. "THERE WILL BE NO FLASHLIGHTS, HOUSE LIGHTS OR OTHER LIGHTS USED. What in hell are *other* lights? THERE WILL BE NO FIREPLACE FIRES, NO LIGHTED MATCHES, NO LIGHTED CIGARETTES, NO LIGHTED STOVES. THIS IS AN ORDER. ADULT FEMALES WILL CONTINUE TO REMAIN, AS PREVIOUSLY ADVISED, IN HOUSEHOLDS OF TWO, PENDING VEHICULAR EVACUATION FROM THE RESERVATION OF SCHOFIELD BARRACKS, CURRENTLY CONSIDERED A MILITARY OBJECTIVE OF THE ENEMY. ALL WOMEN AND CHILDREN WHO HAVE NOT ALREADY DONE SO ARE INSTRUCTED TO RETURN TO THEIR ALLOTTED QUARTERS, EAT IMMEDIATELY, EXTINGUISH AFOREMENTIONED LIGHTS AND FIRES, DRESS WARMLY AND SENSIBLY, AND SIT OUTSIDE ON FRONT STEPS AWAITING FORTHCOMING TRANSPORTATION AND SUBSEQUENT DEPARTURE TO AN UNANNOUNCED DESTINATION. THIS IS A PRECAUTIONARY MEASURE. THERE IS NO NEED TO PANIC."

Sharon, who had been tearing up a Kleenex during the reading and wadding it into little balls, began to cry.

"It gets scarier and scarier," she said.

"No, it doesn't." Dora stacked the Wedgwood cups and saucers on a black tin tray decorated with gilt flowers. "Just more and more practical. They say they're taking a precautionary measure. It never hurts to take precautions."

"That's what my gynecologist kept telling me, but I wouldn't listen." Honey broke the tension, and everyone laughed except Boots and Jean.

"Well, live and learn." Honey dropped the used napkins she'd been collecting into the fireplace. "I'll pay more attention to the peep-show boys after this." She started dumping the cigarette butts in with the blazing napkins. "How do we go about putting out this fire, Dora? If I throw water on it, you're going to have a stinking gloppy mess on your hands."

"The mess doesn't matter." Dora corked the rum as Anna-

Lee headed for it again. "Sharon. Go fill the mop pail and pour it in the fireplace, will you, please?"

"And for God's sake don't leave any sparks!" Jean Workman's voice, speaking to Sharon's retreating back, was nearly as shrill as when she'd been dressing out Raico earlier. "Come *on*, Elaine. We're leaving! Get up on your feet!"

Elaine got as far up as her knees.

"Can Marty spend the night with me?" she asked.

"My-God-don't-you-ever-listen-you've-got-ears." Jean fumbled her purse around under her arm, and I tried not to wonder in which direction the gun barrel was pointing. "The bulletin says *get ready to go!* No one's going to spend the night with anyone."

"That reminds me." Dora pulled the fire screen aside so Sharon could empty the mop pail, and there was a loud hissing as the smell of wet ashes filled the room. "Those of you who don't have house mates had better get them while you're here." I don't know how and when Dora found out who was living alone, but, being Dora, she had found out.

"Boots, why don't you double up with Jean?" she suggested. "And Honey, I'm sure AnnaLee would like to have you over with her. Does that suit everyone?"

Boots and Honey said yes, Jean said she supposed so, and AnnaLee, who had taken off her sneakers to practice the hula, was humming and didn't hear.

"Oh, my goodness." Boots stopped buttoning the gray Bermuda sweater that matched her eyes. "I forgot. I'm almost out of calcium pills. Do you have any, Honey?"

"No, why should I?" Honey lifted her poodle off the mattress by its leash.

"For *teeth*. Don't you want any bones and teeth?"

"I already have some." Honey's levity was lost on Boots, who folded her knitting into her green knitting bag and said: "April, do *you* have any pills?"

"Run over and look in the medicine cabinet. The bottle

with the blue label." I felt a wave of nausea as Sharon emptied the mop pail on the fire again, making the ash smell worse. "Don't worry about waking Liz. I'll have to get her up in a second, anyhow."

Jean, who didn't seem to care whether Boots joined her or not, had gotten as far as the porch. She came pounding back to yammer at Elaine, who'd loitered behind to snitch the frosting off a leftover piece of cake.

Honey pushed Elaine toward her mother.

"Forget the goodies and get cracking, kid," she said. "You're still wearing a fair amount of icing, in case you happen to get hungry later on. Coming, AnnaLee, old girl?"

AnnaLee, making a feint at alertness, stopped dancing and started for the door.

"Oh," she said, "oh, yes."

"Better put on a little footgear." Honey brought AnnaLee her sneakers, saying, "In we go," before she steered her off. Jean and Elaine and Boots had already gone, with Marty behind them, and in a minute or so I followed.

The rain had settled down to a drizzle. As I cut across the lawn, I passed Willard Seymour sitting and swinging his legs in our slit trench, impervious to the dampness and cold. Joey, secure on the porch with Duff, was ranting about some recent misdemeanor of Willard's.

"Liar!" said Joey. "You know darned well you're a liar!"

"That *boy*." AnnaLee Seymour wove a little as she floated home with Honey beside her. "It looks like he's at it again. I tell you, I simply can't do a thing with him."

"Hadn't he better eat?" Honey, surveying Willard coolly, tried not to ignore his basic needs.

"Oh, I suppose so." The smoke from AnnaLee's cigarette drifted up around her nostrils as she worked at putting her feet down carefully on the walk. "Willard"—she pronounced it "Willud"—"come get some soup or something."

Willard regarded her as if she were a car going by. Or a cat or dog. Or nothing.

"I already did." He stayed where he was and went on swinging his legs.

"Shouldn't he have a raincoat on?" Again, Honey wasn't being particularly solicitous, just practical.

"Shouldn't you have a raincoat on, Willard?" echoed Anna-Lee.

"The fact is, no," he replied, and I couldn't help thinking he'd gotten at least one fact right. A graven image doesn't need a raincoat. The devil doesn't need a raincoat. AnnaLee may not have been much of a mother, but even if she'd been the Madonna herself, I don't believe it would have changed things much.

Marty jiggled my arm.

"Can I stay outdoors and play with Willard?"

"No, you can't, and don't ask me for a reason." My answer was rougher than I meant it to be as I pulled her into the house.

Boots had come and gone and Liz was awake. She still acted exhausted in spite of her long sleep. Her color made me think of the white strawberries I had seen growing beside a crater one morning over on the Big Island . . . the strawberries that ripened but remained pale and sickly looking. I don't know why the comparison occurred to me when it did; usually Liz looked healthy enough.

"Are you all right?" I asked.

"Sure, dear," she answered, "if you don't care what you say."

"Meaning what?"

"Meaning if you don't press me for details. I'm bone-weary and I keep having gas pains." She paused. "Otherwise, I'm fit as a fiddle." She clutched her stomach. "A fiddle that's been run over by a truck," she said.

"No wonder you don't feel well." I struggled to keep another fear at bay. "You haven't eaten all day."

"No, and I'm not about to start now."

"You can at least drink an eggnog. I'll fix it."

81

I made her an eggnog with sherry in it and brought her up
to date on the bulletin writer's latest ideas and conclusions. I
found a barracks bag of Lang's and when I thought of how it
belonged to him, how he'd bought and touched and used it, I
stroked it a moment with my hand, the way I sometimes
stroked my wedding ring with my thumb. The gesture was a
sentimental and useless one; it didn't bring Lang back, and it
didn't comfort me. All it did was start me thinking again of
things it did no good to think about; all it did was reinforce
the loneliness I'd been doing my best to ward off. I swung the
barracks bag upward by the looped cord, so I'd know it was
nothing more than a blue and stitched piece of canvas, nothing
more than a carrying case. I filled it with some cans of fruit
juice, a bottle of rye, a Thermos of milk, and the box of
crackers I'd left beside the mattresses earlier in the day. I
asked Liz to try the radio, but she couldn't work it, either. I
sent the kids to use the bathroom, I reminded my sister to use
it, and I used it myself. I shut Duff, along with a pan of dog
food and one of water, on the porch, where he wouldn't wander
or litter the house. I collected a pile of coats and sweaters and
rubbers for all of us, and some head scarves for Marty and
me. (Joey was still wearing his policeman's hat, and Liz—in
a leftover stab at the sartorial splendor depicted in the pages
of *Lovely Lady*—insisted on swathing her head in a striped
turban.) I folded an Army blanket lengthwise on the outer
front steps, and the four of us bundled up and went and sat
on it, reversing our coat collars against the light but con-
tinuous rain, and waited in a tight little row for whatever it
was we were waiting for.

Up and down the street, other women and children sat on
other sets of steps in tight little rows, exchanging comments
or not, acting resigned or not, looking valiant or not. Dora
and Sharon spoke from the right of us, and Honey and Anna-
Lee Seymour waved from the left. AnnaLee had on lavender
velveteen slacks and a sweater of Willard's that was too small
for her. She was smoking and humming to herself, as if she

didn't know there was a war going on, as if she had just decided to wait on the steps until it was time to go to the movies or over to someone's house for cocktails.

Willard wasn't on the top step with his mother and Honey. He was slumped sidewise on the bottom one. I won't say he was facing us—no one ever knew whom or what Willard was facing—but he was facing in our direction.

His face was blank, disclosing nothing of what he felt or thought.

"Graves," he said, just loud enough for us to hear, pitching his voice so it sounded like a wind moaning in winter. "Don't forget about the graves."

"Shut up!" Joey, far enough away from Willard to be safe from possible retaliation, tried to create an impression of authority by batting the crown of his policeman's hat.

"Handcuffs is what I need," he said to Marty. "Handcuffs and a gun. *That* would show him."

"Sh-h-h." Marty started whispering.

I looked at the still-gray but still-daylit world and felt I had to do something besides look at it. I reached into the barracks bag for a pack of cigarettes and lighted one, though I didn't want it.

"What was all that for?" Liz watched me step on the cigarette after a few drags. "Afraid you'll never smoke again?"

"Maybe that's it." I tightened the knot of my head scarf. "Like the condemned man ate a hearty breakfast."

"Don't mention breakfast or any other kind of food." Liz, whose gas pains had either become fewer or less acute, folded her arms across her chest. "I'm trying to forget I ever drank that eggnog."

Someone across the street began singing a hymn, and a second person joined in. The singing had a forced and embarrassed quality to it, and I was glad when it died out after the first verse.

Liz shivered once or twice, and Duff growled uneasily from the porch. Joey straightened the folded-in flap of one

83

of his rubbers while he and Marty whispered together, and —without knowing quite why I did it—I reached over and touched the crumpled petals of the lowest flower on the doomed poinsettia tree.

Then darkness—which comes down like a springless black window shade in the tropics—unrolled in the sky and fell.

Two

THE NIGHT

3

MARTY

Father wasn't at our house that time in the morning when I thought he'd be there, the time when I finally caught up with Mother going after the food. So I guess Joey's hanging onto me in his living room didn't really matter, though I told Mother how bad he'd been and how I'd lost my salamander. She wasn't much impressed, just figured it was one of Joey's and my squabbles, the way Aunt Liz must have figured when the fight was going on. Anyhow, right after that we moved, which gave us all other things to think about.

It seems to me we spent a lot of the day of December seventh making trips to Aunt Liz's. Even after we were meant to be settled down at our house, Mother took Joey and me back again so she could lock the door or something. Coming home we met that lady who seemed so tall to me then, the one named Mrs. Lopez, whose hair was like the fairy hair in my picture books and whose red dress was so thin that the top lace of her underwear showed through. She had a bracelet of diamonds—I guess they were diamonds—on her leg instead of her arm, and she let me walk her Scottie dog. The four of us went to lunch at Mrs. Bendel's, and Elaine and her mother

87

were there, and a Mrs. Daly, who talked about babies all the time. Also Willard Seymour's mother. Mrs. Workman was neater and had her hair piled up in a tower again, but Elaine was still a sight.

"I see Raico never got around to dressing you," I said.

"She couldn't." Elaine plunked herself down on the floor. "Mother sent her away somewhere."

"Too bad," I said. "She was a good maid."

"Yes, she was," agreed Elaine. "She made good popcorn."

Mrs. Bendel didn't have a maid, so Mother helped her serve lunch, and so did Sharon, who lived there. Sharon was in love with that smiling, swimming officer called Sharkbait, and sometimes she worked at the Wheeler Field playground. She used to run and laugh and play with us, acting as if there wasn't anything sad anywhere, back in the days before she began crying so much. The war made her cry. It made other people do other things, but it made Sharon cry.

We didn't eat all of Mrs. Bendel's lunch, though everyone ate some of it, especially Elaine, who stuffed herself on cucumber sandwiches. While Mrs. Bendel was pouring coffee, Sharkbait came around with his men and dug some trenches out front, and Joey and I went and watched him before he moved over into Willard's yard. Our trench, like all the trenches, was pretty wet from the rain, so Mother put the straw matting we usually took to the beach in the bottom of it, trying to make it drier. The matting didn't do much good, though; Joey came out of the trench covered with mud when he fell in. Well, he didn't exactly fall in. What happened was he had on his fire-chief hat, and Willard Seymour said a good fireman could jump any ditch, big or little, so Joey jumped and didn't make it, and then he blamed Willard.

Joey was always blaming Willard. For instance, just before dark, when we were putting a pan of water and a bone on the lanai for Duff, he got all steamed up because of something Willard had supposedly told him about the trenches.

"He says they're not really trenches; they're graves." Joey

was mad, but he shuddered just the same. "He says we're all going to be planted in them. He's a liar. I know he's a liar."

"What do you mean 'planted'?" I thought I knew, but I wasn't sure.

"Planted's bad. Planted means buried. The cowboys do it, kind of on a little sandy hill. They shovel a hole and put a white cross on top, like at Easter, and the men don't talk and those women with the hats that poke out in front of their faces bawl. Buried messes up the movie," said Joey.

"Look." I pointed. "There's Willard coming out of his house. Let's go ask if he was fooling about the graves. I bet that's what he was doing; fooling. Mother wouldn't put straw matting in a grave."

"You go." Joey whacked Duff's bone against the screen. "I'm not going anywheres near him, and if he comes around here, I'll sick Duff on him."

"You won't sick Duff on anyone." Mother wanted to know if I'd go out to the maid's quarters and get the extra blanket off Iyaga's bed.

"The tan one," she said, and I hurried off, partly because I hoped Iyaga might be home from her weekly trip to the cane fields and partly because I'd never seen the inside of her house.

Iyaga was still away, and I was disappointed about that. Also about her house, which turned out to be two tiny rooms with hardly any windows, and a mildewed shower in between.

I took the blanket to Mother.

"I'm glad I don't live where Iyaga does," I said. "Did you know her floor is just dirt?"

"Yes, I know." Mother spread the blanket on the steps. "It's not a very fancy house, but she's used to it. Here. You and Joey put on these clothes. It's getting late."

Joey didn't want to wear his rubbers, but he finally put them on, and after that we all went out and sat on the steps. Everyone was sitting on steps, including Willard, who called and said something about the graves. What he said wasn't much, but it was enough to bother Joey, who began carrying on. Mother told him to hush, or Aunt Liz did, but he didn't really hush, just switched from talking to whispering.

It wasn't very nice sitting out in the rain, especially when the day ended. We couldn't see anything, the night was so black, and Aunt Liz was cold, so Mother decided to get the couch cover off the lanai and put it over her. That was when she went inside and stepped on Duff in the dark.

She let out a curse, and Aunt Liz asked what was wrong.

"Your miserable dog bit me. That's what's wrong." Mother was very cross.

"I wonder why he did that, dear. Are you bleeding much?"

"How should *I* know?" Mother made a series of shuffly thuds that sounded like hopping. "Did you ever bleed in a blackout after sitting in the rain? I can't tell what's water and what's blood. I suppose I'd better go upstairs and get some iodine." The living-room door opened and closed—we could hear that—and after a time it opened and closed again.

Doors, doors, doors, I thought. And stairways and lanais. Saturday and the days before Saturday we used them and paid no attention to using them. But Sunday was different. Someone was always opening a door, shutting a door, walking onto a lanai, off a lanai, up steps or down, and nothing about it was the same.

"My compliments, Dr. Livingstone." Aunt Liz was suddenly talking the new way, the way she and Mother talked ever afterward when they got together during the war, calling each other those funny names they sometimes call each other even now. "I trust your journey through the wilderness was successful and the natives friendly. You weren't gone long."

"Long enough, Stanley." Mother banged the screen door and dropped the couch cover on top of my head instead of into Aunt Liz's lap. "When I got to the lower hall I realized I'd never be able to find anything, including my way, so I turned back.

"Damn dog," she added, and as I handed the cover to my

aunt I found I was no longer surprised by Mother's swearing, any more than I was surprised when she began talking the new way, too: joking but not joking, acting as if she didn't care about anything, but not really that, either. It was mostly a tone of voice, but also an attitude, a defense—I know now —against all painful contingencies, present and to come.

"Hell, I'll just stay here and bleed," she said. "I have nothing better to do."

Joey had to go to the bathroom again, and Aunt Liz told him to stand up and water the lawn.

"Only don't walk forward," she said, "or you might land in the slit trench."

"It's not just water." Joey never left anything to anyone's imagination.

"Now, *there's* one of the less-heralded little wartime problems." Mother made the huffly noise that meant she was either tired or disgusted. "Certainly you can't take him upstairs, Liz; you might trip and fall. And if I go, Duff's apt to get me in the other leg." She huffled some more.

"Though at least I could limp evenly that way," she said.

"I couldn't help overhearing." Mrs. Bendel told Mother to put Joey facing the building with his hands against the screen. "And, Joey," she said, "you slide over here without dropping your hands or stepping backward. Understand?" So that's what Mother and Joey did, and pretty soon I could hear my cousin's hands whooshing away along the screen and afterward whooshing back.

"Did you and Mrs. Bendel have any trouble finding the bathroom?" Aunt Liz shifted beside me, and I could feel her shivering, even with the couch cover over her.

"We didn't use the bathroom. We used the porch. Mrs. Bendel helped me." Joey sat down on my knee by mistake and grumbled, "Watch it," as though it were my fault instead of his.

"Oh, no, Dora!" Mother acted shocked. "Not on that lovely wall-to-wall lahalla rug you just bought?"

But Mrs. Bendel didn't answer. Anyhow not about the rug.

"Look," was all she said, "I think there's something coming."

It was the trucks. We didn't know they were trucks in the beginning, because all we could make out was a long line of double lights, dim and not too far apart, that curved into sight, moving and stopping, moving and stopping. But eventually the line drew up opposite us and we could tell what the lights were: headlights and taillights and a flashlight that finally approached us, throwing a pale circle of brightness on the ground around a pair of walking feet, a man's feet.

A voice above the flashlight said: "I've come to guide you to the trucks, but don't get up until I tell you. I'll take you two by two."

I wasn't dreaming—I know I wasn't because I remember all the talk about Duff and Joey and Mrs. Bendel's rug—but for a moment I thought the voice was Father's. I thought he'd returned to see if things were all right with Mother and me, to make things all right if they were wrong. I thought he was coming to find us, to be with us, before we went off into the unknown darkness without him.

"Father," I called. "Oh, Father!" but just then Sharon called "Adam!" and when the flashlight man spoke again he said, "Sharon, my lovely Sharon," and I knew Father would never have said that.

The light went up and down the Bendels' walk before it came to ours.

"Hi, Mrs. Langsmith, Mrs. Snyder." Sharkbait's ghostly grin came out of the night. "Hi, kids. Who's next?"

"You and Marty, Liz," decided Mother, and my aunt and I went off, one on each side of Sharkbait, and after that so did Mother and Joey.

"I know this bus." Joey climbed over the tailgate onto the innermost crosswise bench where the rest of us sat facing the rear opening. "It's the bus to the Wheeler Field playground. Oh, boy. Let's go."

"Another time, fire chief. The playground's closed tonight." Sharkbait disappeared and returned with Mrs. Lopez, who said, "Hi, kiddo," as she brushed by me. I wanted to say "Hi" back again, but I couldn't get the word out. Not because I felt unfriendly toward Mrs. Lopez but because I felt unfriendly toward everything else.

The twin headlights glittering beyond our tailgate reminded me of two huge lidless blue eyes weeping tears of rain, and I didn't like them. I didn't like the truck. I didn't like the night. I didn't like my wet clothes. I didn't like anything about anything.

"Shouldn't we have left a note for Father?" I touched Mother's arm. "He won't know where we're going."

"Neither will the rest of us till we get there." The words (Mrs. Workman's, I think) came from deep in the truck, and I didn't want to hear them, so I pretended I hadn't. I closed my own eyes to shut away the weepy monster eyes of the headlights and did my best to force a happier picture into my mind. I tried to see my red beach ball resting on the Wianae sands. I tried to see one of my green fishing floats with my bed lamp back of it making it sparkle. I tried to see my orange balloon bobbing against the safe ceiling of my warm, dry room. But the beach ball blew away, and the fishing float wouldn't let the light through, and the balloon hissed and dropped like a little rag onto the floor. And after that I saw Father. I saw him the way I'd seen him earlier at Joey's when I couldn't find my lost salamander. He was walking up and down the Loop with a flashlight, shining it into our house, into my aunt's house, into all the empty houses, saying: "Where's my April? Has anyone seen my Spring Song?" He asked the two questions quietly at first; then I heard him shouting them into the unanswering dark.

The beam of light fell on my face and I opened my eyes.

"Steady there, Mrs. Seymour. You're the last passenger."
Sharkbait lowered the light onto the seat beside me, and I
slid over to make more room. Then he kissed Sharon—not
exactly with everyone looking, because no one could see that
well or cared that much, but with everyone there—and told
us he had to get the rest of the trucks loaded.

"Good-bye and good luck to you all," he said, and swung
himself down out of sight.

Sharon did what I was pretty sure she was going to do:
started crying again. I never heard anyone cry so much.

I was already tired of the trip. It hadn't begun, but I was
tired of it. The seats were backless and hard, and there was
nothing to look at through the door but the headlights on the
next truck. No, that's wrong. There was another light—one
from a motorcycle—that appeared and disappeared, as the
cyclist zipped and roared up and down the other side of the
road.

"Like a damn sheepdog herding his flock," Mother said the
second time he came by. I guess it was Mother. She and Aunt
Liz had taken to talking so much alike it was hard to tell.

Mrs. Seymour, squeezing close to me, had a funny smell
about her. Liquor, I realize now. When I asked her where
Willard was, she said she supposed he was in another truck;
he'd broken away from her and Mrs. Lopez and scampered off.
(She pronounced it "skampud.") Mrs. Seymour didn't seem
to miss Willard much. She began humming, trying to tap her
foot to the song, but she couldn't seem to get the beat right.

"Are you here, Elaine?" I turned around, but I couldn't see
her or anyone.

"Yup." Elaine sounded sleepy. "I'd like to go to bed, but
I can't. I wish we'd go somewhere, though."

I wished the same thing. The way the trucks kept starting
and stopping, starting and stopping, I didn't think we'd ever
get underway. But finally our driver made a sharp turn that
cut off our view of the trailing blue headlights; and when the
next truck turned, too, and the headlights moved back into

their old position, I knew we had to be out on the avenue by the barracks. We crawled along and crawled along, making more turns or not making more turns, until we came to the Kemoo gate, the gate that meant we were leaving Schofield. I knew when we did that, because the motorcycle man whoomed by, lighting up one of the shadowy stone posts as we passed between them.

Afterward we couldn't see anything beside the road for a long, long time except flashes of cane fields, like walls, whenever the motorcycle man went by.

It was boring in the truck, driving and driving and driving. Now and then someone spoke but not about anything interesting. Mrs. Daly was there, still going on about her baby. Though I couldn't see her, I knew who she was by what she said. And I could recognize Mrs. Workman's voice because of the way she yelled when Mrs. Seymour forgot about the rules and lit a cigarette. Once there were things in the sky like big shooting stars and everyone got scared and thought the Japs were back. Mrs. Workman screeched, "Duck, Elaine!" and Sharon—I'm pretty sure it was Sharon—began crying again. And Mrs. Daly kept saying she wasn't going to lose control—it might upset the baby—though she didn't sound half as controlled as Mrs. Seymour, who kept humming through everything, while Mother and Aunt Liz talked together the new way, and some other woman started praying.

" 'The Lord is my shepherd,' " said the praying woman, not quietly to herself but loud and fast like a radio commercial. " 'I shall not want. He maketh me to lie down in green pastures: He leadeth me beside the still waters . . .' "

The praying woman stuck to her prayers even after the motorcycle man came sputtering through the spooky cane-field walls and told us the shooting stars weren't anything to worry about.

Sharon stopped crying and Mrs. Workman bleated, "What next? What next?" and Joey said his eye was twitching; what was he meant to do about it.

"Nothing," answered Aunt Liz.

" 'Surely goodness and mercy shall follow me all the days of my life; and I will dwell in the house of the Lord for ever.' " The praying woman finished her psalm. I knew it was a psalm because I got a gold star for learning it in Sunday school.

"Amen," said the praying woman.

Mrs. Seymour swayed a little beside me and quit humming.

"Amen," said Mrs. Seymour.

We rode on—on and on and on through the blackness—and after I'd stared and stared at the hated blue headlights weeping onto the inky macadam of the road, I grew drowsy listening to the rumbling hum of the wheels and put my head against Mother's shoulder. I may even have slept; I'm not sure. All I remember is that one minute I was staring at the never-ending night, and the next thing I knew we were going over a hill and I could see a great brightness through the arched opening of the truck. A wind had started to blow, not a sustained wind but a gusty one, and I could hear the canvas roof fluttering.

"Has the day come?" I asked Mother, but just then the wind got under the lacings of the truck cover so it rattled and flapped and suddenly flipped up at one side, like a jack-in-the-box lid, before it tore loose completely and bumbled and bounced away into the receding cane fields.

As I sat there with the other women and children exposed to the wind and rain, Mother didn't tell me whether the day had come or not; she didn't need to tell me. I could see the high round oil tanks that meant we were above Pearl Harbor, and beyond them the whole wide sea and sky were alight. But it wasn't the light of a new morning; it wasn't a sunrise.

It was the fleet burning.

The great graceful ships, the gray-and-white ships, the ships we passed whenever we drove to Honolulu, weren't ships any more. Their flames reached upward and outward and into each other, doubling themselves in the mirror of the silver-and-orange sea.

There was silence in the truck, the kind of silence I used to notice in church before the minister and choir came in, the kind where a cough or a shuffle or rustle or squeak became part of the silence instead of interrupting it. I looked at the wet gray faces around me—wet from rain and tears, gray from weariness and grief—and I wanted to shriek, but I didn't shriek. I wanted to say something but I didn't know what to say. I wanted to hear a voice, any voice but most of all Father's, speaking quietly and sanely into the silence. I wanted to hear a sound, any sound except the rumbling hum of the wheels moving along more quickly now that there was light enough to see by.

The first sound came from Mother. She sat stiffly, weeping but ignoring the weeping, and said something to my aunt. A minute later Aunt Liz doubled over, and I noticed there were big drops of water on her forehead that didn't look as if they came from the rain.

She put both hands on her stomach and rocked backward and forward on the bench.

"April!" she cried. "It isn't gas pains. It can't be gas pains. It's the baby. Help me!"

"Oh, no," Mother said. "I mean, yes," said Mother. "How?" she asked and gazed wildly at the ships, away from the ships, around her at the speechless passengers, behind her at the driver no longer hidden from view.

"I'll think of something," she said, but Mrs. Bendel was already on her feet, flagging down the motorcycle man, who signaled the line to a halt and made everyone get out of the truck except my aunt and Mrs. Bendel.

"Drive as fast as you can to the hospital at Shafter," the motorcycle man told our driver.

I don't know why Joey wasn't scared, but he didn't seem to be. He looked more confused than worried when we were all on the highway, standing in little clumps under the fiery sky.

"Where's Mom going?" He watched the truck veer out of the line into the other lane of the road and speed away. "I thought she only had to throw up. She always throws up."

Mother watched the truck, too.

"She's gone away to get some rest," said Mother.

The rest of us crowded into other trucks—with Mother and Sharon and Joey and me in the last one—and the only person I remember noticing once we started to ride again was an older lady all in blue who looked too dressed up for a war. Most of the women had on clothes like slacks and sneakers, even Mother, who'd changed into something sensible just before darkness fell. I don't remember much about the last of the trip except the rows and rows of empty cars beside the road. Sometimes I'm not even sure I remember the cars, because Mother doesn't. I don't remember whether we drove past houses or through pineapple fields or up hills or around bends or under trees. It couldn't have been late, but it seemed later than late; and just when I was wondering if we'd go on riding forever—riding, riding, riding to the edges of the world and over—we slowed up going down a little slope, and the humming wheels stopped.

The motorcycle man rode up and down the line of trucks.

"You can get out now," he told us. "This is your home for the night."

It wasn't much of a home, just a lot of one-story buildings that turned out to be locked schoolrooms with porches.

When the lady in blue asked why the rooms were locked, the motorcycle man said that wasn't his department.

"You're to sleep on the porches next to the inner walls," he said. "End to end or head to toe, whichever way you care to put it. We brought some blankets"—he pointed at several stacks of them on the ground—"and there's a washroom open in the first building, and there'll be a sentry on for your protection." He walked away and to this day I don't know why we slept where we did. Maybe no one had keys to the class-rooms. Maybe there wasn't enough space indoors because of the school desks. Whatever the reason, we did as we were told. We slept, when we slept, on the porches.

At first everyone wandered around. A number of women gathered in the washroom, partly to use it, partly to talk, while others collected their blankets and chose places to spread them. And everywhere there were children, not only from our Loop but also from all over Schofield, who followed their mothers or played tag on the playground or just stood and watched the ships burning. As the fires burned on and on, most of the watchers lost interest and turned away, but a few kept watch-ing, sort of like Joey used to do when he sat through a second show of the movies, knowing there was nothing new to see.

Willard was one of the ship watchers. He was sitting on the ground apart from everyone else, and I couldn't tell if the glow on his face came from the light of the ships or from something else.

"Hello, Willard," I said. "Can I come sit with you?"

Willard didn't say yes or no.

"Isn't it sad about the fleet?" I was doing my best to be nice.

"What's sad about it?" Willard didn't change expression, because he didn't have any expression to change. "The fact is, I consider it a pretty good fire."

"But there were men on the ships." As I started to sit down, I tried to picture the men but I couldn't.

Willard must have seen me through the side of his head, because he told me to find my own sitting place.

"Scram, kid," he said. "This is private property."

I knew it wasn't private property, but I did as he said: I scrammed.

I ran into Elaine in the washroom.

"Hi, Marty," she said. "Want to go play tag?"

"I guess I won't. It's mostly boys and they crash into you too much. I came to find Mother and Sharon."

Sharon was washing her eyes, and Mother was pouring Joey a cup of some pineapple juice she'd brought. Elaine edged closer, so Mother poured another cup for her. I didn't want any.

I didn't stay in the washroom long. Mrs. Workman started fighting with Mrs. Lopez, and I didn't like that, so I went and stood outside the door where I wouldn't have to listen. But it wasn't any better there. A big boy—I've forgotten who—was bashing bugs on the wall with his shoe, and though some of the bugs tried to scurry away, not many of them made it. So I wandered off and sat swinging in one of the playground swings till I noticed Mrs. Workman and Elaine coming out of the washroom. Then I went to join Mother.

I almost bumped into Mrs. Lopez in the doorway.

"I think I'll go find me a jouncy mile or so of floor and stretch out on it," she said.

"Hey, where's your dog?" asked Joey.

"I turned him loose before I left home." Mrs. Lopez dodged around me, patting my head as she passed. "Don't worry. He eats avocados so he won't starve, worse luck."

"Oh, there you are, Marty." Mother swung her laundry bag up by the rope. "Come on, Sharon and Joey. It's late," she said, and we followed her out onto the porches.

It was hard to rest because of the mattressless floors, the swarming mosquitoes, the light from the fleet, the wailing of babies, the whining of the older children, the complaints of the grownups, the weeping of Sharon. Also the prayers of the praying woman—the woman whose voice I can still hear though I never was able to put a face to the voice. And always there were the fears for tomorrow although the night had brought no new dangers, always the wondering about Aunt Liz although she was with Mrs. Bendel. Some people coughed, some moaned, some sighed, some slapped at their faces and necks, and some lay stiller than still, once they'd arranged themselves under their blankets in long single rows, settling down to sleep or not to sleep, to dream or not to dream.

100

I dreamed. I dreamed so graphic and sequential a dream that I remember it even now; I remember it as clearly as the lion dreams that came later, although I guess I really didn't dream all of it. I guess that as I slept and woke and slept again—or else hovered in the twilit place that is neither consciousness nor sleep—I fantasied bits and pieces, afterward fitting them together into something I could bear.

Because when I first slept, slept with the light from the dying fleet flickering across my face, I dreamed that Father and I were swimming through the stained and steaming waters of the harbor, and I couldn't bear that.

"Let's not stay here, Father," I said. "We'll be burned. We'll be burned like the ships!"

But Father only smiled. He smiled as if he knew something and wanted to save it for a surprise. Then he stopped swimming and so did I, which frightened me.

"Watch this," he said. And he held up one arm the way he sometimes did when he was about to drop down to the ocean bottom to see how deep the water was.

That frightened me, too, because as I kept treading water —treading and treading and treading—I was afraid he'd disappear and never return from the bottom of the sea.

Father didn't go down to the bottom, though. He stayed on top of the waves, and as he held up his arm, the fleet suddenly stopped burning, and I saw the fires turn into great, graceful ships again and sail majestically and silently out of the bay.

"See, Marty," said Father. "We're not swimming at Pearl Harbor. We never swim at Pearl Harbor. We're at Wianae."

And he put his hand under my elbow, and I laughed up at him, and we went shoreward under the peaceful blue-and-white Sunday sky, through the foamy blue-and-white breakers, back to the beach where my pretty mother lay curled like a kitten on her straw mat and the sand castles waited square and wet and glistening, with lots of little moats around them to let the water in.

101

4

APRIL

The day of the air raid was traumatic and wearing, but at least we were warm and dry most of the time, and there was light in the world. The night was another matter. As we waited for the trucks to reach our Loop, the moments seemed to stretch into a dark infinity. Joey, as usual, had to go to the bathroom and when I started to take him inside Duff bit me on the ankle, so I had to abandon the trip and call on Dora for help. I thought Dora would take Joey upstairs but instead she let him use her lanai, which made me feel badly until she said: "What's the difference, April? We'll be leaving in a little while, anyway." And, of course, she was right because—again—the rules and niceties of yesterday no longer applied.

The evacuation convoy finally finished collecting passengers from the other sections of Schofield and snaked its way around to where we were sitting, and, when it did, we felt a gratitude of sorts; but the gratitude was short-lived because as soon as we were settled inside the trucks we realized that all we'd done was exchange one set of discomforts for another.

"Well, there goes our last link with the opposite sex," said Honey when Lieutenant Dawson left us.

"You forget. There's always the driver." The voice might have belonged to any one of Honey's critical contemporaries. "Don't forget the driver wears pants, too."

"I sure as hell hope so." Honey made light of the cut. "Otherwise, the poor bastard's going to get mighty cold in the crotch out in all this weather."

"Cold," murmured AnnaLee Seymour. "Right cold." I don't know if she was referring to the driver, the weather, or herself.

"I could swear I felt the baby kick." Boots was at it again. "Wouldn't you call that odd?"

"I'd call it odd as hell." Honey indulged in a bit of casual sarcasm. "Pretty active little embryo you've got there. Better write a letter to Ripley about it."

Just then AnnaLee lit a match, and Jean Workman went into one of her tailspins.

"For the love of God, AnnaLee-or-whoever-it-is"—her voice hit high C—"do you want us all killed? Put that match out! Put it *out*, I say!"

"Sorry. Forgot." AnnaLee huffed out the match.

"Looks to me like the natives are getting restless." I circled my ankle wound with my fingers, trying to ease the pain. "How does the situation look to you, Liz?"

"More and more restless, but what did you expect? A Quaker meeting?" My sister was the only person who seemed to take everyone's emerging inconsistencies and latent characteristics for granted.

"I had a boss once," she told me afterward, "who never hired new salesmen or editors, not even a new office boy, until he'd taken them out on the town and gotten them drunk. It revealed their true natures, he said. Well, dear, drinking may be a fair personality test, but if you want my unsolicited opinion, an air raid beats it, hands down. Most of our merry little companions, with the possible exception of Dora and a few true-blue types, appear to have vanished since the blitz. You notice?"

"Not most of them. It just seems like it. The bad ones tend to stand out in a crisis, or rather their faults do."

"You can say that again." Liz rolled her eyes heavenward. "Even without my little jaunt to the hospital, that get-together on the truck was no joy ride."

I had to agree with her about the truck ride. Jean Workman continued to go in for a lot of paranoid exposition that was unsettling to everyone, and Sharon—so gay and engaging up until that morning—cried all the time, especially when there were tracer bullets in the sky and we all thought the Japs were back until the motorcycle sergeant explained what was happening. And JayJay Murphy, a noisy exhibitionist extrovert who'd spent her fourteen months in Hawaii either giving parties or going to them, suddenly went in for religion and kept repeating the Lord's Prayer over and over and over till I wanted to swat her, while Honey drove me nearly crazy humming "Little Brown Girl" off key. Otherwise, Honey was more of a help than a hindrance. I'd always thought of her as brazen and tough, but she had another side to her. She was a bit nymphy, maybe, and had no conception of what to say or wear, but she turned out to be compassionate as well as thoughtful, and she wasn't afraid of God himself.

It was harder to assess poor AnnaLee Seymour. As always, she was so befogged by liquor that no one knew what went on inside her head or whether anything did, even when she spoke. As for Boots, with her one-track mind, heaven knows she was boring enough before the air raid, going on and on about motherhood as if it was the greatest thing since Coca-Cola, but at least she threw in a remark about the dearth of white fur rugs or brocade slipcovers once in a while. After the bombing, her preoccupation with pregnancy really got out of hand, like a now-and-then cough growing chronic in a drafty house.

104

The trip didn't improve as it progressed, mainly because of the burning fleet and Liz leaving for the hospital. Also because of the way Joey carried on after his mother and Dora went riding off.

"Your mother's going to be okay," I told him. "Everybody's okay with Mrs. Bendel." But for a time Joey was inconsolable. While we all waited to be assigned to other trucks—some of us slouched like rag dolls, some of us rigid as carved wooden figures in the burning night—he said he wouldn't ever see his mother again; he knew he wouldn't ever see her again, and nothing I answered seemed to reassure him. If it hadn't been for Marty, I doubt if I'd ever have gotten him quiet. For some reason he kept clinging to her instead of me, and no matter how hard she tried to shake him loose, he wouldn't let go. Finally, in desperation, she told him if he'd be good she'd give him her pet salamander when we returned to Schofield, a promise that seemed to divert and cheer him. I never understood about Marty's salamander. From time to time she mentioned having one, but if she did I never saw it. She also talked about her father off and on, the way children do. I don't think she was actually worried about Lang's absence—he was gone all day five or six days a week—but when evening came she expected him to be home and kept asking me when he'd arrive.

It was lonely without Liz, and I was pretty certain she'd lose the baby. She began having really severe pains when she saw the flames of the fleet. The sight was heartbreaking for all of us, not only because our last hope of protection was gone—we more or less knew that, even before we counted the few undamaged ships riding wraithlike at anchor in the background—but we were stricken and subdued, thinking of the hundreds of men, alive a night ago, happy or troubled or resting or restless a night ago, who had perished in the flames.

"It can't be, it can't be." Liz, sleeping the day away, had missed the news of the decimated fleet. "First no planes and now no ships."

There was too much tension in the truck, so Liz and I began making flip remarks back and forth. We didn't feel flip, but it was one method of combating the untenability of the situation, the same method that cropped up later in trenches and cockpits and landing barges and foxholes. Our irreverent approach may not have been the best approach in the world, but it kept us from yelling or weeping or just sitting there tied in knots.

"Oh, to be back in Boston." My sister's words filled me with a sudden hopeless nostalgia. "That old port in the harbor would sure look like a port in a storm tonight. About time for Paul Revere to hop on his horse, isn't it?"

"Not unless he borrows one from a mounted cop. They put his old pony out to pasture." I could see Boston: the brick and clapboard houses stately and dignified, the winding streets covered with snow falling like feathers. I could see myself as a child walking home from the park in my red coat and button-on leggings, my red cap and initialed mittens, carrying my silver clamp-on ice skates and blowing steam experimentally in the cold. The clock tower boinged six times—I listened for each "boing" after the first one—and a car drove by with a fir tree tied to the bumper. High strands of evergreen with firefly Christmas lights in them roped the street lamps together, and there were ribboned holly wreaths on all the doors.

I rang the bell, and Fay, the maid, answered it.

"You're late, Miss April." She smoothed her voile apron. "You shouldn't be out after dark alone. Miss Elizabeth's already in and changed for dinner." As she took my wraps I could smell a wood fire in the study grate; I could see candles blooming in the dusk of the polished dining room beyond; I could hear the walnut clock independently and belatedly striking the hour. It was one or any winter evening in the Boston house, where all evenings merged and became a single entity in their separateness, like the crystals on the overhead chandelier.

That was my childhood, I thought. A crystal chandelier where the world came into brightness at the flick of a switch.

"Sometimes I get the feeling Boston never was." As I turned to Liz, the chandelier disappeared but the white New England town hung like a backdrop beyond her and the glare of the terrible tropic waters. "I mean, there couldn't ever have been a real Boston with real avenues and real houses and real holly wreaths on all the doors."

My sister wasn't listening. Her face was no longer her face; it was the face of a stranger, grooved and ghastly in the wavering unnatural light from the sea. She stared straight ahead of her, and her lips started to tremble, then her shoulders, then her body. Then she drew up her knees and screamed.

I couldn't ride to the hospital with her because of the children, so Dora went, and I watched Liz vanish into the night, looking like a raffish, disconsolate Arab in her wilted striped turban.

Sharon kept saying she wished she'd gone with Dora, she felt safer with Dora, and I had to keep reminding and re-reminding myself how young she was, how inexperienced. She didn't mean to be a burden, but that's what she was, always displaying whatever feelings she felt, always revealing whatever thoughts she thought. I wasn't a great deal older or more experienced, as I'd noted earlier, and groping my way toward a stability I'd never had was a demanding job. However, I was working at it and Sharon wasn't. I tried to tell myself that possibly being a wife made me better able to cope, that possibly being a mother had developed my sense of responsibility more than I realized, but I knew neither condition had really imposed any special requirements in the past. I tried to tell myself my New England upbringing had given me a more fortifying background than hers, but when I thought of my dependent growing years in Boston, I rejected that idea, too.

"Shut up, Sharon," I said.

The four of us took another truck to the public school,

where we spent the night, sleeping in the roofed-over outdoor passageways that connected the complex of six or eight buildings. I've forgotten the reason we slept in the passageways instead of in the schoolrooms; probably because they were meant to be safer, though I can't think of anything now to support the theory.

Honey, lying with her head below my feet, spent the better part of the first hour thumping and flailing around.

"Dammit, handsome," she burst forth once when the sentry passed, "what are you doing with the toy rifle? What we need around this place is a Flit gun to fire at these Christ-awful mosquitoes. They're bigger than eagles." She hiked up her dress and whacked at her bare thighs. "I'll bet Lopez has a mosquito net." She spoke her thoughts aloud to anyone or no one. "Not only that, but I wouldn't put it past him to have a brace of dancing girls, complete with fans and fannies."

The sentry honked his nose into his handkerchief going around a corner, and Joey stirred.

"Who blew that horn?" he asked.

"No one blew any horn." Honey cuffed at her ear. "It's just the wild geese going over." She thumped around some more.

"Or the wild mosquitoes." She cuffed again.

"Roll up in your blanket," I suggested, and she tried wrapping it around her lengthwise, then kitty-cornered, but it was too short.

"This bitchy thing fits me like a shawl." She gave up wrestling with the blanket and kicked it aside. "To hell with it." She got to her feet and went off in the direction of the washroom.

I tried to sleep, but what sleeping I did was fitful. The mosquitoes were an intermittently nagging annoyance, but my fears for Liz were a constant and painful source of real anxiety. I knew Bert should be with her, and I wanted to get in touch with him, but I didn't know where to find a phone. I cat-napped once or twice briefly and at widely spaced intervals and finally decided I might as well get up for a while. Sharon and Joey were quiet but Marty was awake and wanted a glass of water, so I took her to the lavatory.

Honey was stooping to see in a mirror as she combed her improbable hair; and Jean Workman, who had purposely stayed awake so the Japs wouldn't take her by surprise, was saying she'd caught the sentry yawning.

"You can't trust sentries." She fastened and unfastened the clasp of her purse with the pistol in it. "I've seen enough of them to know. Most of them couldn't shoot a gun if their lives depended on it."

"No kidding." Honey scratched her armpit with her comb. "I thought it was the Army's pride and duty to train its men."

Boots Daly went by, capping her toothbrush holder.

"If I hurry, maybe I can still get my nine hours," she said.

AnnaLee Seymour emerged from a toilet cubicle and staggered across the room. She must have brought a flask with her because she wasn't just addled; she was dead drunk. She flopped backward into one of the wash basins.

"Chair has no bottom," she announced with a glazed smile.

Marty had stayed on the doorsill to admire the swing-shift activities of Willard Seymour, who had one shoe off and was using it to bat cockroaches on the outer wall.

"Come get your water, Marty," I said.

"Hi, April." Honey heard me and swiveled around. "Did those damn vampire mosquitoes drive you away from your downy innerspring?" She watched AnnaLee struggle ineffectually to light a cigarette, then glanced at Jean.

"You're bound and determined to smoke, aren't you, Anna-Lee?" Jean was working herself into another fit, a bad one. "Even though you know it may bring the Japs back and be the end of us all, you're bound and determined to smoke." She bared her teeth like an animal. "You ought to be horse-whipped," she said.

"I didn't mean to do anything bad." AnnaLee dropped her match folder and began to weep.

"You *didn't* do anything bad." Honey lifted AnnaLee out of

the basin and sat her down on a big sealed carton labeled "Lapham's Lanolin Soap For Gentler Softer Action."

"For Christ's sake, pipe down, Jean," she said. "You know the same as I do that if the Japs want a light to see by, the whole damn Navy's burning. Things were different in the truck. They may be different here tomorrow. But right now if AnnaLee wants to smoke she can smoke." She retrieved the match folder and lit AnnaLee's cigarette. "And there's something else I'd like to say while we're all having this happy little slumber party. If you want to do any more fighting, pick on someone who can fight back." She blotted AnnaLee's tears with the hem of her skirt.

"And who asked *your* opinion?" Jean was bobbing her head around so much that her hairdo quivered like a haystack in a hurricane. "Everyone knows you're nothing but a common floozy, just as AnnaLee's an out-and-out lush."

"Lush, lush." AnnaLee singsonged the words. "Lush, lush, lush." The smoke rose in spirals around her nose.

I thought Honey was going to knock Jean down, but she didn't. She rested her fists on her hips.

"And who do you think *you* are, smart ass?" She voiced the contempt I felt but wouldn't have dared express. "Never mind. Don't answer that question: I will. You're a mean-minded bitch, a stinking, neurotic blabbermouth; that's what you are. However, that's beside the point. The point I'm getting at is this. I outweigh you, and I don't plan to take any more of your lip. Understand? From now on, *lay off* AnnaLee."

Jean opened her mouth and shut it, like a guppy, then flounced out, pushing Elaine ahead of her.

"Yuk. Give me the circus any day." Honey dusted her hands together. "Well, that takes care of one of the bird brains." She waited for AnnaLee to finish her cigarette before she hoisted her off the soap carton.

"Come on, old girl," she said. "Let's you and me get onto our Beautyrests." She spotted Willard. "You, too, demon."

"Says who?" Willard ducked to one side. "The fact is, I'm busy."

"Says me." Honey wasn't about to be intimidated by an unappealing and untractable child half her size. "You may be tough, but I'm tougher. I could mash you the way you're mashing those cockroaches, which I'm apt to do if you don't shake a leg."

"Willard doesn't like to mind people." Marty sipped at her water as she and I headed back toward our blankets and whatever sleep we could manage to salvage.

"Who does?" Honey gripped AnnaLee's waist to keep her from falling. "Listen, Willard, old stoneface. Are you coming, or do you want a good swift kick in the tail?"

Willard wasn't one to want a good swift kick in the tail. He put on his shoe, taking his time about it, and stamped on a last luckless cockroach lying upside down on the ground, impotently waving its threadlike legs in the air, before he strolled after his mother and Honey, with no hint of grudging co-operation, no sign of annoyance, no anything in either his gait or his attitude.

Three

THE WEEK

5

APRIL

It was a long bad night, and when a new and rainless day filtered weakly but inexorably out of the east, most of us continued to lie where we were, reluctant to shake off whatever degree of semiconsciousness or inertia kept our thoughts, our memories, and fears peripheral and only partially real. But when the babies began to cry, when the children began to wake and fuss, one by one all of us sat up, one by one all of us got out of our covers onto our feet . . . physically worn, inwardly despondent, and outwardly frowsy. All of us, that is, except the commanding officer's wife, who appeared out of nowhere around 8:00 A.M. to inform us breakfast was being served in the school lunchroom. If Mrs. Hunter had been the Queen Mother of England making a goodwill tour among the savages, her manner couldn't have been more aristocratic, her hair more impeccably coiffed, her clothes more immaculate. I have no idea where or how she slept. Maybe she hung by her hands from a tree.

"You look like you got measles." Marty viewed Joey's mosquito bites clinically while she scratched her own.

"So do you." Joey clawed at his ankles. "I wonder how Mom is."

I'd been wondering the same thing.

"Get up and take care of the kids, Sharon." I ran after the motorcycle driver as he walked toward one of the far buildings and told him what was on my mind.

"There's a phone in the principal's office." The motorcycle sergeant hit his leg with a loosely rolled sheaf of papers he held in one hand. "I found out about it last night and jimmied the lock so I could call the radio station requesting volunteer housing for all you evacuees. The station sent out a broadcast."

"Any results from it or don't you know yet?"

"Yes, plenty of results." He pushed open a door and motioned me inside. "When I checked with the station this morning they told me nearly five hundred families had offered to open their homes. I guess no one in Honolulu did any sleeping from dusk till dawn, from the look of things; just sat glued to their radio sets. The radio people sent me this list of names and addresses about an hour ago, and I have to clarify a couple of points when you're through talking." He dropped his papers and they fanned out on the desk. "Help yourself to the phone." He sat down by the window and lit a cigar.

I managed to reach Dora at the hospital. She said Liz was doing beautifully and Bert was with her.

"That's good news." I was limp with relief. "Then she didn't lose the baby?"

"I'm afraid the news isn't all good." As Dora spoke my throat tightened. "Yes, she lost the baby. A little girl."

"Oh, poor Liz. She wanted a girl the worst way. Is she crushed?"

"Pretty crushed, but she's rallying." Dora struggled to put a lift in her tone. "Liz is in good hands, so try not to worry. Are the children all right? And is Sharon behaving?"

"Yes." I let the one word answer both questions, because I didn't want to admit Sharon got on my nerves. "Give Liz and Bert my love and tell them we're going to be farmed out around Honolulu for a while. I'll let you know where the four of us go." I glanced idly at the sergeant's list and saw a familiar name. "Hey, here's a Mrs. Fineberg up on Mount Tantalus, with Langsmith and Snyder and Workman written beside it. What does it mean, sergeant?"

"It means Mrs. Fineberg must have mentioned those three parties as possible house guests," he answered.

"Who on earth are you talking to, April? And what are you talking *about?*" Dora asked. "I never heard of any Finebergs up on Tantalus."

I explained that Rebecca Fineberg, who'd grown up with me in Boston, was living in Honolulu now and had offered to take in Liz and Jean and the kids and me.

"Though I don't know why she included that miserable Jean," I said. "They only met once, at a small dinner party I gave last month."

"Rebecca probably thought the two of you were friends. Don't forget Jean was agreeable enough until yesterday. We all were, back in the days when there was no war going on and there were men in our lives to keep us on an evener keel."

"Oh, not Joseph!" I exclaimed.

"*Now* what are you talking about, April? I'm having a little trouble keeping up with your *non sequiturs.*"

"Rebecca's husband. He's a lieutenant commander in the Navy. You don't suppose he was on his ship, do you?"

"Try not to consider that sort of thing," Dora advised. "Remember only part of the fleet was destroyed, and your friend Joseph may have been home yesterday instead of at sea. I have to leave now. Call me again when you get where you're going."

"I'd like to ask a favor." The motorcycle sergeant stubbed out his cigar in a glass of paper clips as I hung up the phone.

"I wonder if you'd tell the women and kids in the lavatory that I want them all in the dining room in twenty minutes. I'll round up the other people."

When I thought of Liz and Joseph—and I couldn't seem to think of anything else, I couldn't seem to keep the rest of the world from slipping into blankness like the fade-out of a movie—I didn't want to go anywhere, I didn't want to speak to anyone. However, the sergeant's request was a small one, so I did as he asked, watching my feet as I hurried across the schoolyard but not seeing them because of a sorrowing sister, because of the offside smoldering ships that stayed in front of my eyes wherever I looked.

"God, God, don't let Joseph's ship be one of the lost ships," I prayed. "Don't let Joseph be one of the lost men." It was a silly thing, praying for something that was already over with, knowing that if Joseph had died in one of the fires at sea there was no god—however powerful or merciful—who could turn back time and save him yesterday.

I relayed the sergeant's message to the women in the lavatory, but I didn't join in the conversation there. I looked in the mirror, but I didn't see my reflection. I had no face or self to matter any longer, I had no interest even in the cursory cleanliness born of habit, because—as hard as I tried to block out the two superimposed images—I continued to see my sister lying white on a white pillow, and a charred log that used to be a man named Joseph.

I've got to think positively, I told myself. Liz is being cared for, and she'll get over the loss of the baby. And Joseph's ship isn't burning, or if it is, Joseph is safe at home with Rebecca. Joseph is home, understand? Joseph is safe.

The world became a world again.

Why, of course, he's safe, I thought. Otherwise, Rebecca wouldn't be opening her house to guests.

I heard a bird sing somewhere out in a tree, and I almost forgot the other charred logs of men. There was a shaft of sunlight on the floor and I rubbed my foot across it, half

118

believing my shoe would stay sun-colored when I moved it into the shadow again. I dampened a paper towel and washed my face; and while I washed someone looked back at me from the glass, a woman watched me as she also washed, and I recognized the face. It was a tired face, an older face than I remembered, but it was my face and I saw it.

I decided to put some lipstick on.

I caught up with Marty and Joey and Sharon in the dining room. Joey was criticizing the eggs (cold storage), the cocoa (made with powdered milk), the toast (burned), and the tomato juice (warm). He and Marty were dawdling over the Red Cross food that ten or twelve Schofield women—pressed into service and unaccustomed to cooking—were doing their best to prepare and serve.

"I hate tomato juice," Joey was saying. "Hey, Aunt April, did you get ahold of Mom?"

"Yes, she's resting and she sent her love."

Sharon gave a little cry of joy.

"Oh, I'm so glad, April." She rushed over to embrace me. "Then she didn't lose . . ."

I shook my head, incensed beyond all reason at the tears that came to her eyes.

I drew her aside on the spur-of-the-moment pretext of needing help with the barracks bag.

"See if you can untie this cord so I can get some juice for Joey," I said, and when she and I had our backs to the table, I expressed my real thoughts.

"Look." My firmness surprised me. "I don't want to see you crying ever again, and when I say *ever* again, I really mean *ever again.*

"It's all very well to be pretty and ingenuous, but it's not enough. You've got to learn when to do and say things and when not to do and say things. The way you've been riding with your emotions, you not only upset yourself, you upset everyone within a nine-mile radius. Take Joey right now. He's concerned over his mother, and he's watching to see if you know anything he doesn't know. He's watching both of us. Yes, Liz lost the baby, and I don't like it any more than you do. But I don't care to discuss it, and I don't want you to discuss it. You're a nice girl, Sharon, but today isn't last week. And if you have any thoughts of marrying Adam Dawson, you'd better stop being a frail and bruisable flower, because Adam doesn't need a daughter or a ward; he needs a wife. And you'll lose him if you keep on being a child."

It was a lengthy speech, but Sharon accepted the reproaches and demands without argument.

"I never thought of it like that. But you're right. I'm not a child any more." She spoke as though she hoped to make the idea a fact by memorizing the words.

"No. I'm not a child any more." She got a glass and poured some juice. "Here. Drink this, Joey. You've got to have something inside you."

"Hey, there's our truck driver." Joey splashed his juice, waving it at a group of enlisted men seated at a far table. "And there's our other driver. I guess they're all drivers. I wonder where they spent the night."

"In their trucks, probably." Sharon shook off a new fog of introspection. "I told you to drink that."

Joey took one or two sips before he was rediverted by the influx of stragglers the motorcycle sergeant had rounded up.

"And there's the motorcycle man." Joey made a rh-r-rum noise and clamped his fists around a pair of imaginary handlebars. "I'm going to buy a motorcycle like that when I get big. Rh-r-um, rh-r-rum." He leaned sidewise in his chair.

The sergeant walked to the serving counter and tapped on it with his pen before he threw his voice above the general hum and clatter.

"Ladies, may I have your attention, please?" He waited for the room to quiet down. "Due to the fact that the island is still open to possible attack, it seems wise not to let large numbers of people, such as we have here, remain concentrated in any given area. Therefore we will be deploying you shortly to private homes around town, where you will reside until further notice . . . that is to say until replacement fighter planes can be shipped in and other military defenses consolidated." He said he would call us up alphabetically and co-ordinate our names with the names of the Honolulu people who had offered to house us.

"Eat as much food as you can," he added, "because it may be all you get till you arrive where you're going, and it's hard to estimate just when we'll have you in the evacuation trucks, moving out." He seated himself at one of the tables. "Will the A's kindly step up now and give me their names and the names of their children, please?"

Mrs. Hunter, who certainly wasn't an A, stepped up first. Then, acting as self-appointed spokesman for whatever other regimental commanding officers' wives were present, she turned and addressed the gathering.

"Ladies and service juniors of Schofield Barracks." She paused to shift her white gloves into her other hand. "We have been thrown upon the mercy of the good citizens of Honolulu in this our hour of trial, and the townspeople have responded promptly and generously, opening their homes and hearts to us. I don't believe I need tell you" (here Honey muttered "Why *do* you, then?") "that I trust each woman, each child among you, to be a restrained, responsible, and appreciative house guest, upholding the honor, standards, and flawless reputation of our own fine regiment and its sister regiments. I thank you."

"Isn't the blue lady pretty?" Marty joined in the dutiful patter of applause as Mrs. Hunter made her exit and went whizzing off in the chauffeur-driven Cadillac of a Dole or Dillingham or someone else of that breed.

Honey snorted.

"Pretty as a picture of Whistler's mother with none of the boys whistling." She clanged a knife. "A good thing she has friends, because she just missed the nine o'clock broomstick.

Well, so much for rank. Let's just hope we can get this show on the road before things get any ranker." She spread her fingers over AnnaLee's coffee cup as Willard reached for it. "Drink your coffee, AnnaLee. And Willard, old lizard-lids, drink your cocoa."

"I always drink coffee," said Willard.

"Not always." Honey clipped him on the wrist as he tried to get at his mother's cup again. "When I say drink your cocoa, I mean drink your cocoa, you cruddy kid."

Willard, to avoid compromising his preferences, bolted down Joey's pineapple juice, while AnnaLee asked Honey, who had commandeered her flask during the night, if she couldn't please add a teensy, tinesy touch of gin to her coffee to strengthen it a little.

"I certainly wish I could control that boy like you do," she added, either from long-standing custom or because she figured a compliment never hurt a good cause. "I don't know how you manage it. Personally, I've never been able to do a thing with him."

"Sorry, no gin today." Honey swelled her bosom and crossed her knees as the truck drivers filed by. "I dumped what was left of it down the drain." She opened her purse and handed the quart flask to AnnaLee.

AnnaLee—looking like the wrath of God and probably feeling worse than she looked—clutched the bottle in its tarnished silver casing and held it to one eye like a spyglass, slanting it upward to avoid hitting the lighted cigarette pasted to her lower lip.

"Why, it's empty," she mourned, when the fact finally percolated into her consciousness.

"Empty as the bed of a whore with hives," said Honey. "Now drink your coffee like a good girl."

AnnaLee laid the flask beside her plate of uneaten breakfast and regarded it in a dazed way, not unlike the way she sometimes regarded Willard . . . as though life, with special examples, continued to overtax and trick her, making it pointless for her to try to keep up with it.

She looped her unwashed hair behind her ears.

"My, what a tryin' time," she said. She waited a minute or so for one of the women to agree, for one of them to sympathize; and when nobody answered, nobody commented, she cast a last forlorn and accusing glance, not at Honey but at her flask—the flask she had filled and corked and carried and cherished—before she pushed it roughly aside, disowning it mentally as she had mentally disowned Willard. Then, having no recourse to oblivion, no recourse to anything reliable inside herself or out, she did what she could to please. She cautiously unpeeled her cigarette from her lower lip and picked up her coffee cup.

When our truck, and the other trucks, moved out of the schoolyard around two o'clock, we were all happy to leave. We made a number of stops in and around Honolulu, letting passengers off, but I don't recall much about the passengers or much about the stops. I have a hazy recollection of crowds in the streets of the downtown area, where some of the food stores were boarded up and others open for business but roped off, with guards in front of them to keep the queued shoppers from overrunning the aisles. Whatever else I saw is muddled with what I later read or heard as we rode to the top of Tantalus.

Rebecca ran from her house to meet us, followed by her six-year-old son, Fritzi.

"How l-l-lovely of you to come." She kissed me in her Rebecca fashion, warmly but not effusively, and there was sincerity and warmth in her inclusive welcome.

"It's a joy to be here." I introduced Sharon, as Fritzi—a small, grave masculine edition of his mother—led the other children inside. "And you know Jean Workman," I said.

"But of c-c-course." Rebecca's stutter, which came and went

in moments of self-consciousness or stress, was the one outward manifestation of an excruciating early shyness she had never entirely conquered. "I'm so pleased to see you again, Jean."

"Thank you." Jean, still nursing her preposterous suspicions of the world and everyone in it, unbent a little but not much. She scrutinized Rebecca's blue-black hair arranged like a ballet dancer's, her classic Jewish features, her tiny graceful body in the unadorned beige dress, which probably cost a mint at some place like Saks or Lord and Taylor's.

"Where's L-L-Liz?" Rebecca seemed unaware of Jean's cool appraisal, but the stutter betrayed her.

"She went to the hospital last night. A miscarriage. I'll tell you about it later. Is Joseph all right?"

"Yes. F-f-fortunately he was home when the bombing started but he took the Oldsmobile and drove to his ship right afterward. And my brother David—remember him, April? The adopted one? He's here now, fresh from Annapolis. He has the other car, which presents a slight problem because there isn't much food in the house." She held open the door. "I tried to get a cab and go shopping this morning, but no luck. Then I phoned the Red Cross, but with all the wounded and homeless taking precedence, I didn't get any satisfaction there, either. I guess we'll just have to manage as well as we can on short rations."

"What a wonderful view." Sharon, thinking about something besides herself for a change, paused on the threshold. "You must love it here."

"We do." Rebecca gazed out over the treetops at the sea. "The house is a little pretentious, but we were fortunate to find it, and it's easy for me to take care of because it's all on one level."

"You mean you haven't a maid?" Jean, pushing past Sharon, hit Rebecca with her elbow.

"No, I don't have a m-m-maid. I like doing my own housework." Rebecca's tone was cultured and quiet but she looked perplexed speaking to the Jean she had never encountered before, the mannerless Jean who had once been an amiable addition to a November dinner party.

Rebecca didn't know, as Sharon and I did, that if Jean ran true to form she was likely to get worse before she got better.

"Golly, this is some house. It goes on forever." Joey appeared with the other children in tow. "There's four bathrooms, one for each bedroom, and you ought to see all the toys Fritzi's got. When do we eat?"

"Soon." Rebecca glanced at the grandfather's clock in the corner. "We have no blackout curtains so we'd better. Here, let me show you around while it's still light." She guided us off to the wing where the dining room and kitchen were, then back through the living room to the sleeping area.

"You'd probably like baths, and it might save trouble if you put on your night clothes afterward." She got us toothbrushes and pajamas, and assigned us rooms, declining Sharon's offer to help with dinner.

"The spaghetti's cooking," she said, "and all I have to do is set the table in the kitchen."

By the time we had bathed and changed, another hour or so had elapsed, and once we got to the table we idled too much, delaying dinner even further.

"Keep eating," Rebecca urged as the night shut down, but the spaghetti kept sliding off our forks as we aimed them in and out of our invisible food, and we found ourselves ramming the empty tines into our chins and cheeks and noses. Joey, making a misdirected jab that knocked over his water glass, was the first of us to give up.

"Me, too." Even Elaine, the mighty eater, was discouraged.

"It looks like we'd better all give up." Rebecca told us to hold hands around the table. "Keep holding hands." She rose and we rose with her. "I'll lead the way to the other end of the house."

Joey, doing his usual share of talking as we walked, ran into the wall and yipped that he'd lost his policeman's hat. Elaine giggled.

"People don't sleep in hats," she said.

"The smart ones do." Joey was quick to defend his idiosyncrasy. "People like soldiers do, I bet. So as to be ready for anything."

Elaine said she'd never heard of a soldier sleeping in his hat.

"Did *you*, Marty?" she asked.

"No, I never did." Marty sounded pensive. "I wonder where Father's sleeping."

"In his tent, most likely." I kept one hand against the wall guiding her into the room and leaving it. "Would anyone like to sit a while?"

Sharon was too tired and Jean said what a silly idea; who wanted to slouch around a dark living room with nothing to see or do.

"I'll come, April." Rebecca, addressing each person by name, finished her good nights.

"Good night!" Jean, like a mad goddess reminding her loose-living disciples of the tribal laws before she vanished in a clap of thunder, issued a final decree.

"And don't you dare smoke, either of you!" she said, and slammed her door.

Rebecca and I discussed Liz, Lang, Joseph, Jean, and the war over a glass of sherry; and in spite of Jean's edict, we smoked. Not just to disobey the mad goddess (which would have been a tempting enough reason) but because we felt like smoking.

"I know what we'll do." Rebecca foresaw and solved the mechanics of the problem ahead of time. "I'll get each of us a cup, and we'll hold our cigarettes in the cups when we inhale, so the coals won't show. We'd better light the matches in the coat closet, though." She found my hand and led me there and back. "You'll get eyes like a cat faster than you think. I learned that last night. Why don't we listen to the radio?" She turned a dial and propped a sofa cushion against the luminous face of the set to hide it. "I'll try the short wave first."

The short-wave discussions were mainly about blackout violators, a fact I found both puzzling and inexcusable. Although martial law had been declared throughout the islands and there was still better than a fifty-fifty chance of the enemy's returning, the willful and negligent continued to do as they'd always done, leaving their lights burning in their places of business or in houses they had temporarily abandoned, taking their keys with them.

"Two more lights burning on lower Berengaria," one tired policeman would say to another. "Shoot 'em out, Charlie. Knock and if no one answers, shoot 'em out. You hear me, Charlie?" And Charlie would answer, "Yeah, I hear you. Any more sandwiches and coffee down at the station?"

"Only egg-olive and the coffee's pretty bad—strong enough to float a girder—but they haven't run out of it yet."

After listening to the informal exchanges of the policemen, we turned to the regular news and learned how Wake Island and Midway were safe, contrary to rumor; how a curfew had been ordered; how, because a siege was still possible, food had been rationed to five dollars' worth per person per day; how gas had also been rationed; how the two-day looting was tapering off; how future blackout violators would be fined or put to hard labor; how the Japanese store owners who insisted on selling only to Japanese customers had been arrested; how blood donors were still needed.

I forget whether it was that night or a later one when we heard President Roosevelt's unmistakable voice telling us we were at war with Japan. The air-raid sirens sounded eerily in the city as he spoke, and Rebecca and I were about to rouse the household when an announcer cut into the broadcast to say the warning was a false alarm.

Rebecca dropped onto the couch again.

127

"I suppose we might as well finish listening to Roosevelt," she said.

"Why not?" I settled back beside her. "I'm perfectly willing to give him a few minutes of my time."

I let out an inadvertent oath, listening.

"You don't mean we're really at *war*," I said to Roosevelt as he and a few of the outlying sirens went on and on. "Now that's what I call real news."

But the President didn't answer me. He didn't hear what I said. He didn't see me sitting, tired and cynical, in the lightless room of the lightless house on the lightless island, where the black earth waited to receive the inland dead, while the ocean dead were either ashes on the waves or swaying like unanchored water plants at the bottom of the black and mindless sea.

The next few days had no routine, no hour-to-hour continuity, so what I recall as happening Tuesday may have really happened Wednesday, or vice versa. Jean howled like a banshee when she found the cigarette butts in the cups Tuesday morning, but, since she did the same thing Wednesday, the details of her dissertations are lost. The children, with Sharon overseeing their activities, played happily together. Rebecca tried the Red Cross on and off without success, and as the food got lower, she and I went in for inventive and economic measures like stretching a single can of tunafish into a passable casserole by adding mushroom soup and cornflakes, or making muffins from the last of the flour when we ran out of bread. The household provisions were—as she'd warned us—inadequate to feed eight people over a period of days. The leftovers quickly disappeared; and when the eggs and milk were gone, we leaned pretty heavily on our oatmeal and Wheatena breakfasts for sustenance, using watered-down evaporated milk to moisten the cereal and sparse sprinklings of sugar to sweeten it, while we still had cream and sugar, and plain tap water and sparse spoonfuls of diluted honey and syrup after that. I'd never gone hungry or even semihungry before, and as the icebox and cupboards grew emptier, my appetite stubbornly improved.

At some hour or moment of one of the days, I remembered —with a happy sense of discovery—the nearly full barracks bag I'd casually kicked under the bed the first night; I thought of the crackers and juice. I even thought of the milk, though I knew it was probably spoiled, and I hurried to add the food to the communal supply.

The barracks bag was under the bed, but only the Thermos of sour milk was in it. "That's peculiar," I remarked to Rebecca, who said yes it was very peculiar. Like her blankets disappearing.

"I wanted to tack the extra ones over the kitchen windows, the way the woman next door did to black out the room, but I could only find one or two," she told me.

Elaine was going by.

"They're down in the cellar," she said; and we went to the laundry room in the partial basement and found the blankets hidden in a hamper and the food in the washing machine.

"I'll give you one guess who's planning to use this place as a personal bomb shelter." I gave a hiss of disgust. "I should have known there was some reason why Jean didn't go in for any of her dogged digging here on the mountain."

Jean, when I accused her, was in her bedroom putting her purse—which she alternately carried and hid—under her pillow.

"And what's so wrong about being prepared?" She raised her penciled eyebrows. "We'll all be down in the laundry in case of another attack, so you ought to thank me for planning ahead. Besides, I was only borrowing the things."

"Yes." I fought for control. "The way you'd borrow the wheelchair of a cripple because you happened to feel like taking a ride."

Jean stomped off, probably to call the clipper people again, unless that was after she reached them. When she finally got a call through, she found the clipper was booked till March, so we had to listen to more of her vituperation.

"It's a put-up job," she insisted. "Anyone can tell it's a put-up job. I don't trust airlines. They always give all their seats to friends and high-up mickey-mucks with pull."

When Jean wasn't overseeing the work of others (for instance, Rebecca nailing the blackout blankets around the kitchen) she stayed in her room a lot, but she was still enough in evidence to keep me edgy and ashamed, so I avoided her as much as possible. I spent a number of hours outdoors picking flowers, and afterward arranging them down in the laundry room, not because we needed any more flowers in the house (which was bulging with them at a time when no one was overly concerned with gracious living), but because I found the occupation absorbing and restful. As soon as the morning or afternoon chores were done, I'd wander out to the garden to selectively pick a blossom, ignore a blossom, or search for a better, brighter one in the sun. And when I forgot where I was, when I turned to the growing plants and buds and blooms for therapy and solace, I might have been gathering flowers in Eden or anywhere. The air was clear, the mountain green and peaceful, and below and beyond lay the ocean, forever there, forever the same.

When I say the ocean was the same, I mean it was the same after the fleet left. I don't honestly know whether or not Pearl Harbor was visible from the top of Tantalus, but I can still see the remainder of the great fleet moving out. I don't recall what day or what hour of the day I saw it go, *if* I saw it go; but since a faulty recollection is often as real as a true one, I doubt if a map of the island or a week of riffling through history books would alter my mental picture of the ships gliding off and away, giving the ocean surface back to the ever-crying gulls who claimed it, the gulls that had more use for fish than navies as they circled down from age-old skies, where birds were more indigenous than planes.

Either Tuesday or Wednesday, a list of our addresses and

phone numbers appeared in the newspaper. I'm not sure how we happened to have a newspaper, but we had one. Maybe it came in the mail (I'm uncertain about the mail deliveries) or maybe Rebecca borrowed it from the woman next door, although the latter seems unlikely because the woman next door wasn't one to lend things. At least, she wouldn't lend us (or even rent us) her car to go down the mountain and shop, and if she went herself, she never invited us to ride with her. She was an unmarried writer, middle-aged and taciturn, who was irked by interruptions and went back to ticking away at her typewriter as soon as she dispensed with whatever meager conversation we managed to elicit from her.

Not long after the list came out, Lang called, and eventually so did Adam Dawson and Major Workman and Bert.

"Are you all right?" I pressed Lang for details, but he hadn't many to give.

"I didn't see your sister's name in the paper, though I saw Joey's," he said. "Was it an omission or what?"

"No." I brought him up to date on Liz. "I talked to her and Dora about an hour ago. Liz is getting around some now, and they're planning to leave the hospital and go back to Schofield when the rest of us go."

"That ought to be by Friday or Saturday. Whenever the fighter planes arrive. Are you and Marty all right?"

"Yes, we're all right. Here, she wants to speak to you." As I handed the phone to Marty, I wished I'd never learned the phrase "all right." I'd said it too often lately. I'd heard it too often.

Is he all right? I thought. Is she all right? Am I all right? Are you all right? Is everything all right?

Yes, he's all right. Yes, she's all right. Yes, we're all right. Yes, everything's all right.

Everything's all wrong, but everything's all right.

I told myself I'd throttle the next person who used the words, but I didn't throttle Marty when she said: "Oh sure, Joey's all right." And I couldn't very well throttle Lang when

I got the phone back and he wanted to know if Joseph was all right. Instead, I answered what I knew, which wasn't much because Joseph hadn't called at the time.

He called Wednesday evening after supper. I remember it was Wednesday because of what came later. I was stirring a stew made from the tag ends of everything in the pantry and icebox, and Rebecca was washing the dirty containers. She dried her hands and went to the phone.

"Oh, Joseph. I'm so glad to hear from you!" She told him what was going on in the house, tactfully omitting the worsening food situation and the troubles with Jean, then listened to what he had to say. When she hung up the receiver she walked to the open door and stood there looking over the treetops for several minutes.

"Is Joseph all right?" Much as I hated the words, I heard myself saying them.

"Yes, he's f-f-fine." Rebecca went back to her dishwashing.

I think that was the evening Jean yakked all during supper about men having the best of everything: plenty to eat, orderlies to wait on them, and no homes or children to slave over.

It was a ridiculous premise, so nobody bothered to refute it. Rebecca and I kept silent, Sharon (either because Adam Dawson had or hadn't called) left the table when her eyes began to drip, and not long afterward the rest of us went to bed.

I couldn't sleep. Whenever I closed my eyes I saw Lang. I saw the way he walked, the way he sat, the way he put his socks on, the way he reached into his pocket for a handkerchief. I saw him driving a car, I saw him dancing, I saw him eating an apple, I saw him brushing his teeth and taking a shower, I saw him reading, I saw him throwing a beach ball. I saw the shape of his mouth, the shape and color of his eyes, the movement of his hands, the black hair on the knuckles of his hands. I felt the ardor and strength of his love-making, and I felt the postponement of love. I heard the grandfather's clock strike nine, then ten, then eleven, then twelve, in the still house. And when I finally made myself stop thinking about Lang by trying to visualize every dress I'd ever worn in my life—a device I sometimes used to empty my mind—I realized the house wasn't really still, that I had been hearing something all along without noticing it.

I walked across the hall to the door of Rebecca's and Sharon's room.

Why, of course, I thought. It's Sharon. Crying again but crying at night this time, because that's when adults are meant to cry. Crying into her pillow to keep from waking the rest of us.

I admired her new restraint, but I was distressed by the ragged pain of her sobbing, by the length of time she had sobbed.

"Sharon," I whispered. "It's April. Don't cry any more. Come out and I'll make you some tea."

The sobbing stopped, but Sharon didn't answer.

Rebecca answered.

"I'm sorry you heard me." Her voice caught as she tried to keep it low. "I thought you were asleep."

"Well, I'm not. And since you're not either, we might as well stay awake together. Unless you'd rather be alone."

"No, I wouldn't rather be alone." Rebecca was already next to me in the hall, and we fumbled our way to the other wing of the house, where I shut the kitchen door and turned on a light.

"It must be something Joseph said." I made the speculation aloud. "But what? He phoned, so he must be safe." A wind was blowing outside, and I could hear the branches of the hibiscus bushes scratching, scratching at the hidden window-panes.

"Yes, Joseph is s-s-safe." Rebecca lowered herself into a chair and sat there bent over like an old woman. "But my brother, David, isn't." She pushed her thumbnail along a crease of the tablecloth in front of her.

"My brother is dead," she said. "He died in the smoke below decks trying to save one of his men. They just identified him."

A board creaked somewhere, and the branches scratched louder at the shrouded windows.

I could see David seven years earlier walking past our house in Boston, a leggy, bright-eyed high-school boy with a sensitive face and hair like a bear. Whistling. He always whistled.

"Remember my brother, David?" Rebecca looked farther back into time than I. "My mother's nephew who came to live with us when he was four after his parents were killed in that train wreck?"

To me, David as a child was just a child; to me, he would always be a high-school boy, a whistler.

"Yes, I remember," I said.

"I'd always wanted a brother." Rebecca gazed at her lap, then at the stove, then at me. "And that's what David turned out to be. My little brother, David." She spoke in a monotone, trying to keep the sobs from breaking through. "My handsome, selfless, lovable, loving, *dead* brother, David," she said, and put her knuckles in her mouth.

"Cry it out if you can." I wasn't sure it was the right advice for me to give; I wasn't sure she'd ever stop crying if she started again.

Rebecca must have sensed my uncertainty, because she pushed herself slowly upright and went to the sink.

"I've cried it out." She splashed water on her eyes and forgot to dry them. "I've cried it out as much as anyone ever cries anything out." She sat again and lit a cigarette.

I got the sherry decanter and some glasses.

"Would a drink help?" I poured us each one.

"It might." She gave a last shuddery breath that sounded

a little like the wind shuddering through a loose screen somewhere.

"I wish the wind would stop blowing. David loved the wind." She drank half her sherry.

"The night David came to live with us, it was March and the w-wind was b-b-blowing." She ran one palm back and forth, back and forth on the table. "I sneaked into his room after the rest of the family had gone to bed and found him looking out through his curtains.

" 'I like the wind,' he said when he noticed me. 'See how it blows the clouds away from the moon?'

"I told him yes; I could see.

" 'I'd like to live on the moon,' he said. 'Everything's nice there.'

" 'Everything will be nice here, too,' I promised him, and it was. 'We'll all love each other,' I said, and we did."

Rebecca's hand still moved on the table, back and forth, back and forth.

"Drink your sherry," I said.

"I am." She finished the glass.

"And then there was the time he gave his new kite to the little boy in the park. You probably don't remember that." Her eyes were agonized and I didn't know whether to stop her or let her go on.

I let her go on.

"I remember he made kites," I said.

"This was a s-special kite." Rebecca, who wasn't a drinker, picked up the wine and poured it herself. "He loved that kite. He spent over a month making it, but the little boy wanted it so he gave it away." She traced the table edge with a forefinger.

"That's why he l-liked the w-wind," she explained. "Because it made his kites fly, and it made his toy sailboats sail. And, well, he just liked it." She studied the window blankets and got up for a moment to tighten a thumbtack.

135

"Of course, that was a long time ago." She finished her second glass of sherry. "But one night last week when he was s-staying with us, last week before the b-b-b . . ."

She tried again, getting the words out fast.

"B-before the b-bombs and b-blankets," she said, "he left his book and coffee after supper and drove and drove all night because the wind was blowing."

She unplugged the decanter and spun the stopper.

"I wish that wind would stop," she said.

I started to say: I think it's dying now, but I didn't want to use the word "dying."

"I think it's letting up now," I said, and Rebecca put her finger beside her nose, listening, while I scraped the floor with my foot to help drown out the insistent rustle and scratch of the hidden hibiscus bushes.

"I hope so," said Rebecca; and she and I had another drink and another drink and went on talking or not talking until daylight.

We had finished a pot of coffee and were getting dressed when Jean woke up.

"Well, *you* two must have slept well." Her tone implied that even our imagined sleep had to be a plot of some sort. "Both of you awake and rushing around at this hour."

We weren't exactly rushing around, but there was no use going into that.

"I plan to walk down the mountain." At breakfast Rebecca began making out a grocery list. "We've got to get food, somehow."

Sharon and I offered to make the trip with her.

"No, not you, April. You might do what L-L-Liz did. But you can come, Sharon, and so can you, Jean. If we each spend our five-dollar quota, we ought to be able to keep going a while longer."

Jean was shoveling in her cereal.

"Well?" I said to her.

"Well what?" Her temper was up. "If you think I intend to get myself bombed strolling down some lonely country road in broad daylight, you've got another think coming. What if the Japs attack again?"

"Oh, for God's sake, you could hide in the trees." My temper was up, too.

"And what about Honolulu proper?" Her voice climbed the scale and broke. "Do you think I'm crazy?"

I almost said yes, partly because I was angry and partly because her eyes were wild. Though I hadn't much knowledge of psychology then, and though I didn't understand the Jeans of the world, I had a faint glimmering of the fact that she was ill, that she had reached the breaking point we all may or may not reach, depending on ourselves and circumstances. But since the glimmering was only momentary, like the flash of a bottle on a stream bottom before the darkness of a wave hides it, my fleeting comprehension was more of an intuitive glimpse than a discovery, and I forgot it almost immediately.

Rebecca asked if I'd like to add anything to the grocery list, and I read it without reading it, like a newspaper headline, and said no.

"Then we might as well be off." She and Sharon began their long walk down the mountain.

The children went outdoors to play, and I carried my coffee into the living room. I didn't want to see or hear Jean, but she tagged along.

"It's all talk, you know." She plunked herself onto a yellow corduroy loveseat and hung her slipperless feet over the side. I was used to bare feet, but the sight of hers repelled me.

"All talk," she went on in the voice I'd grown to hate, "this business of not having enough food in the house." Her matted hair hung half in, half out of Joseph's bathrobe. "You and I certainly keep enough food in the house, so why doesn't Rebecca? I'll tell you why. Because she's Jewish, and that's how Jews are. Frugal." She bit off a hangnail and got a smear of lipstick on one of her front teeth.

"I don't trust Jews," she said.

I dug my fingernails into my palms.

You don't trust Jews, I thought. You don't trust Japs, not even Raico. You don't trust Hawaiians (gooks). You don't trust sentries. You don't trust airlines. You don't trust men. You don't trust women. You don't trust . . .

"And I don't trust stutterers." She finished my unarticulated sentence. "Why does your friend Rebecca stutter the way she does?"

It was all I could do to let her live.

"Because of people like you!" Until December seventh, I had never considered myself a volatile woman, but I was screaming like a fishwife as I stamped out of the room.

I was shaking pretty badly, but I made the beds and was going back through the living room to the kitchen when Jean announced the fighters were in.

"I just heard it on the radio." She spoke as though the information would solve our differences.

"Good." I collected the dirty ashtrays.

"That means we can go back to Schofield."

"Even better." I could hardly wait to see the last of her.

"Well, you're not saying much." She seemed more critical than conciliatory.

"No, but I'm about to." Though I kept my voice under control, she took one look at me and started to get out of her chair.

"Stay where you are." I moved the ashtrays into one hand and pushed her down with the other. "My friend Rebecca took you into her house through the goodness of her heart. She put up with your rudeness, your hysteria, your selfishness. Her brother died Sunday and she was up all last night when she heard about it, but today she walked down the mountain. Think about that. *You* didn't walk down the mountain. *She* did. None of which may interest you, but I'm not through."

Jean edged forward.

138

"I don't have to put up with this sort of thing," she said.

"Right now you do. Just the way I have to put up with you so long as you're in this house. Not any longer than that, though. After we leave here I don't give a hoot in hell where you go or what you do, because I never want to lay eyes on you again."

As she started to rise once more, I didn't bother with dignity, empathy, or even ordinary kindness. I put my foot on her bathrobe so that she jerked to a halt halfway up.

"From now on you're to behave, do I make myself clear?" As I heard myself speaking to Jean as ruthlessly and authoritatively as Honey had spoken to her in the washroom, I felt a strange sense of power coupled with a regret for my lost diffidence and rectitude. "We may be leaving here tomorrow, we may be leaving the next day or the next, but in the meantime you're to act like a decent human being." I handed her the ashtrays. "And you might begin by dumping these and doing the dishes."

"And what if I don't?"

"Then you won't eat." It was a childish and spiteful threat, a threat I probably couldn't or wouldn't have enforced, but that didn't keep me from making it. "I've already neatened the bedrooms and bathrooms and right now I need some fresh air."

I stayed in the sun an hour gathering flowers, and when I went through the kitchen afterward the dishes were done.

Rebecca and Sharon were lucky enough to get a cab back up the mountain, and they returned around four, just as some anonymous minion of the bulletin writer phoned to say a truck would take us home in the morning.

"Will Mom be there?" Joey opened a box of cookies while I relayed the news.

"Yes, I think so." I didn't want to tell him about Liz losing the baby, but I told him.

"Oh, that's okay," said Joey. "Mom loses babies every once in a while. What's for supper?"

139

Rebecca had shopped wisely.

"Everything," she said, and later we had cocktails in the blacked-out kitchen before we ate our meal of scalloped potatoes, meat loaf, peas, coleslaw, biscuits, and cake. I remember the menu because dinner was like a festival that night. We lingered over coffee, stretching the occasion out, and even Jean was temporarily caught up in the gaiety. The food was in, the fighters were in, and God was back in his heaven.

Our ambitions shrink with adversity, I thought. Someone who's cold wants only a fire. Someone who's tired wants only a bed. And we who will probably miss many things again tomorrow—our vanished illusion of security, our husbands, our lost or limbo habit of love in an unthreatened bedroom —tonight want only a meal in our stomachs and the planes in the airfields.

We clinked our liqueur glasses.

"To food and the fighters," we said, and asked no more of life than the basic gifts restored to us that day.

When the truck carried us off in the morning, I was already missing and wanting again: missing the peaceful mountain and Rebecca, wanting Lang and home.

We took the Wheeler Field road into Schofield. The earthen bunkers that should have housed the old fighters housed the new fighters, and the noon sun glittered on the tails of the planes. There were machine-gun emplacements on roofs, on the parade ground, on the bunkers; and soldiers in strange new deep-crowned metal helmets patrolled most of the streets, including the one that ran from Wheeler Field up past the artillery section to Mason Loop. Outside and inside the Loop there was barbed wire everywhere: across alleyways, through fields, around buildings, even around the small and harmless lei shop a short distance from our house. The mynah birds, unimpressed by wire and guns and battle helmets, were back at their old arguments again, flying in and out of the avocado trees or carrying on their raucous councils in the green spots between the slit trenches. I knew then—as I know now—that birds don't think like human beings, but it seemed to me they realized our war was none of their affair; they realized no one would shoot them because no one had ever shot them; that it was an open season on people, not birds.

We, the peace-loving Americans, I thought. And they, the wily but complacent mynah birds. We've always gone about our business believing no enemy would ever stalk us on our native soil and come at us with guns.

In lieu of reprisal, I must have needed a scapegoat, I must have needed some creature lower down in the social order to suffer the same indignities I had suffered, because—as I stepped from the truck—I found myself whispering an inane warning, not to myself, not to Marty and Joey, but to one of the mynah birds.

The bird, an arrogant owner of undeeded property, went zipping past me and lit on a strand of barbed wire where it teetered a while and turned its shiny head to preen one blue-black wing.

"Go on and preen yourself," I whispered, "but just bear this in mind. That perch you're sitting on isn't a clothesline; it isn't a telegraph wire; it isn't the branch of a tree.

"Is this your personal acre?" I asked. "It was ours last week, if you remember. Nobody knows whose land is whose today. Nobody knows whose life, whose home, is safe now.

"Watch out!" I said to the mynah bird. "The world is changing and your day may also come."

Four

THE MONTH

6

MARTY

We had fun at Fritzi's, where we went after we left the school. Not everybody went: just ourselves and Sharon and the Workmans. I don't remember what we rode in, but I can remember driving up, up, up, to the top of the mountain where Fritzi lived, and I can remember Sharon braiding Elaine's hair as we drove. Sharon got better after the night of the bombing and began laughing and playing with us again the way she used to do at the Wheeler Field playground. I guess she got sick of crying.

Fritzi's mother was a friend of Mother's and we all liked her: she had such a soft way of speaking and looked so neat and pretty, like a doll. We liked Fritzi, too, and his house and toys. He had a two-wheeled bike and a model railroad and a microscope and some planes you could wind up so they flew and bubble pipes and a chemistry set; and he gave Joey a white sailor cap, which Joey wore all the time. Elaine and I had fun with the bubble pipes. We used to sit on Fritzi's lawn, blowing and blowing, and sometimes the bubbles bumped into bushes and broke and sometimes they drifted off toward the ocean like little round rainbows before they turned back into air again.

I didn't want to leave the mountain. There were no trenches there, and the beds were all in the bedrooms instead of on the living-room floor and none of the windows had bullet holes in them. I missed Father, but when he called on the phone he said he wouldn't be seeing us for a while.

"I have to stay here at the beach with the other men," he said, and when I asked him if he liked his new beach as well as he liked Wianae he answered no; it was a different kind of beach and lonelier, because Mother and I weren't with him.

"Maybe after we're home, she and I could get in the car and come visit you." I wondered why Father hadn't thought of the idea himself. "Mother could fix a picnic and I could bring my sand pail."

Mother was waiting for the phone.

"Don't be ridiculous, Marty," she said. "Your father isn't where he can have visitors."

"How do you know?" I didn't like her spoiling my plan. "Have you ever been there?"

"No, I haven't. They only let men in trucks go. Say good-bye now."

So I said good-bye and never mentioned visiting Father again, though I thought of it quite a bit and wished I were a man in a truck. And when I found it hard getting to sleep at night, which was fairly often after Willard told me about the lion, I'd try to imagine how to get to Father because I knew the lion would never dare go where he was. I thought and thought and thought about going, and finally I figured out a way. What I did was pretend to take the wings off an old angel costume I'd worn once in Sunday school and pin them to the shoulders of my nightgown at bedtime; and then I'd fly like a bird over the trees and the mountains and cane fields till I found the place where Father was standing all alone by the water staring sadly out to sea. I used to squeeze my fingers together in anticipation at that part, because I knew Father's

146

sadness would end soon; it would end when I landed in one of those little groves of rough and high-branched pine trees that grew along the shores and tiptoed, tiptoed, tiptoed up behind him and suddenly threw my arms about his waist and hollered, "Boo!" When I did that, Father would swing around as if he couldn't believe the wonder of it all, and laugh and laugh and hug me, saying, "Marty, Marty, Marty."

"Where's your mother?" he used to ask me sometimes.

"She had no way to get here," I'd answer. "When they let cars onto the beach, she'll come." And Father would nod and say yes; that was right.

"You were smart to think of the angel's wings," he'd say admiringly. "What's going on at home?"

"There's-a-green-lion-with-a-terrible-tail-and-teeth-living-in-the-lei-shop-and-I-promised-not-to-tell." I'd try to get the worst of it out quickly.

"Don't worry, Marty." Father wasn't afraid of lions; I knew he wouldn't be. "If the lion gives you any trouble, just come here. What else is going on at the house?"

"Raico's working for us now," I'd say, if it was after Raico came, and if it was before Christmas, I'd ask: "Are you coming home for Christmas?"

"Yes, but don't let anyone know. It's a secret." He'd take my hand. "Here, let me show you around."

I'd never seen Father's beach; I only knew it was different, which meant I could imagine whatever I liked there, and every night it was something new. Once it was a pile of gold mussel shells, and once a black cave full of winking fireflies —glitterbugs, Father called them—and once a blue ditch behind a giant rock where dozens of little yellow-and-black-striped fishes flipped in the sun.

It was strange getting back to Schofield from Fritzi's. The earth had hardened into little hills beside the trenches, and wire was twined in metal coils around the lei shop where the women usually sat weaving their flowers.

147

Aunt Liz met us on our front walk. She didn't look any bigger around than Joey as she stooped to kiss him.

Joey hated being kissed.

"You're smashing my sailor hat," he said.

"Hi, dear." Aunt Liz straightened up to speak to Mother. "Those slacks of yours have about as much shape as a pair of gym bloomers."

"I didn't intend to spend six days in them." Mother took my aunt's arm. "When did you get in?"

"About ten minutes ago, and the way things are I'd just as soon get out again."

I understood what she meant when we went onto the lanai. Although Uncle Bert had managed to feed Duff once in a while he hadn't done much else.

"Whew." Joey pulled Duff outside.

Whew was right. The house smelled as bad as the lanai, with the flower arrangements sagging in their silver bowls of black fetid water and the garbage moldering in the kitchen sink.

Mother made Aunt Liz lie down in my room while she cleaned the place up. She chose my room because all the windows in the other upstairs rooms had been painted black while we were away. One of my windows was still broken, but Mother said at least it let the light in and made things pleasanter for Aunt Liz.

Aunt Liz rested most of the time, either upstairs or down, and at night she and Uncle Bert slept in Father's and Mother's room with Joey on the chaise, and Mother and I slept in the guest room. We didn't use my room because we couldn't turn on the lights there after dark.

"Where is Father going to sleep when he comes home?" I asked the first night.

"Here with me," Mother answered. "You'll have to sleep in your own room or down on the living-room sofa."

"On the sofa," I decided, because I didn't want to wake up

in the morning and look out at the lei shop where the lion lived.

Willard told me about the lion the afternoon we got back to Schofield. I was feeling sad that Iyaga hadn't returned, and I went over after lunch to tell him about it.

"I don't know why she's staying away so long," I said. "They painted her windows black, like ours, so she could come."

Willard was standing beside his trench, where a yellow cat ran from wall to wall trying to get out.

"Iyaga's a Jap, isn't she?" He didn't seem to care about the cat or Iyaga either. "I call it good riddance."

"But Iyaga isn't one of the bad Japs. She's a good Jap." I hoped I was right, but I wasn't sure.

Willard looked as if he knew more than I knew. He picked up a stick and dropped it on the cat's head.

The cat thrashed and mewed.

"That's mean, Willard," I said. "Let the cat out. Isn't that the cat that sits under the awning with the lei-shop women? They'll wonder where it is."

"Not them." Willard watched me carefully as he spoke. "The fact is, the women are gone and won't ever be back. Didn't you see the wire around their shop?"

"Yes, but there's wire in lots of places." I kneeled down and tried to reach the cat, but I couldn't.

"Where did the women go?" I asked, and that was when Willard explained how a lion had eaten them, biting their heads off first, then crunching the rest of them slowly and quietly arm by arm and leg by leg until there was nothing left but the women's shoes. According to Willard, the lion was living in the lei shop and could see through a crack in the wall as he held up his heavy maned head in the windowless darkness, restlessly twitching his tufted, slashing tail. He knew how to open the door with his teeth and was waiting there with his eye to the crack, ready to spring through the door and over

149

the wire and catch anyone else who happened to wander by. Especially little girls.

"He likes girls about your size," said Willard, and the only expression on his face was a growing glint in his marble eyes.

"Girls with curly red hair," he added thoughtfully, "like yours."

I covered my ears as he finished explaining about the brown and smiling women who had threaded blossoms into necklaces all day long, every day, in the sun. But I was too late. Willard had said what he'd said.

"We could at least save their cat," I told him, and I slid into the trench, forgetting that then the cat and I would both be trapped.

The cat stared at me with its scared green eyes and clawed me when I tried to pick it up, so I had to drop it.

"Help me, Willard!" I cried, but Willard didn't.

Mrs. Lopez finally heard the noise and rescued me, and after that she rescued the cat. She took it by the scruff of the neck and heaved it over the trench side, and the last I saw of it was as it streaked away between the houses across the street.

"You ought to be strung up by your thumbs, you stinking kid," she said to Willard. "I hope Santa Claus puts coal in your stocking."

"Aw, lay off it." Willard didn't sneer outright, but a sneer was implied. "I'm not a five-year old like *her*, still dumb enough to believe in Santa Claus." I wasn't surprised by Willard's cynicism; he didn't believe in much of anything. And since he never told me what he got for Christmas—I mean coal or not—I never learned how Santa felt about his nonbelief. All I know is that Joey and I got some nice things. I got a One O'Leary ball and a jump rope and a toy cooking set and a game of Parcheesi and a gold bracelet, and Mother gave me some queer-looking black shoes with square toes because my sandals had worn out. ("You'll need them for the trip back to the mainland," she said. "I couldn't find any others." So I put on the shoes and wore them even though they hurt my feet.) Joey got some roller skates and a baseball and a couple more hats he wanted, including a policeman's one with a whistle to go with it. (He swiped a star off the tree for a badge.) With all the decorations Mother had strung around (mainly to cheer Aunt Liz, who didn't seem to be getting well very fast), the house looked gay and bright even with the curtains and pictures and things put away in the barrels the packers had left. It was hard on Mother doing everything for everyone and she got pretty tired until Raico came. I've forgotten how Raico happened to come, but I went to the door one afternoon, and there she was.

We couldn't get a real Christmas tree, so Raico said how about using the potted palm on the porch. She giggled as she said it, and she giggled even more when we put the ornaments on, because it was such a funny tree. Elaine came by while we were stringing popcorn for it, and ate so much popcorn we had to keep popping more.

Elaine was mad at her mother for not taking Raico back, and I didn't blame her.

"I never can fix my hair or do up my buttons," she complained, "and there's no one to talk to."

"There's Mrs. Daly," I answered, though I knew Mrs. Daly wasn't much help because she stayed out of the house most of the time, and when she was in it, she and Mrs. Workman sort of talked at each other without listening, while Elaine moped around by herself.

After we opened our Christmas presents, we went to Sharon's wedding when she married Sharkbait in the chapel, and I was flower girl. I wore a headband of red hibiscus flowers and a green velvet dress of Mother's that Mrs. Bendel cut down for me. Sharon looked pretty and everyone said I looked pretty, too, so I left my outfit on after the wedding to show Father when he came home.

Joey and I were playing Parcheesi on the living-room floor as the clock struck twelve.

"Do you suppose Father will be here pretty soon?" I said to Mother, who was having a predinner drink with Aunt Liz and Uncle Bert.

"What do you mean?" There were two new little lines between her eyebrows. "Your father's not coming today. He can't. He's having turkey in his tent with the other men."

"Your move," said Joey.

"But he promised to come." I spun the Parcheesi spinner without really seeing it.

"Not that I ever heard about, and I've spoken to him nearly every night."

Joey had to put his oar in.

"Uncle Lang was dopey to be a soldier," he said. "If he was a doctor like Dad, *then* he'd be home."

"Father *isn't* dopey." I wanted to say Uncle Bert was dopey, just to get back at Joey, but I couldn't in front of everybody.

Uncle Bert told Joey to tend to his Parcheesi game.

"Be patient, Marty," he said. "Your father has to wait his turn to leave the beach, but he'll be coming to see you any day now."

"Your *move*," said Joey.

"No, today!" I didn't care about Parcheesi any longer. "Father's coming *today!*"

"What makes you think so?" Joey didn't like my holding up the game.

"Because that's what he told me! He said it was a secret, but he was coming home for Christmas!"

"That's enough, Marty. Lower your voice." Mother was always disturbed when I didn't act ladylike. "Your father never said any such thing."

"See?" Joey didn't notice how mad I was getting.

"He's coming *today*." I raised my voice instead of lowering it. "He *is*." I raised it even more. "He *is*, *he is*, HE IS!" And when Joey mumbled, "I'll bet he isn't," I hauled back my arm and slapped him across the mouth as hard as I could slap him.

There was a second of quiet before Joey let loose. Then he really bellowed.

"Serves you right," I said, and Uncle Bert said the same thing, but Mother told me to go to my room, anyhow.

"I won't stay in my room!" I kicked over the Parcheesi board, getting up. "I hate my room! I hate my window! I hate everything!"

"Your room's perfectly pleasant, and your window isn't all that bad." Mother thought I meant the window toward Willard's house, the window with the missing panes. "You heard me, Marty. Scoot." She must have remembered it was Christmas, because she toned down her sternness a little. "You can take one of your presents if you'd like."

I took a doll Mrs. Bendel gave me, not because I wanted to take it, but because Mrs. Bendel came in just then and I had to. I didn't play with it, though; just carried it up and threw it on my dresser. Then I hung a towel over the window facing the lei shop and lay down on my bed with my back in that direction. I knew I was crushing my flowered headband, but it didn't matter any more because Father wasn't going to see it. Father was having turkey in a tent. Father was staying at the beach.

Father wasn't coming.

Someone else was coming. Someone or something else. Something I didn't expect.

The green lion.

The lion was coming with a smile around his mouth that showed his pointed and fearsome green teeth, coming with his long tail lashing like a hard green pine bough in the wind. He had gotten sick of waiting in the lei shop—waiting, waiting, waiting with his eye to the crack in the wall—and had broken out through the door, snapping the thorny silver wire like thread. I could see him walking softly across the field, walking carefully like a cat, walking with the green grass bending to flatness under his padded green feet. Walking fastidiously over the fallen green avocados. Walking toward our house. Walking, walking, walking.

"Oh, no!" I cried. "*No-no-no-no-no!*" And I put on my angel's wings as fast as I could and barely got off the ground in time. The wings kept coming unpinned, but I held them on with my hands and flew over the trees and mountains and cane fields to the place where the stripy, flipping fishes used to be, and the firefly cave, and the shiny gold mussel shells all in a pile. But nothing was there, no one was there, at least no one I could see. I could hear voices, though, coming from a row of tents in back of the beach. I could hear men laughing, and I could smell turkey cooking.

"Wake up, Marty." Uncle Bert's words came through the laughter. "Dinner's ready, and we're all waiting for you. I saved you a drumstick." He sounded concerned, like Father. "Haven't you got that towel on the wrong window?"

"The sun got in my eyes." I didn't like to lie, but I couldn't tell him the truth. "I'll be down in a minute."

"Good." He smiled the tired smile he'd been smiling lately. "We miss you, and your mother always feels unhappy when you're unhappy."

"I'm all right now." There was no use being angry any more. It didn't help me, and if it upset Mother, what was the point? Mother wasn't like Father; she didn't understand me the way he did, but until Father came home she was all I had.

I sat up as Uncle Bert went clacking down the stairs. Clacking again. Too much clacking.

You're not my father, I thought, listening to Uncle Bert's footsteps. You sleep in my father's bed and you carve our turkey, but you're not my father.

I realized it was an unfair way to think. I realized someone had to carve our turkey, and it didn't make much difference who slept in Father's bed so long as Father couldn't be in it.

Uncle Bert's okay, I thought. He's a nice man. He hasn't done anything wrong.

He's mostly done things right, I thought. Being a doctor is doing things right. Doctors come home once in a while.

"I don't know why you didn't figure things out a little better," I said to Father, wherever he was, because it seemed to me he had slipped up somewhere. I knew he was the best father and the strongest swimmer and the smartest sand-castle builder. I knew he was kind and gentle and handsome and wise and good and brave and always kept his promises, or always had in the past. But though something in the back of my mind kept trying to tell me he hadn't actually said he'd be home, kept trying to tell me his being a doctor wouldn't have solved whatever needed solving, I didn't want to listen. I didn't want to do any more sorting out.

I concentrated on the sounds from below, the Christmas dinner sounds, and reached a kind of peace by evasion.

"I'm going to have turkey, too, Father," I said, getting off my bed.

"A drumstick," I said, smoothing my velvet dress.

"Like always," I said, starting to brush my hair and hitting the brush against my crumpled headband.

I took the headband off. It was nothing Father would have cared to see even if he could have seen it, so I dropped it into the wastebasket before I went downstairs.

7

APRIL

Liz was waiting outside our house when Sharon and the kids and I returned from the Finebergs' to Schofield.

"The place is a shambles, dear," she said, and she was right. However, Bert had put the mattresses back where they belonged, which was a help, because Liz was meant to keep quiet. She lay down on one of the twin beds in Lang's and my room almost immediately, and I let her stay there because it was a better bed than the one in the guest room. Also, Bert frequently spent the night and Lang didn't, so it seemed a more sensible arrangement. The only thing I really minded about the guest-room bed was sleeping in it alone, and that would have happened wherever I was. Marty seemed comfortable on the chaise beside me, and I put a cot in the upstairs hall for Joey.

Dora had to give up her bedroom, too. She owned the only double bed on the Loop (unless Mrs. Hunter, the C.O.'s wife, occupied one, which I doubted) and every time a husband was home on pass, his wife pleaded so hard for Dora's more intimate and luxurious sleeping accommodations that Dora, being Dora, didn't have the heart to refuse.

156

"A typical day," she said once, coming in from our lanai through the packing boxes. "A morning of rationed shopping and wrapping china and an afternoon with my customary eviction notice. I can't keep up with the dirty sheets."

"Who's the lucky couple?" Liz, whose health precluded any sexual relations, was lying on the couch in the only nonmaternity housecoat she owned, a yellow taffeta affair that she couldn't spare long enough so I could launder it.

"Honey and spouse," Dora answered. "Not that the names matter about now. There's a constant turnover, and Sharon and I haven't time to keep a guest book."

"Well, there's nothing like learning to run a legalized bordello, dear, in case you want to go into war work later on," Liz said. "It pays better than rolling bandages, and don't let anyone ever tell you it isn't a worthy cause." She fingered the sleeve of her housecoat. "My own worthy cause is out of the wrapper by Christmas. This robe couldn't be more disgusting."

"Christmas!" I'd been trying to forget the day and all it meant. "Do we need to have Christmas?"

"The children do." Liz scratched at a coffee stain on the front of her housecoat, knowing it wouldn't come out. "Don't get the idea you can hurdle the season like a fence and suddenly be on the other side of it."

"I suppose not, but that doesn't mean I wouldn't like to." I thought of the armed garrison around me that had once been a peaceful community, and for a moment or so I was afraid my old nausea would return. I thought of the barbed wire and the painted windows and the laundry whistle that continued to sound its authoritative toots from time to time, ordering us into the slit trenches to wait in renewed panic for the all clear. I thought of the rumored native uprisings, of the recently issued .45 revolver under the mattress of the bed, where I slept a restless sleep when I slept at all. I thought of the limited food and liquor, of the unstocked city department stores where there was little or nothing to buy even if we

157

could get the gas to go there and buy it. I thought of the chore-filled hours that left me too depleted at the day's end either to anticipate or to fashion a proper holiday. I thought of the Japanese, still waiting perhaps, waiting somewhere beyond the range of the sentinel bombers, somewhere out where the winds came from, gathering their dark armada to surround the islands and cut off our food supply, leaving us nothing to live on but frugal portions of poi and avocados and fruit and fish, until the last taro root was gone from under the earth, the last pineapple and papaya and mango and avocado from on top of it, and the last passing fish from the blue encircling seas.

"Christmas," I said, and I didn't say it pleasantly. "Peace on earth. Joy to the world. We'll be lucky if we even get a silent night out of it."

"Oh, hush, April." Liz tried to get a little dash into her outfit by turning the back of the collar up, but the cloth was too limp. "Don't get carried away. You're just tired from packing and riding herd on the kids and putting all that blackout paper around the kitchen. Even if it's a makeshift affair, Christmas will still be Christmas."

"Maybe for you, Pollyanna, but not for me." I yanked a needle of excelsior out of my little finger. "I'll go along with the farce if I have to, but mark my words, nothing good will come of it."

I was wrong. Quite a lot of good came of Christmas. Since there were no firs or balsams available, I decorated a potted palm while Liz looked on and made suggestions. She was out of her housecoat but she wasn't strong enough to move around much, so Bert and I saw to it that she followed a restricted program of activity. She and I wrapped ten-cent presents for Marty and Joey and brightened up the house with sprays of red hibiscus and paper chains. And Sharon got married, and we all sang Christmas carols. And Raico came to work for us. And Dora got a new lease on life. And Honey's poodle straggled home from wherever he'd been. ("Wouldn't you know?" Honey remarked. "His chances of survival were bad enough living on avocados, but God help him living around Willard. Still, I suppose Lopez will be pleased.")

A number of years later, when I was describing my 1941 Christmas to a friend, the friend thumped her forehead with the heel of her hand.

"One thing at a time," she said. "I've forgotten who Raico was. Begin with Sharon, and go on from there."

So that's what I did, gazing back across the rolling hills and level plains of time at the far-off island that was home once; not at the yellow-hot town of Honolulu but at the temperate inner part of the island, the part where the gray-green mountains looked down on the arsenal of Schofield, looked down on the poinsettias blooming taller and redder and more beautiful than ever before. And as I gazed I saw Sharon all in white in a white church, Sharon with her scared expression gone, Sharon looking calmer than Dora, while Dora—in a green velvet dress she'd borrowed—looked almost as vulnerable as Sharon.

Adam Dawson married Sharon at 3:00 P.M. in the post chapel. Bert sat down at the organ in the too-quiet church and played "Clair de Lune" for a wedding march; also as background music during the ceremony and for a recessional after that. It was the only piece he knew and it was better than nothing, so no one criticized. He and the groom and the chaplain were the only men at the service because the others couldn't leave their battle stations; but all the women were there.

Sharon wore Boots Daly's wedding dress, which Dora tenderly removed from its yellow tissue paper and rehemmed while Liz refurbished the veil with some white satin candy-box ribbon. Marty wanted to be flower girl, so Sharon let her, even though the only flower-girl costume I could find was a cheesecloth-angel one left over from a nativity play the previous year. Marty said she didn't like the tinsel headband, it

159

pricked too much, so I anchored a poinsettia to her head with bobby pins, burning the stem of the flower beforehand so the juice wouldn't leak out and gum up her hair.

The bride looked properly radiant and Adam properly proud coming down the aisle, and later they spent their twenty-four-hour honeymoon at Dora's and Dora slept on our couch.

When Sharon had shaken hands with everyone she became practical.

"I'll be sure to wash the steak pan tonight and the sheets tomorrow," she told Dora.

Dora couldn't seem to stop crying.

"Oh, you know I don't care about pans and sheets," she said through her sodden handkerchief. "There's wood in the fireplace—you can use it in the morning even if you can't use it tonight—and I finished blacking out the downstairs while you were getting dressed, and I moved the champagne—that bottle Mrs. Hunter sent—higher up in the icebox where it would chill faster, and I put a can of mushrooms on the kitchen table and the salad's in a damp bag, and for dessert I made some of that *crème brulée* your new husband likes." As she said "husband" she went into another spasm of weeping.

"Stop *crying*, Dora. Hey, where did you get that dress? It looks great on you. The thing is, there's no *reason* to cry, I mean, you don't have to *worry* about me any more, Dora, because I'm grown *up* now. I'm married."

Dora tried to smile, but she couldn't.

"Well, I love you," Sharon said, "but I can't stay here any longer. Adam and I have to get on home."

"Yes, we do." Sharkbait—that is, Adam—spoke in his easy way. "I'm outnumbered by all you ladies and, lovely as you are, I think my wife and I are ready to leave now." He bowed to Sharon.

"My queen"—he offered her his arm—"your coach awaits."

The two of them ran off to the car in a modest shower of

torn-up tinted toilet paper that Honey had brought and distributed, while Joey—resplendent in a red-tissue Santa Claus hat he'd made especially for the occasion and stubbornly refused to remove during the service—rang a silver dinner bell he'd smuggled out of our dining room. At the curb, Mrs. Hunter, who was the picture of a commanding officer's wife in her fawn-colored suit and tolerant expression, called out: "God bless you, children," and prodigally threw the contents of two boxes of rice in the air before she disappeared, as befitted her station in life, into the back seat of a vehicle driven by someone else.

"Thanks, old Hawknose." Honey salvaged as much of the rice as she could salvage by brushing it into her scarf. "Confetti today, curry tomorrow is what I always say. Looks like the festivities are over for us single girls."

Liz, out for the first time, drove back to the house with Bert while the rest of us walked and sang carols.

AnnaLee Seymour liked "Good King Wensyclaus" best, and though Jean Workman (with whom I had a temporary and teetery truce) kept correcting her and saying it was "Good King Wenseslouse," AnnaLee preferred her own version.

"We'd better hurry and get home before dark." Jean, wearing a gas mask around her neck and an idiot feather hat on her updo that made her hair look like a nestful of birds, forged mistrustfully ahead, trying to outwit the night in case it planned to sneak up on her in midafternoon.

Elaine dragged behind, partly for the usual reasons, and partly because her gas mask weighted her down.

"I like your angel costume, Marty," she said. "You were a good flower girl."

"Thanks, Elaine." Marty, to whom angeling and flower-girling were a natural combination, dodged as Willard whipped by.

"Let's sing 'Away in a Manger,' " she suggested.

"You mean 'Away-in-a-Manger-No-Crib-for-His-Bed'?"

161

Elaine gave a little hop of pleasure and her gas mask clanked against her right knee. "Yes, let's."

We all began singing.

Boots Daly stopped in her tracks at "The cattle are lowing; the poor baby wakes."

"The baby *did* kick," she said, and for a second I thought she meant Jesus. "I know he did. Let's see," she rattled on. "Christmas. That's over three months. Going on three and a half. He *might* have kicked, though they usually don't that early."

AnnaLee Seymour, who was having a little difficulty staying on the walk, finished singing "Away in a Manger" and began on "Good King Wensyclaus" again. Her cigarette bobbed up and down in her mouth like a misplaced baton as she sang.

"I don't know where in the devil she stashes the booze." Honey made the aside to me. "She must have bought enough hard stuff for an army before they froze the liquor supply."

Willard put out his foot to trip Joey, and Joey—running into a bit of Christmas luck—clobbered him in the eye with the silver dinner bell.

"That'll teach you," Joey said.

Boots walked briskly along, the way the book said, full of the responsibilities of motherhood, while Jean Workman, a good six houses ahead, screeched for Elaine.

"Darn it, Marty, I always have to leave." Elaine, hampered by the gas mask, stumbled off like a hobbled horse to catch up with her mother.

"Well, this is our stop." Dora paused in front of our house. "Merry Christmas to all and to all a good night."

"Likewise, I'm sure." Honey exaggerated the roll of her hips as Bert came out the door. "Say Merry Christmas, Anna-Lee."

"Murray Christmas." AnnaLee lost her balance as Willard whizzed an avocado past her ear.

"Are you hurt?" Honey squatted beside her.

"Nope, not hurt." AnnaLee, leaning back on both hands in a defeated yet spry way, scrutinized the ground for her fallen cigarette which Marty, remembering the fire rules, had stamped out.

"That boy," she said. "That terrible, terrible boy. Always chunking avocados at someone even on Christmas Eve." As Honey helped her up she went on with her litany.

"That boy." She looped her hair behind her ears under the hat she was wearing, a puce-and-green-satin creation from God knows where. "That terrible, terrible boy."

"I wish I was *really* Santa Claus. I'd put coal in his stocking." Joey clanged his dinner bell for emphasis. "That would fix him."

"Don't bank on it. He'd probably use it to burn the house down." Honey told AnnaLee to brace up.

"Oh, I *am* braced up. Whatever made you think I wasn't braced *up?*" AnnaLee bent with great care to remove a piece of grass from the toe of one shoe and slowly straightened herself into an upright position by walking her hands up her legs. Then she smiled a vague, secret smile, perhaps one of accomplishment, and floated away toward home to the renewed strains of "Good King Wensyclaus."

Dora was a little less lachrymose while the children were still up and around, but about seven-thirty she began crying again. She'd washed her hair and tied the sides of it on top of her head with a piece of turkey-tying string, instead of anchoring it into the usual bun at the back of her neck. I'd never noticed before that her hair was wavy, even curly, with gold lights in it, or that her eyes were as big and green as Sharon's were big and blue. Not only that but her lashes, darkened by the tears, were about half an inch long.

Liz was as impressed as I.

"You've really been hiding your light under a bushel, **Dora,** dear," she said before Bert took her off to bed.

Dora eventually ran out of tears, and she and I stayed up

till after eleven—a late hour for our sunrise-to-sunset existence—stuffing a turkey and baking cookies and tarts. Marty smelled the cooking and left her bed to come down and investigate; and the sentry must have smelled it, too, because when he rattled the door to make sure it was locked, he seemed to know someone was still up.

"I'm going off duty now," he called, "but another man will be on. Merry Christmas."

"Come have something to eat," I called back. "Here. Wait, and I'll turn off the light so I can let you in."

When he was inside I switched the light back on and gave him a chair and a cup of coffee, telling him to help himself to the cookies and tarts.

"I'm sorry the apples are canned," I said, "but we couldn't buy any other kind. I come from New England, where we have lots of apples on the trees in the fall, all red and sweet and polished. You ought to see them."

"I wish I could and maybe someday I will." The sentry was a Negro, who introduced himself as George Jackson. I don't know how he happened to be where he was, because the army hadn't yet been integrated and Schofield had no Negro battalions. But I remember his face and his name and the way he held an apple tart in his hand. Marty also remembers these things but not in the same context, not in the same way.

"I wasn't born in apple country," he said. "I was born in the South, and I'd have lived and died in the South if I hadn't joined the Army. I'd of bought me a mule and lived and died behind that mule. But one day I said to myself 'There must be something more to life than a mule, George Jackson, and there must be something more to the world than the South.' "

"Well, I guess the South isn't so bad if you're used to it." I thought of Alabama, which I'd visited once. I thought of the red dirt, the heat, the squalor, the racial inequality, the stupidity, and I didn't believe a word I was saying.

Neither did the sentry.

"The South isn't so good," he replied, "and you don't have

to stay somewhere just because you're used to it. There's a lot of hate in the South." He bit into a second tart.

"I'm a gentle person," he said, "and I don't like to hate, but sometimes I do." He looked to see that his words weren't bothering Marty, who was saying, "Eeny, meeny, miney, mo," over a cookie sheet.

"There's hate all over the world, corporal." I could tell George Jackson was truly a gentle person, as I'd been a gentle person before December seventh.

"I don't like to hate, either," I said, "and I didn't used to think I was a hater, but I'm one now. I hate the Japs, so I don't see how you can stand white people like us, after all we've done to you and your race."

"I can stand you and your friend here," he said, "and you can stand me, and that's where we have to start." George Jackson spoke quietly, thinking as he spoke. "I don't mean broader conditions won't have to change, because they will, but not the past conditions; no one can change those. It's the present and future conditions we've got to really work on.

"I do a lot of reading," he continued, "and I don't imagine the Greeks liked being slaves of the Romans or the Romans liked being taken over by the Gauls. But that's over. That's history. I may have anger in me against some of the present whites, as you and I have anger now against the Japanese, but I won't fight over who made my great-grandfather a slave because whoever did it, it wasn't you, any more than it'll ever be you who yells nigger.

"I'll fight those people," he said, "those present and future people, once we've all fought the Japanese. I'll fight the people who want to make *me* a slave and call *me* nigger."

"I'm sure it must be bad." Dora spoke in her Dora way, causing no offense because she meant none. "Still, I'm Irish on my father's side and I don't get upset when I'm called a Mick."

"It isn't what you're called; it's how you're called it." The sentry finished a cookie and rose. "As I say, I do a lot of reading and here's how I understand things. Originally some of the blacks came from Nigeria and were labeled Nigers, which got corrupted to niggers, so it isn't the word itself that's the problem." He wished Marty a Merry Christmas as she went off upstairs with a tart in one hand and a cookie in the other.

"I wonder where Mick came from," he said. "I'll have to look that up. Thank you, ladies, for the food."

"Thank Mrs. Bendel here, not me." I gave him some extra cookies I'd wrapped. "She's teaching me to cook, now that my maid's left."

I thought of Iyaga.

"It's very confusing," I said. "I say I hate the Japs, but I don't hate the ones I know, even though I'm not sure where their loyalties lie. I don't hate my maid Iyaga, and I don't hate Raico, the Workmans' maid—everyone on the Loop loved her —but both of them disappeared after the air raid, and no one has any idea where they went."

"I can't answer for Iyaga." The sentry halted at the door before I switched out the light. "But I know a little about Raico. I saw her this afternoon while all you ladies were at the wedding. She was going into her house to get her clothes. She's pregnant by a white soldier, so her family won't take her back, and I gather Mrs. Workman won't."

"Where is she now?" I could see poor Raico wandering from place to place—or, even worse, from soldier to soldier.

"She's nowhere." Corporal Jackson's voice came out of the night. "But I may run into her going there."

"If you do, bring her here, please," I said, and when Marty went to open her stocking in the morning she came racing back up to tell me Raico was at the door.

"Should I let her in?" she wanted to know.

"Certainly," I answered. "Forget all that silly talk of Mrs. Workman's. Raico's our friend."

So Marty and I hurried downstairs laughing and Dora sat up on the couch and rubbed her eyes and laughed, too, as

Raico—in a blue kimono with white butterflies on it—walked softly into the room and broke into a giggle of delight when she saw the potted-palm Christmas tree.

"Guess what! It's my turn in the double bed. Jack just phoned to say he had an overnight pass." Dora came into the kitchen where Liz was sitting in a chair sorting silver while Raico and I finished the dishes.

"He's coming at four and it's two now. Do you mind if Sharon takes my place here on the couch tonight, now that *her* honeymoon's over?" Though Dora was glowing, she was back in some kind of dreary print dress and her hair was straying out of its moorings again.

"Certainly Sharon can stay here. How wonderful about Jack." I thought of Dora's stocky balding husband with his long nose and whimsical eyes. No Adonis except to Dora, but a nice man with a vibrant voice and a quiet sense of humor he didn't push.

Liz laid a couple of spoons down on the table.

"I think we'd better go somewhere and have a little conference, Dora, dear," she said.

I told Marty, who was blowing bubbles in the living room, to go to her room and play.

"Take Joey with you," I said.

"We'll play in the upstairs hall." Marty gathered up her bubble-blowing equipment. "I don't like my room."

"Why not? It's a perfectly good room, and you've always liked it before. If there's too much air coming in the window, stick a pillow in it."

I guess Marty was out of sorts from all the holiday excitement.

"Come on, Joey," she said. "Let's go play in the upstairs hall."

As things turned out, the two of them might as well have stayed downstairs, because Sharon came dreaming her way in, and Liz decided to transfer the discussion to Dora's house.

"Now, Dora." My sister lighted the Bendels' lights against the daytime darkness of the blacked-out room. "I have a few things to say, and I hope you'll hear me through. It's time you stopped going around looking like someone's laundress."

"Isn't that an exaggeration?" Dora didn't ask the question in a defensive manner or a resigned manner. She asked it squarely and unself-consciously, wanting to know.

"Maybe. But look at you in that awful sparrow get-up with your hair yanked back into a hunk and no make-up on those simply fabulous eyelashes or that sensuous mouth, and your eyebrows every which way. It's criminal. Here you are about to launch yourself on a big night of sin and revelry, and something's got to be done about your appearance. I mean being staunch and sturdy is all very well but it isn't enough."

"So it's as bad as that," said Dora. "Well, I can tell you something. I hate being staunch. I hate being sturdy. I hate being good old sensible overweight Dora, but that's how it is." She flexed her capable peasant's fingers.

"That's how it *isn't*." Liz punched a sofa pillow. "Take my word for it. You're just not making proper use of your assets; that's all. Sure, you could lose a little weight, but I spent six years in the beauty business and I've got a few ideas about the other things." She shut the front door. "Well, first problems first. I want to make a few mental notes on your over-all setup before I go to work, so let's get on with it.

"Strip, dear," she said.

"Gee, Liz, do I have to?" Dora was a modest woman.

"Oh, for heaven's sake, don't act so *young*. There's no one here but April and me, and we're not about to put up bleachers and sell tickets. You heard me. Off with the wren costume."

"All *right*." Dora looked exposed before she was exposed.

"Oh, well." She crossed her hands over her bare breasts. "I suppose there's no need to feel foolish. What's here is here."

"Drop your hands and stand up straight." Liz clicked a fingernail against a front tooth. "Now walk to the hall and back and walk tall."

"But I'm *not* tall." Dora slumped.

"Quit that. It's *feeling* tall that counts. Now start walking."

Dora walked. She didn't walk as well as she might have walked, but she walked.

"Just as I thought." Liz could have been studying a map or a blueprint. "Ankles heavy. Upper thighs heavy. But luckily that's the worst of it. Hips rounded. Waist firm. Breasts sturdy."

"Wouldn't you know the breasts would be sturdy along with everything else?" Dora slumped again.

"Count your blessings. You can get into a wrapper now." Liz led the way up to Dora's dressing table. "I'm going to accent all your good points, beginning with your hair. Walk *tall*, I told you."

"Oh, stop riding her, Liz," I said. "Maybe Jack likes her the way she is."

"He'll like her better when I get through with her, so mind your business, April. If you want to be useful, run get my bottle of Shalimar and my make-up kit and a sexy black nightgown if you own one. Oh, yes. And my long jade earrings."

"Right away, Miss Arden." I curtsied. "Will that be all, Miss Arden?"

"As a matter of fact, no. Find those pink damask sheets of yours and a decent bottle of wine."

"What?" I said. "No stringed trio? No squab under glass?"

"Glad you reminded me. Have Sharon and Raico work on dinner and put it down in the kitchen. Canned vichyssoise out of the reserve cupboard, leftover turkey in patty shells . . . oh, they can figure it out."

"At your service, Miss Arden. I didn't know you were going into the restaurant racket on the side. You'd better not stay on your feet too long, or we'll all catch it from Bert." I rushed off like a proper slavey.

I didn't have a black nightgown, so I brought back my green chiffon one with the negligee to match.

169

"Will this do?" I held it up after I'd dumped the other stuff on the dressing table.

"Couldn't be better." Liz finished her barbering while Dora watched in the mirror. "How do you like the new curly coiff?"

"Perfect." I meant what I said. Dora's face looked almost elfin and her eyes were bigger than ever. "You're a first-rate hair-hacker, Miss Arden."

"With hair like this, any moron could be a first-rate hair-hacker." Liz laid the scissors down and picked up the eyebrow tweezers. "What's *your* opinion, Dora, dear?"

"Oh, thank you, Liz." Dora took a hand mirror and swung around on the dressing-table bench. "It does make a difference. A big difference."

"Don't tweeze too many of her eyebrows," I said. "She'd look ridiculous with just a thin line."

"Who's in charge of this Cinderella job, you or me?" Liz told me to run the tub and make the bed.

"Now for the face cream and a hot soak and the nails and make-up." She finished the tweezing. "Into the bathroom, Dora, dear. And my God, let's not forget to shave your legs. You look like King Kong from the hips down."

Dora had given up arguing. When I went in to make a progress check a while later, she was sitting on the toilet-seat top, pink from her bath, holding her fingers obediently apart so her nails would dry, while Liz wielded the mascara and lipstick.

"Oh, good, April. You brought the rest of the siren equipment. Here, Dora, dear, let me take your place so I can sit and rest a minute, while you go get a peek at yourself in the long mirror."

Dora went to the glass on the bathroom door and stood in front of it. She didn't stand naked although she was naked.

"My golly," she said. "My golly." She let me slip the night-gown over her head. Then she took the jade earrings and screwed them on.

170

"My golly," she said again, and jutted her lower lip, practicing provocativeness.

"Don't jut your lip," Liz ordered. "It'll work by itself if you let it alone. Those earrings are glorious on you. Give you a nice air of wantonness. Don't you agree, April?"

"Truly an inspiration, Miss Arden." I handed Dora the Shalimar and she began dousing it on herself.

"Not so *much*." Liz's tone was pleading. "Good God, Dora. You'll smell like payday night at the brothel." But Dora was communing with her reflection.

"The world may end tomorrow," she said to the mirror. "But there's never a world yet that hasn't ended sometime. And tonight Jack's coming home.

"Imagine"—she let me rescue what was left of the Shalimar—"just imagine. Me in my own double bed. Little old tousle-topped green-eyed seductive me." She held out her skirt like a dancer.

I gave Liz a long look.

"Maybe you went too far, Miss Arden," I said. "Ever think of that?"

"Nonsense." Liz quit biting her lip. "I just did what I could for the cause. Me, the barefoot cobbler. The nun at the waltz." She went in for a final metaphor. "Or, better still, the champion boxing coach who never gets a chance in the ring." She pushed herself upright. "Well, that takes care of the preliminaries. Let's skip along home before the main bout begins."

"After you, Miss Arden." I followed her from the Temple of Beauty back to the house, where we all had eggnogs and turkey sandwiches, and Sharon said how wonderful for Dora and Jack, and Liz said how wonderful for Dora and Jack, and I said how wonderful for Dora and Jack.

I said it more than once, and the last time I remember saying it was just before I went upstairs and cried myself to sleep.

• •

171

Lang got a couple of daytime passes during the next two weeks, but Marty wouldn't let him out of her sight, so we were never alone.

The first overnight pass he got was on January ninth, which is an easy date to recall because we left Schofield January tenth, Liz and the kids and I, going out of the house for the last time and walking in a ragged little troop across the echoing lanai into the golden afternoon. As the screen door banged, a spray of doves—startled in the midst of their mournful and meaningless lament—rose from our roof and disappeared round the corner past the faded flowers on the poinsettia trees. And a lone mynah bird cocked his head sidewise as he paced up and down like a sentry beside the trench that might have been part of the lawn forever.

While Lang was starting the car, Raico—who had gone to work for the Bendels—stood on the walk crying, and so did Dora and Sharon.

"Aren't you coming with us?" Marty asked.

"No. This boat is only for women like your mother who expect to have babies," Dora answered. "And women like your Aunt Liz who need a good doctor."

"But Dad's a good doctor," Joey said.

"Too good, if you ask me." Liz had seen her husband oftener than any of us, but I suppose in some ways her agony was worse. ("I mean, who can go on holding hands forever," she said when her health failed to improve. "It's enough to make a girl join the Carmelites.")

"Is Mom right?" Joey asked his father. "*Are* you too good a doctor, like she says?"

"I'd say not good enough." Bert climbed into the car. "I'm not a lady's doctor, and the man on the ship is meant to be an expert with expert medical equipment and a well-trained medical staff."

The sky was very calm and blue when we drove out of the Loop and down the avenue and through the Kemoo gate. And the water in the harbor was very calm and blue when we

172

reached Honolulu and I went with the others to the pier, doing my best to survive the good-bye by ignoring the future and pushing away the past, especially the recent past of the previous night with Lang. For even though in the following months I was able to hold onto the memory, I couldn't hold onto it walking up the gangplank away from him. If I had held onto it then, I couldn't have walked.

A good-bye time is a nowhere time, I thought. It's like the "equals" point in a horizontal addition problem: this + that = ?

There have been nights behind, I thought, and there will be nights ahead, but now we are hung in nothingness.

Lang and I had spent our last hours together at the Bendels', alone in a house that was silent except for our lovemaking. We lay in the double bed—the silly, sensible, used double bed—and went to the moon and back. And when Lang fell asleep, I tried to memorize his face, his hands, his body, everything about him, as he slept and I sat beside him with the cold tears running down between my breasts.

"Sleep well, my love," I whispered, and kissed him. And he woke up reaching, reaching and finding, and the moon grew nearer again, nearer and nearer in a great blaze of light that blinded us both and shut away the stars (if a place as high as that has stars) and we went up and over and past the moon —crying, clutching, sobbing—before we tumbled downward once more through space, downward out of the blaze and back to the world we'd come from, and were still.

I don't know what we said afterward or whether we said anything, lying there with nothing and everything to say and only that time to say it in. I don't know whether we slept again or didn't sleep. I don't know when we arose or how we acted when we arose.

But I remember the night was over before it was over; it had to be over so both of us could face the new day. I remember we were apart before we were apart, breaking our together-edifice down into separate boards and laths and timbers, because our land was no longer our land and our home had to be dismantled, had to be moved. And——however hard we tried to save the pieces——some of them would be lost, some strewn, some broken, and the others carried off in hope to somewhere, somewhere . . . since we possessed no sheltering warehouse where they could be safely (and perhaps interminably) stored.

Five

THE SHIP

8

MARTY

Though Father didn't come home for Christmas, he came a couple of times before we left Hawaii: once around New Year's, and once the day before we went to the boat.

"Marty kept insisting you'd be here Christmas Day," Mother said the first afternoon he came, and I was cross at her for saying it, because I wanted to forget all that.

"Yeah." Joey went past as I untied a handkerchief full of special shells Father had brought me for a present. "I told her you should have been a doctor like Dad, and she had a temper tantrum."

Father said he'd never had enough money to be a doctor and he hadn't come home for Christmas because none of the men were allowed to leave the beach that day.

"Maybe you just wished it, Marty," he said. "Sometimes wishing things are true can make them seem true. Is that what you did?"

I nodded. Father had a way of knowing about thoughts that no one explained to him.

"I used to do that when I was your age," he said. "I used to wish a lot. I'd wish I had magic boots and could jump the orphanage wall and run to a lovely green place by a river, where a big strong father played ball with me and a mother with a beautiful kind face knitted me sweaters and socks that matched as she sat and watched. The river was deep and clear, and sometimes after the ball game my father and I took a red boat out onto it and fished, and when we came back all three of us swam for hours, laughing and having water fights, before we opened the huge picnic hamper and ate and ate and ate.

"I never really went to the river," he said, "but I was sure the river was there and my mother and father were there and the picnic was there. All I needed was a pair of magic boots to get to them."

"Why, that's just like my angel's wings!" I said, and I told him about the wings.

"Keep the wings," said Father. "The pretend wings. And go on dreaming your waking dreams along with your sleeping dreams; we're all of us dreamers. But try to remember this, Marty; you have to know what's real from what isn't real. You have to know a sleeping dream is only a sleeping dream and a wish dream only a wish dream. You have to know what's honestly happening from what has never happened or what may never happen. Does that make sense to you?"

"Yes, Father." I wouldn't have put it that way, but I could see what he meant. "I guess I always knew I couldn't really fly with a pair of paper wings."

I wanted to talk about the lion, as I'd done in my wish dreams, but I didn't dare because—although I hadn't been near the lei shop since the air raid—I never questioned the lion's existence; I never doubted the peril that waited inside the door. And I was afraid that, if I tattled, the lion might hear my words and eat me as soon as Father left.

("The fact is," Willard had said, "the lion likes best of all to eat little girls who are tattletales.")

It was too great a risk to run, so I kept quiet. Before the air raid I might have taken a chance on telling; I might even have wondered if a green lion was possible, since I'd never seen an animal that color. (There was a picture of a green villain lion in one of my storybooks, which is probably where I got the idea in the first place.) However, after the air raid anything was possible, because that was when everything stopped being usual and right; that was when everything changed. That was when the Japanese planes roared improbably out of nowhere into the safe everyday skies over our roof in Hawaii, with the goggled, helmeted men sitting in the cockpits and the round red suns painted on the backs of the planes. That was when horror came to stay and the lion came to stay, both biding their moments, both waiting to spring out and devour anyone who happened by.

The morning we went to the ship I spoke to Willard for the last time.

"Good-bye, Willard." I dropped my voice to a whisper. "I kept that secret like you told me."

"What secret?" Willard stared through me.

"The lei-shop secret. You know. The one about what's hiding there."

"Oh, that." Willard's smooth little stone eyes began to pick up the light. "So the fact is you kept the secret. What of it?"

"Only that pretty soon we'll be going across the ocean where the lion can't go. To a place called Boston, Mother says. I guess I'm safe now."

Willard had one shoulder in the direction of the lei shop. He took a long time looking over the shoulder and back. Then he lifted one side of his mouth a little, only a little, but enough.

"I wouldn't be too sure," he said.

Father and Uncle Bert took us to the ship. For some reason I thought Father was going to Boston with us, though he couldn't have said so. We'd gotten our sailing orders the afternoon before, right about the time he arrived from the beach, and the coincidental timing of the two things must have made me think as I did. And with everyone busy planning and packing and running around, it's possible no actual discussion of

179

the subject ever came up. All I remember is the bustle of getting ready to leave and the talk about not having enough warm clothes to wear, and Mother putting a bunch of stuff into the laundry bag again; not only food and cigarettes, but extra sweaters and toys and books for Joey and me, even our life jackets. I remember some of the neighbors stopping by, including Mrs. Workman, who was furious not to be going along with us. ("I've *got* a child, even if she's not in my stomach," she said. "I only wish she were, about now." And I looked at Elaine and decided she'd be a mighty tight fit.) It was pretty mixed up—the afternoon, I mean—and at the end of it, Father and Mother went over to eat and sleep at the Bendels', and Aunt Liz and Uncle Bert had trays in their bedroom, and Joey and I ate in the kitchen with Raico, who cried quite a bit and kept apologizing, which was silly of her because, once the war started, people were always crying, the grownups more than the children. The day was all kind of unreal and queer, and so was the night, but not bad in any way, not scary; and with Father next door ready to take us away to a new and warless place, I wasn't bothered by the lion; I didn't ever expect to be bothered by the lion again, no matter what Willard said. Everyone had eaten breakfast when Joey and I woke up in the morning, and after he and I ate, Sharkbait—who always seemed to be loading something— loaded our luggage into a truck, and then there were a lot of good-byes, and we all drove to Honolulu. We must have talked during the twenty-mile ride, but none of the talk comes back to me, no mention of Father going or not going with us across the ocean. To Boston, wherever Boston was.

Father parked the car near the dock and carried me in his arms to the ship.

"Even without your angel's wings, you can always come to me in your heart and mind," he told me, "just as I'll always be with you in mine. But try to remember what I said about the wish dreams, Marty. Try to remember what's true and what's not true."

I had a moment of uneasiness.

"Aren't you going on the ship with us?" I asked, and Father said yes; of course he was going on the ship; he could hardly wait to look it over. But an old bald-headed sailor with black teeth was standing at the top of the steps and wouldn't let him on board, wouldn't let any of the fathers on board, so I had another bad moment until the sailor explained.

"We won't be sailing today." The sailor mopped his splotchy head with a red kerchief before he put on his squashed blue cap. "So why don't you and the other men come back tomorrow?" And Father and the other men said they would, which seemed all right, even though Aunt Liz acted kind of peculiar, standing on the steps in the new striped turban she'd made to match her traveling dress, and holding onto Uncle Bert as if she thought she'd never see him again.

"Take care of yourself," she kept saying, until the black-toothed sailor made her move because she was blocking everyone's way. "Take care of yourself, Bert." And she kept on saying it when she was leaning over the rail and Uncle Bert was on shore.

"I will," Uncle Bert answered, "and you do the same, Liz. Go lie down now." But Aunt Liz was stubborn; she just stayed where she was, telling Uncle Bert to take care of himself, until Father interrupted.

"I'll take care of him, Liz," he called up to her. "I'll take care of Bert. That's a promise. We're going now, but do as he says and we'll see you tomorrow."

So all day while Joey and I were walking round and round the place Mother called the main deck, or peering into the windows she said were portholes, or examining the little wooden sheds with entrances at the sides that she told us were blackout doors, I didn't worry about Father not being on the ship. I didn't worry while we were eating our meals in the big room where the sailors ate and the tables were nailed to the floor—or later when Mother and I were getting ready for bed in our stateroom on the upper deck. I brushed my

181

teeth in the tubless bathroom we had and asked where I was meant to sleep: on the couch or in one of the single beds.

"On the couch." Mother was trying to wash her face in the sticky water from the tap. "No matter what your aunt thinks, I'm sure we'll need the other bed tomorrow, and there's no point in switching back and forth."

I didn't mind the couch. A little smiling, monkey-faced man who said his name was Arthur brought me some sheets and things, and I was perfectly comfortable except for the heat, which couldn't be helped once the wooden blackout window was over the porthole. And I didn't notice the heat particularly when I thought about Father returning the next day and hurrying up the steps in the yellow morning, with all sorts of happy plans for Boston in his mind. The sailor had asked him to return, and Father had said he would, so I wasn't doing any harm when I pictured him getting onto the ship . . . really and truly getting onto it, not just pretend getting on, not just being there in a wish dream. I lay and thought and thought of tomorrow coming and Father coming until I fell asleep. And sure enough after the long night, tomorrow came and so did Father. But Father was too late.

I cried when I saw him. I stood on the main deck—a railed platform that seemed higher than smokestacks, higher than planes or birds—wearing my yellow pinafore with the white forget-me-nots embroidered on the hem of the skirt, and I cried and cried. Mother was waving and calling, and Aunt Liz and all the rest of the women were waving and calling, too, crowded together in a thicket at the rail, where the other children and I were as dwarfed among them as lantana under the mango trees, existing hardy but hidden below their branchlike arms, unable to see either over or out. I kept pulling and pulling at my mother's dress, trying and trying to tell her about the steps, but she wouldn't listen. She just stood there, smaller and prettier than most of the women but equally tired-looking, with her copper hair falling straight to her shoulders and shining in the sunlight, while she called and called and waved and waved and didn't notice what I said at all. She didn't notice the steps moving away.

Mrs. Lopez picked me up.

"Don't cry any more, Marty," she said. "Wave to your father and throw him a kiss. He feels just as badly as you do."

"But he's late!" I said. "He shouldn't have been late!"

"We sailed early," she answered. "Nobody could help that. Come on, now. Do as I tell you. Your father wants to remember you looking happy, not sad."

I didn't think what Mrs. Lopez said was true. I didn't think Father would want to remember me looking happy going away from him; I didn't think he'd expect it. But then I thought that if the ship had sailed early, Father would just wait and catch the next one, so I threw him a kiss and waved until Joey wanted a turn, and Mrs. Lopez put me down.

Uncle Bert had brought Duff to the dock with him, and Joey kept swirling his arms and yelling.

"Good-bye, Dad," he yelled. "Good boy, Duff!" and once or twice he got mixed up in his words and said, "Good-bye, Duff; good boy, Dad," by mistake.

"Dad says Duff can go to Boston when there's room on a boat," he told Mrs. Lopez. "Is someone going to send your dog when there's room on a boat?"

"Perish forbid," she answered. "If they do I'm going to join the list of missing persons." And when Joey roared another "GOOD BOY, DUFF," she added, "Go easy on the noise, kid. My eardrums are beating like tom-toms."

I wiggled my way through the crush of calling women and found a leaning place next to one of the blackout sheds. My square-toed shoes hurt me, and there was a hole in the front of my pinafore where some lady had bumped me with her cigarette. I tried to smile back at the bald-headed sailor as he went by, but it wasn't much of a smile.

"Ninety women with kids on one ship," he said, shaking his head, "and ninety stowaways." He circled one hand out around his stomach, but I didn't understand what he meant.

183

"Going to sit next to me at lunch?" he inquired then, and since he was a friendly old man, I said I guessed so. I wanted to ask him why his teeth were black, but I was afraid of sounding rude.

"Attagirl." He winked at me as he went off. He was a great winker.

There were five or six gulls in the sky, swinging among the paper-cutout clouds, and when they wheeled away toward shore, I wondered if Father could see them coming instead of going; whether he watched them, as I watched them, returning to the land where I was gone and he was staying . . . at least, staying until he could catch another boat. I wondered if he could hear their cries growing louder, not fainter, across the blue stretch of widening water. I meant to ask Mother about it when she and the other women wandered away from the rail, but she seemed to be thinking her own thoughts, so I decided to wait. Besides, by then you could hardly see the gulls; they were just little scraps of blowing cloth in the distance; and the dockful of people was only a gray blur in front of a flat toy town pasted on a scalloped strip of toy mountains. And pretty soon even the town and the mountains disappeared, and there was nothing anywhere around us but sky and air and sea and a lone black gull, lost from the others, that followed our lone ship as it cut its way through the slap and chop of ever-darkening waves and finally joined a line of other ships.

There wasn't enough room for Aunt Liz and Joey in our stateroom, but the two of them moved in anyhow. After lunch, Aunt Liz kicked off her shoes and lay down on the bed that should have been Father's. I pointed out the cigarette burn in my pinafore, but no one seemed interested.

"Call me when we get to the Golden Gate Bridge, dear." Aunt Liz watched Mother hang her red plaid skirt on the bathroom door and pull on a pair of slacks that were getting too tight to zip. "You were right about my leaving that hell-hole downstairs, but where on earth are you planning to put Joey?"

"He and Marty can sleep together on the couch," said Mother, and that's what we did for one night, which was one night too many, so far as I was concerned. Joey sprawled all over me, and besides, he wet the bed, so from then on I bunked with Mother, even though we were too crowded.

"Playing sardines?" Mrs. Lopez asked the next evening, when she stopped by around bedtime. "I tell you I'm going loony living over there with Earth Mother."

By Earth Mother Mrs. Lopez meant Mrs. Daly, who couldn't ever stop talking about her baby, although all the other women on the ship were just as pregnant or more so, except for Aunt Liz. It was that kind of a ship. It was also a boring kind of ship for Joey and me, because none of the other children aboard it lived on our deck, which meant we had only ourselves for company. Mother didn't like us to walk on deck without her, and, once the sea got rough, she wouldn't even let us downstairs into the slippery hallways where the sailors went in and out all day in their wet raincoats and boots. Joey and I got sick of our toys pretty fast and sick of our stateroom . . . even sick of Aunt Liz and Mother.

There was a little roofed balcony in back of where we lived, and he and I used to go sit on it every morning until the weather grew too cold. We'd count the other ships to make sure none of them had disappeared since yesterday, and then we'd wait for the airplane to fly off the cruiser and afterward watch the plane hum round and round over the water until it finally landed back where it belonged. And each day we'd search the ocean and sky to see if the black gull was anywhere in sight, and sometimes he was and sometimes he wasn't. Joey and I did quite a bit of arguing about where the gull slept at night or whether he did. I liked to think of him flying and flying through the darkness, zigzagging along over the zigzagging row of ships, but Joey thought he probably perched on a

185

smokestack somewhere with his black head tucked under one of his black wings. Joey said that's why the gull was the color he was, from sleeping up in the dirt and smoke and all. But I knew that wasn't the reason because the dirt would have washed away whenever the gull lighted on the waves, which he did every so often. Once in a while he even lighted in front of us and rode proudly between our ship and the next, looking like a tiny ship himself or maybe only trying to look like one, so as not to feel out of things.

I asked Mother once why the gull was staying with us and she said he probably needed a change.

"You mean he's tired of Hawaii so he's going to Boston?" For the hundredth time I tried to imagine what Boston was like and couldn't. I knew it was different there and we were meant to visit my grandparents, but I couldn't picture my grandmother at all, or my grandfather really, although I figured maybe my grandfather looked a little like the old sailor with the black teeth.

"No." Mother began explaining about the various places we'd be seeing. "After we get to San Francisco we have to take a train to Boston."

"Do you suppose the gull will follow the train?" I didn't want to lose the gull, maybe because he was my last tie with the only land I'd ever known well enough to remember.

"I don't think so." Mother stared at the sea appearing and disappearing outside the porthole. "Gulls don't usually leave the water, so this one probably only wants to see San Francisco."

"I'd kind of like to see it myself." Aunt Liz gave one of her seasick moans.

"And Father. I'll bet he'll be glad to see it." I still had the idea Father was going to Boston with us, though I'd shied away from saying so for reasons I hadn't examined. "I bet Father's on another faster boat this very minute, hurrying to meet us."

"You have too much imagination, Marty." Mother made

her huffly noise. "I doubt if we'll be seeing your father till the war is over, though we can always hope."

Hope, I thought. If we can always hope, I'll hope Mother is wrong, and then I won't think about it any more.

"I'm going out on the balcony with Joey," I said. "Maybe Arthur's there."

Joey and I liked Arthur, the little monkey-faced steward, who used to join us now and then and tell us stories about a far-off place named Manila. And if Arthur wasn't around, sometimes the black-toothed sailor would halloo at us from the wider deck below, shouting up things that were getting harder and harder to hear above the racket of the wind and waves.

Joey and I got to be pretty good friends with the sailor, because we sat with him at meals until Joey dawdled so much Mother decided we'd all better move. That didn't happen right away, though. We stayed at the sailor's table long enough to learn about his teeth.

"How come they're black?" Joey wanted to know. "Were you born like that or something?" And the sailor answered no; his teeth had gotten the way they were from eating betel nuts.

"A mark of beauty in some parts of the world," he added, winking one of his old sky-blue eyes at me and mopping up his gravy with a folded-over slice of bread.

"Oh, beetle nuts." I was wondering if beetle nuts were shaped like beetles or only black like beetles, when Joey decided to find out.

"What are beetle nuts?" he asked, but the sailor didn't have time to explain just then, because Mother made us leave before we ate dessert. She had all Momma Duck's children with her and got sick of waiting around. Momma Duck wasn't any more like a duck than betel nuts—when we finally learned about them—were like beetles; Mother only called her that to amuse Aunt Liz, when she took the children back to our cabin.

As we all crowded through the door, Aunt Liz gave a wan

smile and raised her head a little but not much. She was getting too weak to raise it much. My aunt kept getting weaker because she wouldn't leave her bed or eat anything except tea and toast. George Jackson—a Negro waiter friend of Joey's and mine—used to take her special things from the kitchen, trying to tempt her, but she wouldn't touch them. And the doctor kept urging her to walk on the deck, but she wouldn't do that, either.

"Is the man off his rocker?" said Mother one time after the doctor left. "Advising someone with your particular problem to stay on her feet?"

"Not to mention staying on them with the damn boat pitching around like a match in a washing machine," said Aunt Liz.

My aunt hated the doctor but she liked George Jackson.

"I'd eat if I dared," she told him when he brought her a plate of apple tarts still warm from the oven. "I'm sure the tarts are delicious."

"I'm sorry the apples are canned," he said, "but we can't get any other kind." And, to take her mind off herself, he began telling her about a mule he'd had once in the South and how he'd left the mule when he moved away. I think the mule's name was Niger or something like that.

"I've got a home in New England now where there's lots of apples on the trees in the fall," he said. "All red and sweet and polished. You ought to see them."

"I wish I could and maybe someday I will," Aunt Liz answered, and she and Mother started talking about how they'd both come from apple country and were going back there after we left the boat.

Joey and I finally ate the tarts, all except for a couple we gave to Arthur when he came in to change Aunt Liz's bed, which he did each day when he realized she didn't intend to leave it.

She wouldn't even leave it the afternoon of the lifeboat drill, though she must have been as scared as the rest of us. A whistle blew, much the way the air-raid-alarm whistle used to blow at Schofield, and Mother's hands shook as she bundled Joey and me into our few warm clothes and let out the straps of our life jackets. She threw Aunt Liz her wraps before she put on her own.

"Come *on*, Liz. This may be the real thing." She dropped her laundry bag and tried to pry my aunt from her bed, but Aunt Liz wouldn't budge.

The drill was just a drill, but it was a bad day all around. While we were standing by our lifeboats getting drenched and cold, Joey kept saying he wouldn't ever see his mother again; he knew he wouldn't ever see her again, and nothing anyone said would quiet him. We thought things would be better when we got back to our cabin, but they weren't. We were just changing out of our wet clothes when there was a sudden explosion overhead that sounded like the roof being blown to bits, and we were sure it was the Japs until Arthur said no; it was machine-gun practice. The machine gun went off only once, but we kept waiting for it to go off again, just as we used to wait for more air raids after the first air raid, although one never came. We were jittery all day, and that night when the ship's engines skittered and stopped, as they frequently did, Mother and Aunt Liz began discussing the Japs having submarines—boats that swam under the sea like fish, she told me when I asked—so I went on being jittery. And though I finally dozed off in the queer rocking silence, I was certain the lion had gotten onto the ship and was bumping about in the dark unexplored places below where I lay.

I think I may have called for Father, but all I heard myself saying as I woke was, "Willard was right. Oh, help me! Willard was right." And when Mother told me to forget about Willard—he was enough to give anyone nightmares—I decided I hadn't told the secret.

"Has she done it again, dear?" Aunt Liz must have been referring to my nightmares.

"Yes, and I'm frozen." Mother turned on the lights and got a bathrobe. "The next time I take one of these little scenic cruises, I hope it'll be more restful."

"You and me both." Aunt Liz covered her eyes against the brightness. "And while we're hoping, let's hope to God this floating obstetrics ward docks sometime before Easter."

Hope, I reminded myself. If the grownups keep hoping, maybe I'd better do the same thing.

So that's what I did. I hoped. I hoped Aunt Liz would feel better soon, but she didn't. I hoped we'd get to San Francisco in a day or so, but that didn't happen either. And when we reached San Francisco I hoped the black gull would stay around, but he joined a flock of other gulls as we entered the harbor, and that was the last I saw of him. And though I hoped and hoped my father would stride up the steps in the sunlight when the steps of the boat rattled into place once more, there was no sign of sunlight over the unfamiliar dock and no sign of Father. So I wasn't surprised when he didn't appear at the railroad or afterward in Boston.

I didn't think much of Boston when I saw it. The houses were too close together on the gray streets where no flowers grew, and the high sky was colorless and lifeless. My grandparents were nice enough. My grandmother had on velvet boots and a furry hat and she smiled as she kissed me, but she was no one I knew. And my grandfather wasn't at all like the old sailor; he was tall, with white hair and white teeth and a white mustache, and he never winked. Their house was all right, I guess, but instead of Iyaga or Raico opening the door in a bright kimono, a maid in a white cap and apron opened it, while a nurse who was white all over led my aunt off to bed. Mother and I bathed in a big white bathroom before we went down to dinner at the long table with the heavy white tablecloth and all the white napkins and china. And afterward, when the grownups were having coffee in little white cups in the parlor, my grandmother showed me a skimpy white poinsettia she had, but it didn't look like any poinsettia I'd ever seen. The house had too many white things in it, and when I went up to my room with the white bedspread and curtains, I suddenly remembered my orange balloon and wondered where it had gone.

Grandfather took Joey to his bed and let me go on to mine alone.

"Girls are all right with their mothers nearby," he said, "but a boy needs a man around."

I couldn't see why Joey needed a man around any more than I did, but if that was how things were going to be, that was how they were going to be. Boston was Boston, and Mother was Mother, and though both of them were reliable and well-meaning enough so far as day-to-day surface needs went, I wouldn't have chosen to fall back on either of them in a pinch; and as I lay staring out at the night, I didn't look forward to whatever lay ahead. Through the window I could see a flock of little white moths flittering around in the lamplight and I watched them until I realized they weren't moths, they couldn't be moths; there were too many of them tumbling bigger and bigger and faster and faster beyond the sill.

I slid to the floor and ran down the carpeted stairs to the parlor.

"Mother," I cried, trying not to trip over my white nightgown, "the Japs are here in Boston and they're throwing something bad and white down out of the sky!"

While my grandmother laughed, bobbing her white head above her pearls, my mother pulled the curtain aside.

"That's only snow, Marty," she said. "We passed through plenty of it on the train. Didn't you notice?"

"No." I'd noticed the ground was white in places and brown or red in other places, but I'd never seen anything filling the air like this.

"The snow's really very pretty," said Mother, watching it cover the streets and roofs and trees. "You'll get used to it, Marty."

But I didn't want to get used to it. I didn't want to get used to Boston. It was all too new and strange, and I needed someone to show it to me slowly, explaining it bit by bit, someone who could see the newness and strangeness my mother couldn't see.

I thought of Father as I went back upstairs. I thought of all the miles of land and water between us—the miles I couldn't cross now that my angel's wings were no good any more, and he couldn't cross until the war was over.

"I wonder when we'll see each other again, Father," I said before I fell asleep, but all I did was wonder. And, though I spoke the words to Father, it came to me that I was really speaking them to myself; that I was tired of expecting him to come, tired of always getting fooled. True, his coming for Christmas had been a wish dream, his boarding the ship a misunderstanding, and his meeting us in San Francisco a hope, none of which was his fault. But a disappointment was a disappointment, and I'd had too many of them.

"I'll always be with you in my heart and mind," my father had said, speaking the truth because he always spoke the truth. But the truth wasn't enough. It wasn't enough when I had the lion dream that night, where the lion was different from the way he'd ever been before or ever was again.

He was just as big and fearsome as he came padding noiselessly into Boston, leaving his deep soft tracks in the cold unpeopled streets of the town. But he wasn't a green lion; he was a white one. Only his glowing covetous eyes were green as he paused by our doorstep and lifted his heavy maned head to locate my window. Only his white-lidded eyes were green as he lay on his back in the circle of lamplight. Only his eyes as he rolled and he rolled and he rolled in the fresh-fallen snow.

9

APRIL

The trip home from Hawaii wasn't like our arrival trip two and a half years before. The small, stripped-
down transport ship on which we sailed had no recreational
facilities—not even a common room where we could gather—
and it was winter, so there were no languorous days, no easy
evenings of laughter under the stars, no men except for the
minimal staff and crew who ran a lottery on which women
among us would give birth before we reached San Francisco.
We moved in a convoy of eleven ships: a white cruiser carrying a sentinel airplane on a hoist, two outrider duenna destroy-
ers, a hospital ship with a red cross painted on the side, a
Dutch tanker, a Norwegian freighter, and I've forgotten the
others. Ours was an unlikely fleet, with its strange cargo of
fruit and oil and wounded men and pregnant women; and because only memories linked us with the past and nothing at
all linked us with the future, our interval on the water was like
a world between worlds, a world we cared neither to examine
nor to assess. We lived in it (or through it) letting it go at
that, and by laughing over what wasn't laughable and complaining about the inefficient and alien mechanics of interim

193

existence, we were sometimes able to ignore the possibility of a sea attack along with our equally brutal but less definable fears.

We stayed in the harbor three days and two nights before we sailed, and the nights were the worst. The round-the-clock *skreek* and *thwomp* of the cargo-loading were bad enough in the daytime, and so was the heat of the Honolulu sun, but at least we could get out; we could walk the deck or visit together or make comments on the barrels and crates being swung into the hold. But after dark we were confined to our cabins, and—even though a set of floodlights shone all night on the rear of the ship—a dockside blackout order forbade us to remove our porthole covers between the hours of 5:00 P.M. and 6:00 A.M., so we were closeted till morning with the clinging leftover heat and persistent, merciless noise.

During the forenoons and afternoons, visitors came and went, including Rebecca, whom I'd phoned before leaving Schofield. She stood at the top of the gangplank—which was as far as she or any other visitor was allowed to come—and the darkness under her eyes was the only reminder of her continuing grief.

"I'll be joining you in Boston soon," she said, "so this isn't good-bye."

"I'm glad of that." I made a silent vow never to say good-bye again, and I didn't say it for a long while. I didn't say it when Lang appeared with Bert the day we sailed.

Instead I said things like "Don't forget to put gas in the car," and "Be sure and write," and "Promise me you won't be a hero" . . . all useless admonitions. Lang never forgot to put gas in the car, I didn't need to remind him to write, and I already knew, in my limited fashion, that the road to heroism isn't always a rejectable road with available detours, even when it happens to be marked with a sign saying PASS AT YOUR OWN RISK.

I don't like to remember the afternoon of January twelfth, though I remember it. I remember the stone in the chest, the vise around the throat, the needles behind the eyes, the sword-thrust of conjectured finality in the mind, and the Honolulu sky as blue as ever above the latticed rail of the moving ship. I remember Liz—in a red plaid skirt that had come unpleated in the rear from being sat on so much—saying she never expected to see Bert again; and I remember Bert's and Lang's backs as they turned away. I remember Boots Daly shouting, "I'll let you know if it's twins," and Honey Lopez, collared in a carnation lei she'd gotten from Lopez, refusing to throw the flowers overboard, as tradition dictated.

"Leave that to the schmucks who want to return," she said. "Personally I've had a bellyful of this tropic paradise." And while she waved at her husband with one hand, she waggled the fingers of the other at the ship's doctor, who was walking past.

"Don't look so prim, April," she said. "Lopez is gone, and a man's a man. What's next on our busy little social agenda?"

I told her I was moving Liz and Joey, who had spent two nights in the upper bunks of a dormitory over the engine room, up with me.

"I really don't have space for them," I said as we went upstairs. "But Liz has no business doing all that climbing."

"Let Marty come across the hall and use my extra bed," she said, but in ten or fifteen minutes she took back the offer.

"Guess what?" She banged into our room with fire in her eye. "I don't know how or when she got permission to move, but I've just acquired the worst roommate on the boat."

"Who?" Liz, already queasy, peeled off her rumpled skirt and asked me to hang it on the bathroom door.

"Earth Mother." Honey slapped the metal arm of our only chair. "Pregnant Polly." She blew on her reddened hand. "Otherwise known as the Walking Womb." She rubbed her palm against her hip.

"Oh, Boots." Liz sighed herself onto the bed. "That ought to make for an interesting trip, watching her go through her Daly Dozen from here to the Golden Gate Bridge."

195

"I don't plan to watch," Honey answered, but she didn't get off that easily.

Boots, with no wartime-maritime section in her pregnancy book, insisted on abiding by the old landlubber rules, most of which proved a trial to herself as well as everyone else. She stoically walked her daily mile of deck even though she developed a nasty cold and fell twice. She trustingly replenished her supply of daily calcium pills at the dispensary, ignoring the fact that the corpsman in attendance didn't know aspirin from arsenic. And though her shoreside quota of water came up almost as fast as she drank it, she went on grimly gagging down her daily eight glasses.

"I wouldn't mind so much if the glasses weren't so hard to count this way," she said once when she reeled from her cabin to give Honey, who had fled the premises, her bedtime orders.

"Don't forget to open the porthole, Honey." Her face was a chalked-in mask above her neat blue bathrobe as she went gulping off.

"Holy Hannah, how could I forget?" Honey sat awhile longer with us, looking like a flashy latter-day Rubens in her transparent leopard-cloth pajamas. "One more night of this and I'm going to heave Earth Mother into the drink or nail the damn blackout window in."

The ventilation problem bothered us all. The square wooden porthole covers, which fitted into grooved slots at the sides, were easy to slide out in the dark but almost impossible to reinsert, which meant we had to choose between an airless night or a lightless one. Boots's choice of a lightless one was as arbitrary and unworkable as most of her choices, since she made no allowance for after-hours seasickness (the pregnancy book only dealt with *morning* sickness on *land*) and took so long finding the bathroom that she always threw up en route.

"And always in my bedroom slippers, no matter where I move them. I tell you it's uncanny." Honey eyed her bare feet morosely and chipped a little silver polish off one toenail. "A good thing Lopez can't see what's going on. Those marabou

196

slippers set him back a week's pay, and right now they look like a pair of molting roosters in a rainstorm."

Liz and I opened our porthole in the beginning, but when Marty—who disliked the splashing, topless toilet and therefore put off using it—started wetting the bed I had to keep the window shut or risk pneumonia, so we settled for the luxury of lights. I still can't understand how Marty managed to stay asleep through the bed-wetting and also to ignore the reason for her damp clothes when she awoke, but somehow she managed to close her mind to that particular reality. She even thought she moved in with me because Joey was at fault and that Arthur, the Filipino steward my sister called "Art with the big heart," changed both beds each day as a matter of course, which wasn't the case at all. He used to wash the old sheets himself and smuggle the new ones in, grinning his white grin and ducking through the room in his compassionate, conspiratorial fashion, trying to ease my discomfort a little and boost my sister's morale at the same time. And then he'd go to the kitchen for things he hoped Liz would eat and return, saying, "Missy, at least eat the ice cream; at least, drink the tea."

"Has she done it again, dear?" Liz used to ask me each night when Marty flooded the mattress and I woke up cursing. "Well, back into what the well-dressed woman wears to a war." And she'd wait for me to turn on the lights and change into my old chenille bathrobe, barely dry from the previous night, that served as a blotter of sorts. "That bathrobe's going to be able to walk off the boat by the time we reach San Francisco." One night when I saw her pillow was wet again, I told her not to cry any more.

"Bert's going to be all right," I said.

"I wish I believed it." Because her continuing weakness and immobility distorted her perspective, Liz couldn't seem to get Bert off her mind.

"He'll never take care of himself." She'd gaze at her red skirt swaying on its hanger, not because she cared any longer

—as she had at first—about how she was going to get the pleats ironed back into it before we reached San Francisco, but because it was the one spot of color in the room and her eyes were automatically drawn to it. "He'll take care of everyone else, but who's going to take care of him?" And, in my own exhaustion, I'd try not to give in to the contagious despair that hovered offside; I'd try not to wonder who'd take care of any of us if Liz got sicker, or I got tireder. And then I'd start worrying about what I'd do in case of shipwreck or submarine attack or illness of my own.

I knew my thinking was compulsive and useless, that the problems had many or no solutions that might or might not be arrived at in a real situation; but in my predawn introspection I kept going over and over the eventualities, like someone taking a watch apart with no idea of how to put it back together.

No sleep, no sleep. That was the trouble. No sleep, except in hour-or-so snatches, for more than five weeks now. Enclosed in the bleak cell of my mind, I'd thumb through my rosary of complaints: important ones, trivial ones. I'd lie and search my memory for one night, just *one* night since the war began when I'd slept in even a semirelaxed state for any sustained period of time; and the only night I could recall and isolate was the last night at Rebecca's when the food was in and the fighter planes were in. Otherwise, something always prevented me from sleeping or woke me and kept me awake, if it was only a nagging apprehension or recollection, a nightmare of mine, a nightmare of Marty's that set her to sobbing, a moan of Liz's. And the longing for Lang was always with me, the remembrance of my night with him at the Bendels'; the night that gave and took away like the Lorelei luring you to destruction with the enchanted impermanence of song, the night when I sat naked beside him with the cold tears running down between my breasts (did we sleep? did we sleep at all?) and the moon, the moon. Was there ever really a moon where lovers journeyed, crying and embracing? I have a husband. We used to live together once. He has black hair on the knuckles of his

198

hands, but who can see the hands now? Who can feel the hands?

On and on went the thinking; disproportionate, exclusory, obsessive. On and on it went, night after night after night.

When a new day arrived and I forced my heavy but weight-less body upright once more, I tried to believe bed rest was as good as sleep. I tried to push the awesome possibilities of the present back into temporary oblivion as I reminded myself I'd done all I could do to foresee and sensibly prepare for whatever contingency might arise. The barracks bag full of emergency rations was within easy reaching distance, the life preservers were ready in their rack overhead, and the unfash-ionable but usable assortment of winter wraps was piled in a corner near the couch, where Marty used to restack them from time to time. (Marty's cold-weather costume consisted of a red sweater of mine that had gotten shrunk in the wash, a purple wool head scarf of Sharon's, a pair of Joey's faded rust-colored knickers, and a green suède jacket donated by Fritzi Fineberg. I can't remember what she wore on her feet.) She and Joey—forbidden to leave the upper deck unaccom-panied—weren't about to fall overboard, Liz was as comfort-able as I could make her, and I myself—having no illness other than my ever-increasing fatigue—had no real reason to fear any direr affliction than a dwindling effectuality in my day-to-day, tread-water efforts to cope.

Now, making a belated attempt to judge the trip from an uninvolved and unbiased distance of twenty-eight years, I realize our circumstances, though unusual, were only note-worthy because of their particular time and place in history. I realize we merited no special medals for tenacity or gal-lantry, even though death lurked inside us and outside us and death was new to us. Our dilemma of private hopelessness was no different from the dilemma of anyone facing a distaste-ful and immutable situation in a world where all trials are personal and relative.

In short, our journey was our own journey, and I'm not

trying to insist we experienced any overt drama that could, in all honesty, be dignified by that name. Even so, it would be wrong to say the possibilities weren't possibilities, and I was grateful that none of the husbands, none of the concerned fathers-to-be, knew the haphazard state of affairs that existed. I was grateful that none of them had gotten aboard to view the accommodations that cramped our minds as well as our bodies, because we had nowhere to go, nothing to do and no way to fight back at anything; I was grateful that Lang and Bert hadn't checked the inefficient medical setup or met the sleepy-eyed dilettante doctor. ("I hear he doubles as the coroner," Liz said of him before she said worse things.) The captain's orientation bulletin, distributed our first day at sea and again several days later was, if anything, an understatement of the conditions.

Liz launched into a series of ironic and interruptive comments when I read the repeat bulletin aloud.

"THIS SHIP NOW MOVING IN CONVOY FROM THE PORT OF HONOLULU TO THE PORT OF SAN FRANCISCO IS NEITHER A HOSPITAL SHIP NOR A PLEASURE SHIP." "No *fooling*," said Liz. "OUR SERVICE STAFF IS SMALL." "Thank God for Art with the big heart," she said. "OUR CREW LESS THAN ADEQUATE." "Did the big blabbermouth have to *tell* us?" "AND ALL SHIPS IN THIS CONVOY MUST PROCEED AT THE SPEED OF THE SLOWEST SHIP. FOR THAT REASON AND OTHERS WHICH NEED NO EXPLANATION HERE, WE CANNOT ESTIMATE OUR DATE OF ARRIVAL." "June 2, 1980," guessed Liz. "IN ORDER TO AVOID POSSIBLE SUBMARINE ATTACK, WE WILL BE DOUBLE-TRACKING AND ZIGZAGGING FROM TIME TO TIME AND THE SHIP'S ENGINES WILL BE TURNED DOWN ON OCCASION, WHICH SHOULD IN NO WAY ALARM THE PASSENGERS." "Who's afraid of the big bad subs?" Liz intoned listlessly. "BED LINEN WILL NOT BE CHANGED DURING THE TRIP." "Thank God for Art" again. "ATTENDANCE AT LIFE-BOAT DRILLS IS COMPULSORY." "Not for me, dear"—she pulled the sheet over her face—"frankly, I'd rather drown."

200

"AND MEALS WILL BE SERVED THREE TIMES A DAY AT THE POSTED HOURS FOR THIRTY MINUTES ONLY IN THE DINING SALON." "They call that grimy hole a *salon?*" she marveled. "Remind me to wear my gold lamé tomorrow night at the captain's table." "WE WOULD LIKE TO WARN YOU THAT, IN THE EVENT OF A WOMAN OR CHILD FALLING OVERBOARD, THIS SHIP WILL NOT STOP." "Is will not stop still underlined?" She sat up in bed, then dropped back onto her pillow. "WE WILL DO OUR UTMOST TO MAKE YOUR CROSSING A SAFE AND COMFORTABLE ONE." No comment except a look of incredulity as the ship's engines shuddered and she ran to throw up again. "BUT SINCE WE WERE NOT APPRAISED AHEAD OF TIME OF THE CONDITION PREVALENT AMONG OUR ADULT PASSENGERS AND ARE NOT EQUIPPED TO HANDLE ELABORATE MEDICAL EMERGENCIES, WE ASK THAT YOU KEEP YOUR MEDICAL NEEDS AS MINIMAL AS POSSIBLE." "That may take a little doing for some of these girls in their ninth month." "HOWEVER, WE ARE HAPPY TO INFORM YOU THAT THERE IS A DISPENSARY ON THE MAIN DECK AND A COMPETENT PHYSICIAN AT YOUR DISPOSAL."

"Then let's dispose of him," Liz said as I crumpled the bulletin. "They have a lot of nerve calling the dispensary a dispensary or that curly-headed quack a physician. I wonder where he got his medical training. I'd have more confidence in a dropout from dog school."

Honey was the only person who liked the doctor.

"Well, 'like' isn't really the word," she said during one of her evening visits. "I know he's a lousy doctor, but he's built along the lines of Errol Flynn, with pretty much the same extracurricular talents, and there's a need for more than medicine now and then." She went to the bathroom mirror. "I wish to hell I could dye the roots of my hair. I'm getting to look like a badly blended cross fox fur."

"I'm not exactly a cruise ad for the Matson Line myself." I ran my broken fingernails through some of my own grubby hair, "or an ad for personal daintiness either." I rubbed my shoulder blades, itchy from a salt-water bath in one of the communal tubs, against the chair back. (Don't ask me why there was no fresh water.)

" 'She's young. She's lovely. She uses Pond's.' " Liz put some cold cream on her cracked lips and offered the jar to Honey. "None of which has anything to do with Errol Flynn. How can you bear to sleep with that unctuous bore?"

"Who said anything about sleep?" Honey balanced herself on the edge of Liz's bed and rolled up her pajama bottoms.

"But doesn't Lopez mind?" As I glanced to make sure the children weren't awake, my words seemed to echo naïvely and prudishly out of my New England past.

"He and I don't ask each other questions." Honey moved her hand clockwise, massaging cream into her left knee. "We're together when we're together and when we're apart we fry our own fish. If I know Lopez he's already made other arrangements, and though motherhood may cramp my style a little, I don't plan to sit around leading a neuter life till the armistice is signed. Because that may be years from now," she said.

Years from now. It was a veiled thought I'd pushed away before and pushed away again.

"You're a slave to your Victorian upbringing, April," she added, which irked me because I'd been mentally criticizing the nineteenth-century tenets and mores of Boston that made no allowance for change in a changing world.

"It's not so much that." Perhaps the upbringing had been a factor in the beginning, just as it had been a factor in my earlier judgment of Honey, my earlier judgmentality, but that wasn't the whole picture. I tried to compare the reasons for Honey's promiscuity with the reasons for my lack of it.

"It's just that Lang's all I've ever wanted in a man and all I'll ever want," I said.

Lang, I thought. Lang. Lang. Don't let it be years from now. Months maybe, but not years.

"There's a big difference between wanting a man and hav-

ing one." Honey thwacked some cream onto her other knee.
"That's something I learned growing up in one of the rattier
residential sections of Pittsburgh, with a tired bird of a
mother who got gray at thirty wanting sex and attention, and
a mealy-mouthed ex-professor of a father who majored in
women and expected his wife to overlook it."

"You mean your father's a *professor?*" I'd noticed that
Honey never made a grammatical error and that her allusions,
though a bit overly graphic and earthy for my taste, were
usually intelligent and apt.

"Ex-professor," she corrected me, "which means 'bum' even
if it's written in Greek or Sanskrit. The old man got bounced
from teaching because he couldn't keep his hands off the coeds,
and now he hangs around the bistros patting the waitresses
while my mother sells stockings. At least, I imagine that's
what they're both still doing. I ran away from home at fifteen
and haven't checked in eight years." She stretched, and her
finger tips made a series of smudged dots on the septic ceiling. "I had my father's appetites but not his dishonesty." She
screwed the top on the jar. "And my mother's appetites but
not her cowardice." She got up to cover Marty. "So much for
home life in Pittsburgh," she said.

"But where will you go from here?" I asked, and I thought:
Where will any of us go if the war's a long war? Places are
only places.

"Not to Pittsburgh, that's for sure. I'll latch onto a hidey-
hole somewhere around Frisco till the kid's old enough to
farm out; then I'll rustle me up some kind of patriotic job like
working in a night club till Lopez comes marching home, at
which point I'll maybe settle down.

"*Provided*," she said, "he doesn't come marching home with
a little slant-eyed beauty on one arm, which a lot of our brave
boys will doubtless do."

The idea was new and didn't apply to me, but I heard the
words.

"Lopez wouldn't do that." I'd seen small aggressive Lopez,

the swarthy ex-boxer from the Bronx, galloping around a dance floor with girl after girl, but always his eyes went back to her. And always her eyes went back to him.

Lopez plays around, I decided, because he's scared silly of losing her and thinks the only way to hold her is to act as if he couldn't care less. And Honey plays around, not because she's nymphy, but because she has some crazy notion it keeps her free.

"You're not fighting Lopez," I said. "You're fighting your father, and that's no longer necessary." In my own discomfort I tried to dispense with unfaithfulness by breaking it down into disposable components of cause and effect, error and the results of error.

"You can't love Lopez very much or you'd stop all this fooling around," I said, and when Liz rebuked me with an "Easy there, April; people have different ways of doing," I realized I hadn't spoken for Honey's benefit; I'd spoken because she had a workable—though, to me, unacceptable—solution for dealing with uncertainty and loneliness, and I had none.

I apologized.

"That's okay." Honey got up to answer a knock at the door. "If that's that damned Earth Mother organizing the air currents again, I'm going to let her have it from the floor. Oh, it's you, Art." She took a florist's box from Arthur and opened it as he melted away.

" 'Will wait for you in my cabin with a warm welcome and a cold bottle.' " She read the card aloud and handed the box to Liz. "What do you think of *these* for a little come-on present?"

"Gardenias." Liz raised her head, looking intrigued, although it took an apocalyptic happening to make her raise her head and almost nothing intrigued her. "What did Errol Flynn do? Send a runner to the mainland for them or have them flown in by fast sea gull?"

"Neither. He grows them in his cabin." Honey held the flowers to her hair. "Guess I'd better slide into my raincoat and go thank him. I'm pretty good at thanks and pretty bad at life with Earth Mother, so it ought to be an improvement all around . . . me sipping champagne in low-lamped leisure while Boots dreams about pushing a pram in Westchester, between vomitings. See you tomorrow, celibates."

It wasn't meant to be a cruel remark.

"She doesn't know about your last weeks with Bert," I told Liz but I don't think she heard me.

Her eyes were fixed on the bathroom door.

"I believe the pleats are coming back into my skirt," she said, and while we were discussing the pleats to avoid discussing anything else, Honey came stamping back through the door in a pair of gold wedgies and slid out of her wet raincoat.

"I took the goddamned gardenias back to that goddamned Errol Flynn," she announced, and glared at me. "I hope you're satisfied," she said.

"I hope *you* are," I answered, meaning I needed her approval more than she needed mine; meaning I needed her forgiveness, though I didn't deserve her forgiveness.

Because I knew she'd done what she'd done to keep peace, not to show she'd changed either her mind or values. I guess I also knew I'd taken all the joy out of her gardenias.

"Let's see. Who haven't we talked about?" Sometimes I asked the question and sometimes Liz did and sometimes Honey did after she stopped—or didn't stop—seeing Errol Flynn. (None of us ever mentioned the relationship again.) "I have a new theory about AnnaLee Seymour's drinking. I'll bet, back in her heyday, she was one of those eye-batting Southern girls—great at the come-hither but really frigid— who thought she could go on dancing and flirting forever. And when she discovered what marriage was all about—no playing 'Drop the handkerchief' any more—she took up drinking and that supercilious, supervirile husband of hers took up polo."

"I don't call him virile. His sideburns are too long."

With nothing newsworthy happening on the ship except

205

when the machine gun was fired or we had another poorly attended lifeboat drill (the crew attendance proved as optional as our own), the three of us fell back on long dissertations and debates concerning our former Schofield women acquaintances and, eventually, their husbands.

"I still can't understand about Major Workman," Honey (or Liz or I) might suddenly say. "I mean how a smart man like that, a Rhodes scholar and all, ever got taken in by a witch like Jean." And after we'd given the Workmans a going-over, speculating as to what Jean's more recent forays into paranoia might be, we'd move on to Boots and her pink-cheeked boy-scout husband, hazarding a few lewd guesses about the nature of their love life, after which we might vilify the Hunters a little, ending up with an apathetic argument as to whether or not Colonel Hunter had false teeth.

"Thank God for gossip." Liz spoke a truism, because the hours from dawn till dark and dark till dawn had to be filled somehow. And since our thirteen days on the water (counting our predeparture time at the Honolulu dock) had nothing to separate them, nothing to make any of them distinctive, we had no compunction about lapsing into the habits of the idle and elderly, taking an outsized interest in personalities and finding events memorable that were memorable only because of our isolation from anything of real or alterable consequence.

Each day Liz made some comment about her red skirt: maybe that the color was beginning to look faded, maybe that she'd noticed a place along one of the side seams where the plaid was mismatched. Each day she made some repetitive reference to Boots's Daly Dozen and inquired about the health of the little sad-faced woman who was always trailed by her flock of preschool children, the woman I named Momma Duck, back in the days before we sailed. A couple of the more pregnant women on the ship, both overdue—Tweedledum and Tweedledee, we called them—evoked her continuing, fingers-crossed sympathy, and after each meal she used to ask me if they were still taking nourishment or whether their luck had finally run out and they'd fallen into the so-called professional clutches of Errol Flynn.

A black-and-white gull followed our convoy—Joey used to make daily reports on its whereabouts—and every now and then Liz and I invented stories about the gull.

"Once upon a time," I'd begin, "there was this Hawaiian sea gull who got fed up with the islands.

" 'I've about had it here in this bombed-out beauty spot,' he said. 'I don't like the crowd I've been going with, and there isn't a fish around that doesn't taste like every other fish, since some damn fool set all those rotten fires on the water. There must be a better world somewhere.' "

"Jaded," Liz would put in. "Jaded. That's what he was. Couldn't he have learned to eat pineapples or something?"

"And risk a five-hundred-dollar fine? You must be mad. No," I'd say, "he decided to see San Francisco instead. He decided to move to a city where there was a more sophisticated milieu and a lot of good gourmet garbage floating around."

And she and I would go on with the gull game till we grew tired of it.

Our first and last nights at sea are the only nights I remember specifically and only because they were the first and last nights.

The first one was when I went to get Liz some nausea medicine and left the children in the dining room because the dispensary hour coincided with the supper hour. ("That's what I call real planning," Liz said.)

The nurse and the corpsman were dancing, with the motion of the ship making for greater challenge and intimacy as they jerkily hummed "God Bless America."

"Excuse me," I said to one or both of them. "I have a sister who isn't well. I came to get her some seasick pills."

The nurse let go of the corpsman and repinned her cap.

"Everyone's sick but us, Fred," she said. "Get the lady what she wants."

"Right, Lieutenant." Fred saluted and poured some pills into an envelope.

"And a hot-water bottle," I told the nurse. "That might be nice, too."

"Hot-*water* bottle!" She acted as if I'd asked for a bucket of opium. "We don't carry hot-*water* bottles."

"But you must," I insisted. "In case one of the women needs preparation for a delivery." And when the nurse looked blank I added: "A hot-water bottle's the same as an enema bag."

"*I* know." If the nurse knew anything she didn't know much, and neither did Fred.

"Were those seasick pills I just gave her?" I heard him ask as I went out the door, and when the nurse replied, "Search me," I flipped the envelope over the rail into the sea.

Back in the dining room, a number of sailors and children had managed to get to dinner, but only two women: Boots intently stuffing down her daily dietary requirements at a far table, and Momma Duck—surrounded by her flock—at mine.

While I was spooning up my cold soup, I asked the waiter for the rest of my food and he said the kitchen was closed.

"Better be prompt hereafter," he admonished. "We're low on help." And as he spoke, Momma Duck—who wasn't faring well—raised her eyes to mine. She didn't focus them, just raised them and, flipping one hand at me in a gesture that somehow made the little ducks my responsibility, choked and ran from the room too fast for her unalerted flock to string along.

"You'll have to take these kids out," the waiter told me. "Captain's orders. We need the dining room for briefings and like that."

The crew played poker in the dining room.

"But they're not my kids," I said.

"They're not mine, either," he answered, which pretty well settled that.

"Come with me," I said to the duck children, and they came, followed by Marty and Joey.

208

"My God, where did you find Hamelin in mid-ocean?" Liz had taken to profanity more than Boston was going to be prepared for. "I mean, here you are, dear, acting like a female Pied Piper, as if we were living in a ballroom instead of this oversized closetless coat closet. Did you get my pills?"

"No." When I described the events of the evening, including what had happened on my abortive visit to the dispensary, she began saying she wished she'd gotten some pills from Bert; it would have been so easy.

"Easy or not, you *didn't*." I was put out because I'd missed supper; also because I'd been hoping to get my first real night's sleep since the night at Rebecca's.

"Sit on the floor," I told the children and they sat. "Play pat-a-cake," I said, and a couple of them did. "What's your name?" I asked, but they weren't talkers. One of them mumbled something that sounded like Merple or Ferple, and the oldest boy started sucking his thumb.

"*Now* what?" asked Liz, and I didn't have an answer. I could have gone knocking at doors on both the lower decks, saying, "I'm looking for Momma Duck," or I could have taken my problem to the captain if I'd known where to locate the captain, but I was fairly sure Our Leader wanted no truck with the housing problems of individuals.

As usual it was Art who came to our rescue and returned the children to Momma Duck, allowing me part of another night's sleep before Marty moved in with me. And it was Art who reassured us our final evening at sea when the ship's engines stopped just before dark and we lost the convoy.

"It's a broken rudder, but we'll have it fixed in a few hours," he promised, "so don't worry. We can get along without the convoy now because we're almost to land. I know because there's been a gull with us and it disappeared this morning." (Joey had already told us the gull wasn't around.)

And exactly as Arthur had promised (God bless him; God bless him and keep him, wherever he is), the engines started again just before midnight, and the next day we saw the cables of the Golden Gate Bridge looped in the thinning, gilded fog that the morning sun was burning off the bay.

"We're here," Liz said, as I helped her into her red skirt. "We're really here." She swayed as I piloted her onto the deck where Art had put a chair for her. "What are we waiting for?" She looked at the lowered gangplank. "Oh, yes. The luggage inspection. But where's the luggage?"

A last terse bulletin from the captain had hinted, in a polite way, that one of our group might be trying to sneak some highly suspicious item on and off his floating purgatory, though what kind of item he had in mind is hard to say. ("A set of secret papers vital to the enemy?" guessed Liz. "A live rat carrying bubonic plague? A time bomb to blow up San Francisco?")

IT IS ABSOLUTELY MANDATORY FOR SECURITY REASONS, the bulletin stated, THAT ALL PASSENGERS WAIT ON DECK BESIDE PERSONAL LUGGAGE UNTIL SAID LUGGAGE CAN BE INSPECTED AND CLEARED. But somebody hadn't read the bulletin, because the luggage was already on the pier. And the guard at the top of the gangplank, unaware of the tie-up, was only interested in keeping us where we were until he received orders to release us; so it was another hour before we were allowed to disembark, the more deserving of us disembarking first.

There was loud congratulatory cheer as Tweedledum and Tweedledee, making the V for victory sign, lumbered off the ship, with Momma Duck and her flock close behind.

Boots, met by the California branch of Westchester, yoo-hooed her way toward the waiting arms of a correct-looking couple attired in the standard suburban uniform.

"Yoo-hoo, Debby and Michael," she called out. "The trip back was an *experience*—I was sick the whole time—but everything's okay now."

"Everything except my marabou slippers. I chucked them out the porthole." Honey watched Boots buzz off the ship like a fly she'd never gotten around to swatting. "Don't ever tell

Lopez about those slippers. He was proud of them." She asked what I'd done with my chenille bathrobe.

"Out the porthole, too. Stop it, Joey." Joey kept sniffling because he couldn't find the white sailor hat he'd picked up somewhere during the voyage.

"Yeah, hats come and go, kid." Honey wiped his nose. "So why don't you try getting a little air on your head for a change?" She turned to Marty, who had had a bad night and still looked glum.

"Cheer up, chickie." Honey had spent a fair amount of the night sitting in our cabin. "I used to have nightmares myself, but they're like warts. They go away."

She reached out a steadying hand as Liz, momentarily perked up by the sun and excitement, tried to rise from her chair too quickly, and tipped sidewise like someone with a leg missing.

"I don't mean to play the heavy philosopher, friend," she said, "but as one old bleeder to another, I'd advise you to lie down again gracefully and stay lying down until you're really able to get up. It'll be easier on both you and the night nurse in the long run."

I was grieved—that's the only word for it—deeply and truly grieved, at the thought of losing her.

"Come with us to Boston." I made the offer impetuously, knowing it would never work.

"No, thanks." There was a gardenia in the buttonhole of her sateen coat and she took it out and gave it to me. "I figure I'll stay around here and cover the waterfront like I planned and maybe improve my mind by going to night school." She smiled, whatever the smile meant.

Then she kissed each of us without looking at us, and with a hand on one of her rolling hips and her mottled hair brushed and swinging, she walked down the gangplank, while three or four admiring sailors, belatedly swabbing the dingy decks, rested their chins on the tops of their mopsticks and whistled.

.   .

211

Nothing and everything was blowing in the onshore wind from the west, the wind that came and went, came and went, like an unresolved worry.

"Where's Father?" Marty spoke as if she expected Lang to be just around the corner somewhere.

"Staying in the islands." I didn't like the wind because it blew from the place where I had been, pushing me, pushing me, toward places where I had no wish to go.

I told Marty to watch Liz, while Joey and I went on a luggage search. The search took awhile, but we finally located all but one of the suitcases and dragged them over to the packing box where Liz was sitting.

"I can't find the tan satchel with my coat in it," I said, "but I guess I can get along with what's in the barracks bag, which I'm glad to say is a good bit lighter without all that food I left with Art." I glanced at the ship, thinking Arthur might be somewhere in sight, but he wasn't. Nobody was. Seen from the unfamiliar perspective of shore, the ship might have been any ship, might have been a ship deserted, except that as I watched it a piece of yellow paper drifted out of a port-hole in the pilot house and spun waveringly down onto the gritty edge of the pier, where the same wind, the wind from the west, turned it over twice and then abandoned it.

East, the wind said. East to Boston.

I rubbed a hand across my eyes.

I'm getting lightheaded, I told myself. Winds don't talk.

But the wind kept saying: East; go east.

I'd better get some rest, I thought, or pretty soon I'll be hearing voices in the floors and walls.

The covered area that stretched from the dock to the street was full of volunteer Red Cross women in white gloves, carrying bright aluminum pitchers of cocoa and sporting crisp new hairdos to go with their crisp new overseas caps.

Everything so new, I thought. The uniforms, the job, even the cocoa pitchers. Everything so new and ourselves so old.

One of the women came over to our packing box.

212

"The Motor Corps will drive you to your hotel," she said. "I'll let you know when we have an empty car." ("Vehicle," she probably called it.) And when she returned in thirty or forty minutes to refill our cups, I asked if a car had shown up yet.

"No, but one will," she answered, and I told her I thought we'd just take a cab, thanks.

The woman (a good woman, no doubt, but hardly a glittering example of perceptive empathy) was shocked at the idea of our falling back on the impersonality of public transportation.

"But the Motor Corps will be right *here*," she insisted, and when I said we'd really better go because my sister hadn't been out of bed since we left Hawaii, the woman turned brightly to Liz, who looked as if she'd been hit over the head and then propped up.

"Why, my dear, that must be why you look so rested," she said.

We were ahead of our time.

We were ahead of the clinging couples weeping and waiting in crowded stations, in crowded airports, on crowded docks. We were ahead of the other newly nomadic women with the worn faces and sad eyes, journeying back from somewhere to nowhere; ahead, but only a little ahead, of the collective wartime woman who moved automatically on heavy feet, often with a baby in one arm and a small child beside her gripping the other, and no third arm to swing a reaching hand into the well-planned pocketbook with the train money in it or to elbow the callous stranger muscling ahead of her in the ticket line who had knocked the cold formula onto the floor, after she'd already lost her place twice taking junior to the john where he really didn't need to go, while she grew more and more lightheaded because she'd passed up the lumpy scrambled eggs six hours earlier in Chicago in order to change the baby, believing she and junior could eat later between

213

trains which they couldn't because there wasn't time, or else in the diner on the next train but there wasn't any diner, so she fed the baby out of the bottle with the dirty nipple and when junior said what was *he* going to eat she gave him the last ten arrowroot crackers to last him three hundred miles, wishing there were twelve arrowroot crackers so she could have a couple herself.

We took a cab to the hotel and I got through the rest of the day and finally lay down to rest on a bed of my own, a wide dry bed set on a floor that didn't rock.

Sleep, I thought. Now I can sleep.

But I was too tired to sleep.

In the morning, Liz took her mink jacket out of storage and went to shop for a suit, while I cashed travelers' checks and arranged about train tickets and returned to the dock a couple of times to inquire after my missing suitcase, which the attendant assured me was bound to turn up and never did.

"I'm finally on my feet," Liz boasted that evening while room service was clearing away the supper dishes. "I never thought the day would come when I'd actually be clothed and clean and fed and upright again, but I'm finally on my feet." She lay down. "Tomorrow I think I'll have my hair done."

And after breakfast, she had her hair done and later collapsed in the railroad station, and I had to get a porter to load her onto the train and into our drawing room.

I didn't tell her I'd fainted, too, trying to buy a coat while she was at the hairdresser's, and had regained consciousness terrified for fear Marty and Joey might have wandered out into the unfamiliar streets of the town alone.

I should have known better. Marty was standing over me with Joey, watching the saleslady fan me with the newspaper.

"The lady says it's nearly noon," said Marty. "Isn't that when we're meant to meet Aunt Liz?"

"Yes." I thanked the saleslady for her trouble and said I guessed I'd have to get a coat another time.

"Wars are certainly tiring," I heard myself saying. "I never realized."

The saleslady did her best to humor me.

"Oh, but we don't need to worry about wars *here*," she said. "I mean it's not like we were in England or somewhere. Don't forget your purse."

When we reached the station, Liz looked very chic and in command of things, ordering redcaps to do this and that, and dashing sveltely about in her new suit and new coif and her mink jacket with the matching hat.

She saw us and waved.

"Hi, April. Hi, kids," she called while we waved back. "See, I'm still on my feet." And before we had time to answer she crumpled into a little heap of fur and finery on the station floor.

Six

THE YEARS

10

MARTY

Boston wasn't exactly exciting but at least it was bearable during the winter. Joey and I played games or built snowmen in the back garden, and Mother and Aunt Liz had each other for company. But when Aunt Liz finally got well— sometime early in March, I believe it was—she moved away to New York, taking Joey with her. And though my grandparents didn't go on their yearly spring trip to Aiken until a little later than that, they were always running off to parties or the theater, so I didn't see them much.

"You're going to have a baby brother in a few months," they used to tell me, "so don't ask your mother to take you to the park. Make her lie down. She won't mind us." Beginning in San Francisco, when people kept fainting all over the place, everyone depended on me to help, and my grandparents were no exception. "We know you'll look out for things," they'd say, and off they'd go again, leaving me to wander from room to room alone or—if I was lucky—talk to Fay, the maid.

"Couldn't we *do* something, Fay?" I'd ask on her days off. "Mother's asleep and I could go to your church group with you."

"You'd have no way of getting back in time for supper, and anyhow you wouldn't like it, Miss Marty. We sew for the missions, which ain't the kind of thing you're used to."

"I'm used to everything," I told her, because it seemed to me I was. "I'm used to everything since the morning the Japs came."

"I'd never of let them Japs anywheres near me." Fay touched the place where her thinning white hair was combed carefully crosswise under her hairnet. "And, if you want my opinion, your pa shouldn't ought to of let them anywheres near you."

"I don't *think* it was his fault."

"I ain't saying it was nor wasn't." Fay had a gold cross on a chain around her neck, and she polished it with a tea towel. "I'm just saying we're all of us sinners, some worse than others and some a fair shake better, thanks be to the Saviour."

"Who's the Saviour?" Watching her blow dust from the velvet flowers of her church hat, I wondered if real flowers ever were gray.

"Our good Lord who gave his life for the wicked." She touched her hair arrangement again before she eased her hat onto it.

"Your hair's getting thicker," I said, because that's the sort of thing I was learning to do, trying to please people because they seemed to expect it. "At least, it looks thicker to me."

"Worldly things." Fay gave a sniff, but I was pretty sure she liked what I'd said. "Hair is worldly things. Cook's off, the old tyrant, so don't forget to wake your mother when it's time. Get these dishes out of the icebox *here*, like I showed you, and turn on the oven *here* when the clock strikes five." She buttoned her black cloth coat and went out the back door, murmuring, "Thursday again, thanks be to the Saviour. One more blessed afternoon away from Cook."

I didn't know Cook very well. Nobody did. She was a big woman with a voice like a bugle and black eyebrows that

220

grew together in the middle, who guarded the kitchen like a dragon in a fairy-tale book. She waved a knife at me the first time I tried to visit her. She was only slicing onions, but I didn't like the look of the knife.

"I'm not here for children." She pinched my arm, marching me in to my grandmother. "I'll feed them, but if they come into my part of the house, I'll give notice. I can always find other situations. The McElroys still want me, and I could make twice as much money there." She eyed my grand-mother's parlor scornfully. "What's more they travel and not just to places like Aiken and Bar Harbor."

I asked my grandmother who the McElroys were.

"They're nobody," she answered. "Just rich people." But Cook thought differently.

"*One more time*," she warned me before I quit trying to sidle through the swinging door, saying I liked her earrings or her new apron. "Just *one more time*, and I go to the Mc-Elroys."

"Stop bothering Cook," my grandmother told me one night. "If she gives notice, we won't eat."

"Can't you cook?" I asked her, and she looked the way she looked when she spoke of the McElroys. Not exactly outraged but as if some things weren't worth discussing.

My grandfather, very neat and handsome in his black-and-white dinner clothes and his nighttime shoes with the little bows on them, held out her white velvet wrap.

"Come along, my dear," he said. "Alfred's already brought the car around, and you always enjoy lobster night at the club." He opened the door for her. "Marty will see to April."

The reason I had to see to Mother wasn't that she was sick. She just kept getting tireder and tireder. So much so that when my grandparents went to Aiken, taking the servants with them, she could hardly stay out of bed long enough to cook the meals, which meant we didn't eat very well until the rest of the household got back.

"I can't seem to ever get enough sleep," Mother kept saying, and she'd doze off again. The new little lines between her eyes were deeper, and when she moved she moved slowly and clumsily. She didn't even read to me at bedtime any more because it was too much trouble.

I don't mean that she neglected me or that my grandparents did. They bought me new dresses and patent-leather shoes and a gold locket to keep my father's picture in, and they took me to church with them on Sunday. And one day in May—it must have been May because they were back from Aiken and hadn't gone to Bar Harbor yet—my grandfather took me to the zoo.

"That's a lion," he explained, stopping outside a place with high curved bars where a yellow lion was pacing, pacing; and I answered yes, I knew.

"I don't care much for lions," I said, "even yellow ones."

"Why not?" My grandfather let me tug him off toward the part of the zoo where the birds were. "A lion in a cage can't hurt you."

Or a lion in a lei shop, I thought. So long as he stays in the lei shop.

For that's where the green lion was again. He had left Boston before the snows left Boston, and the last time I'd dreamed of him he was back in his little locked house on the faraway island where the barbed wire was and Father was and the war was, when there was a war.

"We don't hold with wars here in Boston," Fay said. "Not since the Tea Party, anyhow."

Fay was nice to me sometimes. She helped me memorize nursery rhymes out of a book she found in the attic and taught me how to tell time, and she answered Father's letters for me when he wrote, printing out the words I asked her to say.

"I know you're being a help to your grandparents," my father wrote. (Yes, I am, Father.) "Be sure and take special care of your mother while I'm gone." (Yes, I will, Father.) And—after Jill was born—"I'm sure you'll look out for your baby sister." (I always do, Father.) He kept asking me to do things that sounded easy and weren't, but I did what he said. I did what everyone said.

Fay showed me how to knit, too, and when I made a bumpy scarf for the missions she carried it off saying, "Don't fret, Marty. Them Africans ain't too fussy." She also told me what to do when I woke up at night and couldn't get back to sleep. I don't mean I was having bad dreams then; it was just that I'd moved into the bed next to Mother, and every time she moaned I'd jerk awake wondering what was wrong. I could have stayed in my own room and gotten more rest, but I was pretty sure Father wouldn't want me to be so far away from Mother when the two of us were alone upstairs.

"Think up names for your baby brother," Fay suggested, "in case your ma decides not to name him Vernon." And I'd lie and think of Randolph (my grandfather's name) and Willard and Joey and Bert and Sharkbait and Fritzi. My grandparents went to Bar Harbor in early June, a couple of weeks before Jill was born. They took Alfred and Cook with them and left Fay to help Mother and me, but she wasn't much help. She got the meals and then went rushing away to her church group, whether it was one of her afternoons off or not.

"People are getting barer in the missions," she explained, "and right now we're up to our necks in underwear for Africans. I won't be gone long." And she'd put on her hat, even though it was summer, and disappear out the back door.

It was a good thing Mrs. Fineberg arrived in town when she did, because I didn't feel too happy when Fay wasn't around.

"Grandfather said to call Fay if I needed anything," I told Mrs. Fineberg when she first came to see us. "Only how can I call her if she's never here?"

"You can't and you don't have to." Mrs. Fineberg walked quickly up the front staircase, followed by Fritzi and me, and shook Mother awake.

223

"You can't let this kind of thing go on, April." Mrs. Fineberg hugged Mother, but she didn't waste much time on hellos. "It isn't right for either you or Marty."

"Let what kind of thing go on?" Mother rolled over onto her other side.

"This relying on a child while Fay's off making aprons for the Eskimos or whatever."

"It's underwear for Africans." I bounced the ball Fritzi had brought me. "Here, catch," I said.

Mother was glad to see Mrs. Fineberg, but she yawned and didn't get up. I guess it was too much effort.

"All this big house," she said. "All this big house, Rebecca, and who *is* there to rely on except Marty? Besides, even if Fay didn't take extra time off, the baby could always arrive on a Thursday or Sunday, and it would all amount to the same thing."

"Is your suitcase packed?" Though Mrs. Fineberg looked as fragile as a doll, she wasn't.

"Yes." Mother stretched and her dressing gown came apart over her stomach. "Marty and I packed it. Marty, mostly. And I told her how to call the ambulance."

"Now listen, April." Mrs. Fineberg's voice was firmer than I'd ever heard it. "I want you to get out of that bed and put on something halfway decent while I go home after Fritzi's and my clothes, because we're moving in." She asked if Fritzi needed any special toys and he said maybe his roller skates.

"And your microscope," I told him. "So we could look at grass and leaves and things through it. And your bubble pipes if you brought them here to Boston with you."

"We brought them," said Mrs. Fineberg.

Fay didn't care much about feeding two extra people ("And them not even Christians"), but she put up with it, saying there weren't any trials that went on forever, thanks be to the Saviour.

"And, truth to tell, I'd as lief not have all that care of your ma on my shoulders," she added, though I couldn't see that she'd had much, and she certainly didn't have any when Jill started to get born, which was on a Thursday just after supper. Mrs. Fineberg didn't want to leave Fritzi and me home alone, so we all rode to the hospital in the taxi. I didn't like the way Mother looked or the way she cried out every few minutes—it was too much like when Aunt Liz lost the baby and began to be sick so long—and though Mrs. Fineberg said not to worry, everything was going to be all right, I'd heard people say that before and a lot of times everything hadn't been all right. I don't mean in Boston. There wasn't any actual trouble there, but what with my grandparents going off and Fay spending all her free hours with her church group, there wasn't much support either until Mrs. Fineberg came. And if Mrs. Fineberg decided to go somewhere or anything happened to Mother, where would *I* go? Who would look out for me? Maybe Father would come if there was reason enough, and then again maybe he wouldn't. Mother had tried to explain how he had to take care of his men, whoever they were, and how he would probably leave Hawaii soon to go to another place where the war was, none of which made any sense to me because I couldn't see why anyone would go to a war who didn't have to. I couldn't see why, if Father moved anywhere, he didn't move back to Boston, where there weren't any wars. Still, my grandparents had ways of doing and so did Fay and Cook, and I'd gotten to know about their ways, although I didn't understand them. In fact, as the weeks went by, Boston and the people there seemed realer than Hawaii, realer than sand castles or blue seas or trenches or bombs, realer than the ship with the black gull following it, even realer —some of the time—than Father, though I kept answering the letters he wrote, and I prayed for him each night, which pleased Fay, who said it was only right to pray for the lost and misguided. "But my father's not lost," I told her. "What's misguided?" "It's them as don't do the simple duties the good Lord asks," she answered and, though she didn't mention any

225

names, her words set me thinking. "Be sure and take special care of your mother while I'm gone," my father had written, and I'd tried to, but how could I take care of Mother now when a nurse had wheeled her away somewhere, leaving Mrs. Fineberg and Fritzi and me on a kind of porch with windows where there was nothing to do except look at a bunch of old magazines I'd already seen?

"Wait here." The nurse shut the windows where a twilight rain was beginning to blow in before she rolled Mother away in a wheel chair, saying: "Try to be brave, Mrs. Langsmith; the pain will all be over soon."

I watched the rain battering the black glass behind Mrs. Fineberg's head while the thunder growled in the distance like an angry animal moving closer.

"Mother's been gone a long time," I said. "I'm scared."

"Don't be." Mrs. Fineberg told Fritzi and me about Goldilocks and the three bears, but I didn't hear much of the story.

The nurse came back.

"It's a girl," she said. "Where's the father?"

"He's overseas and couldn't come," Mrs. Fineberg answered.

"Oh, overseas." The nurse's words were probably just words, but to me they sounded like a judgment.

"My father never does come," I told Fritzi as we looked into the glass room where my new sister lay shrieking and jerking her arms. "No matter what happens, he never, never comes."

"But, Marty, he can't." Fritzi said what I was supposed to know, but that night I didn't believe it and I don't think Mother did.

"Your new daughter's beautiful, April." Mrs. Fineberg let us peek through Mother's door.

"Yes, she is, though somehow I expected a boy." Mother tried to smile at us. "Rebecca, will you cable Lang and ask him what to name her?" She brushed at her matted bangs with the back of her hand. "Tell him we're both fine," she said. "Tell him . . ." She didn't finish.

226

"Oh, Rebecca," she said. "It isn't *right* for Lang not to be here. Why isn't he here when I need him more than I've ever needed him?"

But all Mrs. Fineberg answered was. "Hush, April. Try to get some rest now." And after that we left.

"And you get some rest, too." Mrs. Fineberg kissed Fritzi, who was sleeping in my room, and then she kissed me. "Everything turned out fine," she said. "Didn't it, Marty?"

"I guess so." To me, everything hadn't turned out fine, just some things. I didn't like to remember Mother lying all worn and white in the hospital, lying there alone and lonely longing for Father. And I didn't like the storm growing worse outside my window. I didn't like the flashing and the crashing and the trees twitching back and forth beyond the square of glass. But the storm went on. It went on until my bed became the deck of a ship and my window changed into the silhouette of a little locked house, a house I recognized. And when I recognized it, I knew the lion was still in it. He was in it twitching his tail like the trees, rumbling his voice like thunder; and I could see lightning in the watchful, green-lidded eye he held to the crack in the wall.

"Wake up, Marty." Fritzi was standing over me. "You're having a bad dream."

"I'm awake," I told him.

"That's good." Fritzi, who was gentle as a girl though he didn't look or act like a girl, didn't like anyone to be unhappy. "You were yelling a lot," he said.

"About what?"

"A ship, I think, or a shop. It was hard to make out which." He went back to bed. "Which was it?" he asked. I trusted Fritzi as much as I trusted anyone.

Not enough, though.

"It could have been either one," I said and that was all I said.

• •

My grandfather made a quick trip back from Bar Harbor to take a look at the new baby, but my grandmother didn't. She told me over the phone she couldn't very well leave something she called her bridge tournament. "Anyway, you don't really need me with Fay and Mrs. Fineberg there," she said.

"And I have to get back in time for my Wednesday golf game," my grandfather said as he finished his Sunday-morning coffee. "A pity the baby wasn't a boy, but I don't suppose it can be helped now." He rolled his heavy white napkin into its heavy silver ring and stood up, glancing down at the nursery book I was showing to Fritzi. "What are you planning to name your new sister?"

"Me? Why should *I* name her?" I studied the pictures as I turned the pages.

"Well, someone has to, and your mother can't make up her mind. What's more, we haven't gotten any help from your father, which I must say I find rather surprising."

I couldn't see what was so surprising about it. " 'Jack and Jill went up the hill to fetch a pail of water . . .' " I wanted to show Fritzi I'd memorized the verses.

"A name." My grandfather drummed his fingers against his chest, as he lingered by my chair. "It's only decent for the child to have a name."

" 'And Jill came tumbling after.' " I waited for my grandfather to move, but he didn't, so I said: "Jill's a nice name. Why don't we name the baby Jill?"

"By heaven, that's not half bad," my grandfather said. "Especially under the circumstances: Jill came tumbling after. No, that's not bad at all."

And later that day when Mother called from the hospital, she said: "Yes, Marty. You're perfectly right. We'll name her Jill." So that's what we did. And when Jill was two months old, Mother bought an old farmhouse in New Hampshire, and the three of us moved away from Boston up to where Pearlette was.

We moved shortly after my grandparents returned from Bar Harbor. We moved thanks be to the Saviour, as Fay would have said. If I had missed anyone when we went (and I didn't) it would have been Fay.

"Though I can't be there myself, at least I know you're in good hands," my father wrote just before we decided to leave. But we weren't in good hands and even Fay knew it. She shook her head when she read me the letter.

"Them Japs musta got to him," she told me, "or he'd never have said like what he said."

"Mr. and Mrs. hire good," she went on, "and myself, I don't complain. But your grandma don't know her little finger from a baked Alaska. She don't know," Fay said, "a daughter from a clock striking nine." She pushed a loose pin back into her hairnet. "And your grandpa don't know his toothbrush holder from the Harvard club or a baby from his shirt studs.

"Too bad," Fay said, "that the Saviour didn't hand out brains when he was handing out the Blue Book." She fingered her gold cross, trying to be kind. "Of course, we ain't none of us getting no younger, and that makes a difference." She gazed skyward as if she and Heaven were in cahoots.

"Even the Saviour," she said, though she must have known better, "even the good Lord, who came into the world to save the wicked, found it a trial getting old."

Pearlette was my best friend in New Hampshire. She lived across the road and we went to first grade together.

Pearlette was pigeon-toed and smaller than I was but with more muscles; and her hair, which was slow in growing, stood out from her head like the fluffed-up fuzz on a baby chicken. Her father was a farmer, like most of the other fathers in the neighborhood.

"Where's *your* father?" She wanted to know when we got off the bus after our first day at school. "Divorced?"

"No, away," I answered. "He's a soldier."

"A soldier?" As she raised her forehead—not her eyebrows

because she didn't have any—her eyes reminded me of some goldy glass buttons on a church dress of Fay's; they were the same color and shape, even the same size.

"My father fights," I said.

"Fights what?"

"Well, nothing yet." From all I could make out, Pearlette only listened to answers so she could ask more questions. "But he will when he has to, because that's what soldiers do."

Pearlette set her lunch pail on the grass as a couple of cats, one white and one yellow, came bounding across the road to meet her. She took the white one in her arms.

"I should think your father would rather be home," she said.

"He'd *rather* be home"—I didn't want her believing Father stayed away on purpose—"only he just can't be."

"Why not?" She stroked the white cat while the yellow one purred and swirled itself around her legs.

"Because he has all these men to take care of." I still wasn't sure who the men were. "Like Sanderson, our orderly." I hurried on before she had time to ask what an orderly was. "Or like my uncle." I remembered my father standing on the Honolulu dock telling Aunt Liz he'd take care of Uncle Bert.

"I have this uncle who's a soldier and a doctor, too," I explained. "He and Father are together."

"They are?" Pearlette didn't sound very interested. She reached down and brushed a piece of dead leaf from the yellow cat's whiskers.

"My father and uncle are helping to get the war over with." I echoed some words of Mother's. "They're keeping the Japanese away from here."

"The Japanese haven't ever been here, so what are they wasting their time for?" She gave me a mistrustful look. "They sound worse than the Burnside boys."

I didn't get a chance right then to ask who the Burnside boys were, but later I learned they were the only men in the area who had forfeited their farmer's immunity to go into service (ostensibly because they were bad with cows and

230

"itchy") and their sketchy letters from Fort Benning were the neighborhood's one link with the remote beginnings of war. There were newspapers, of course, but Pearlette's father didn't subscribe to one ("Nothing in it worth reading but the weather," he said), and the radio meant nothing to him because all day every day he worked outdoors, and at night he was too sleepy to listen. Pearlette and her mother liked the serial programs—the ones my mother called soap operas—but that was about it.

Pearlette draped the white cat around her neck.

"What does your father look like?" she asked.

"He's tall and dark." I couldn't seem to remember much else at the moment, so I asked if she didn't want to jump rope or something.

"I can't." She undraped the white cat and cradled it in her arms. "I have to go see my pet calf and feed the hens and clean out the cat box. This cat's Snowball." She put her nose against Snowball's nose. "She's had fifty-eight kittens and she's about to have more any minute. This other one's Butterball." She rubbed the yellow cat's back with her foot. "Don't touch him. He only likes me." She looked me up and down. "How come you've got that white ribbon in your hair?"

"For school. All the girls wear them in Boston." On request, I described Boston as well as I could.

"Any cows or cats there?" she asked. "Any chickens?"

"No. Not where we lived."

"Well, *any* kind of animal?"

"Not really." I didn't think the ones in the zoo counted.

Pearlette gazed up the hill at the cows in her father's pasture.

"Then what do people *do?*" she asked.

I thought of telling her Fay was busy with her church group and Alfred drove the car and Cook liked some people named McElroy and my grandparents were always going to Aiken or Bar Harbor, but I changed my mind.

"They don't do anything," I said.

231

"No wonder you moved." Pearlette shifted Snowball into one arm in order to pick up Butterball, who was mewing. I found out later she always carried a cat or two. It was one of the few loving things about her.

I told her we'd only lived in Boston for seven months; before that, we lived in a place called Hawaii, with my father.

"Oh, him again." Pearlette knew all she wanted to know on one subject at least. "What was the other place like? The place with the funny name?"

"Pretty," I answered. "Pretty as anything before the bombing." I decided not to go into that. "Full of sunshine with blue seas all around it and a beach where my . . . where some of us built castles in the sand, and the sky was always blue like the seas, and there was never any winter, never any snow, and the poinsettias—that's a kind of flower—used to grow as high as the second-floor windows at Christmastime."

I could see Pearlette didn't believe me and, after my months in Boston, I should have known why. *Every* year there was winter in New England and snow to go with it; and the only plants that grew at Christmastime were plants like ferns and begonias and stunted geraniums, and they grew inside.

Pearlette reached a finger to hook up her lunch pail and said she guessed she'd better be getting on home.

"No animals there either, I suppose," she said.

"Well, in a way." I didn't want to lose her. "I mean, yes," I corrected myself. "There was this one animal, only don't tell anyone because it's a secret." I would have asked her to cross her heart if she hadn't been hanging onto the cats.

"I forget what the animal was called." I didn't dare come right out and say it was a lion. "But it was big and furry with a long tail and mane and sharp teeth, and it lived in sort of a little closed-up building where people used to sell things." Instead of saying a lei shop, which would have led to a whole batch of other questions, I groped for a term Pearlette would find more acceptable and remembered the place where Mother bought groceries and things.

"Like a general store," I said, which must have satisfied her because she went on to ask how big the animal was.

"Big." I stretched my arms. "As big as a cow, only he didn't look like a cow." I watched Butterball yawning. "He looked more like a cat. A big green cat."

"*Green!*" Pearlette wasn't prepared for green.

"Bright green." I wasn't going to lie.

Pearlette thought the idea over and decided to give me the benefit of the doubt. Maybe because, like one of the characters in a soap opera, a green animal—however implausible—was somehow interesting enough to be possible.

"Come on over to my house for a doughnut," she said. "Here, you can hold Snowball if you're careful." She fixed her lashless goldy eyes on me.

"I'm glad you finally told me something *real*," she said.

The lion may have seemed real to Pearlette, but he didn't seem particularly real to me that year, though at some point after Christmas I dreamed about him once or twice. Father had moved to a new island by then, and Mother walked the floor night after night or painted woodwork or refinished furniture. I used to wake up to go to the bathroom or cover Jill and notice the bed across the hall was empty, so just to make sure nothing was wrong, I'd wander around peeking into the other rooms till I found where Mother was, and if she saw me I'd say I was on my way to get a glass of milk or a cracker. Aside from that, everything went along fairly well. Aunt Liz and Joey paid us two or three visits, traveling from their apartment in New York to our new-old farmhouse, so my aunt could share and assess and try to forget her hopes and doubts with Mother. Once, I decided to ask the two of them about the lion, sort of casually, and though they listened to me in the mannerly, nonlistening fashion that grownups frequently use with small children, I could tell they didn't have any idea what I was talking about, so I stopped talking, which was just as well. That's when I first learned that memory, right or wrong, is a subjective thing. The lion hadn't been part of their private war, any more than had the bald-headed sailor with the black teeth or the square-toed shoes that hurt my feet or the burn in my yellow pinafore.

I liked school, where I was learning to read and write, and Pearlette gave me one of Snowball's kittens in the spring, and Jill started to walk, and Mother planted a big garden. And the house kept getting nicer and nicer because of all the work Mother was doing on it, even sawing shelves and hammering and putting up wallpaper.

"I can't hire anyone else to lift a hand," she said.

"Did your mother always wear boots and coveralls and have that straight short hair?" Pearlette, whose mother had a tight permanent and wore cotton dresses and flowered aprons, kept noticing things I only half noticed or didn't want to notice.

"No, not always," I said.

"Was she ever pretty?"

"Isn't she now?" I knew she wasn't, but I didn't like thinking about it. Her hands were rough from chopping wood and gardening and the rest of it, her face was usually sunburned or chapped depending on the weather, and she never wore lipstick or nice clothes.

Mrs. Patterson from next door, who used to clean and cook for us, tried to make Mother stop working so hard.

"That's a man's work, Mrs. Langsmith," she'd say. "You ought to have a man around." Mrs. Patterson said it over and over, but Mother didn't pay any attention, any more than she paid attention when I asked her to put on a dress once in a while.

"Why bother when there's no one to see me?" She forgot that Jill saw her and Mrs. Patterson and Pearlette saw her, and so did anyone else who happened to come by.

"I'll fix myself up when your father gets home," she said. "Right now it's more important getting his house in shape. He's always wanted a house of his own, and I'd like him to be pleased." From the way she talked, it sounded as if the house didn't belong to anyone but Father, which kind of annoyed me, but I didn't want to say so because I knew it would only make Mother unhappy and she was unhappy enough as it was, with Father going into more and more battles all of the time.

One day when Pearlette and I got back from picking blackberries, we found her in the kitchen reading the newspaper and crying. She didn't even admire our berries; just told me to watch Jill, who was wandering around, and left.

"Your father again, I suppose." Pearlette said "suppose" a lot, making even her statements into questions.

"I suppose." I could read fairly well by then, so I glanced at the newspaper headline. "A bunch of soldiers just landed on another island. I guess he's one of them. Mother says the men need him more than ever now that he's a colonel."

Pearlette knew even less about colonels than I did, and I didn't know much.

"Come on," she said. "Let's go catch frogs."

She forgot I had to baby-sit until I reminded her.

"All you do is baby-sit." What Pearlette said wasn't true —I'd just been berrying—but, not having any brothers or sisters of her own, she could pretty much do what she wanted when she wanted.

"When are you ever going to be able to *play?*" she asked.

"I do play," I told her, but she was mad at me. And when she was mad she could be mean.

"And don't tell me everything will be better when your father comes home," she said.

"Yes, it will." I tried to believe it would. "Everything will be better for everybody then."

"*Everybody?*" Pearlette raised the eyebrows that she didn't have. "I'll bet he won't even know *you're* around he'll be so ga-ga over Jill." She waited for me to act hurt and when I didn't, she added:

235

"After all, he's already seen you and he's never seen Jill. Ever think of that?"

"Yes," I answered, because I'd heard it often enough.

"Your father will certainly want to see your baby sister," people were always saying to me. Or else they'd say to Jill: "Just wait until your father sees you. That'll be a mighty proud day all around." And while Jill, who didn't have any idea what a father was, smiled and looked cute, I'd think about Father rushing through the door and over to her and never even noticing me.

"Well, so long," said Pearlette, and went off to catch frogs.

After she'd gone, I sat a long time in the old wicker rocker Mother had painted red. I sat there while Jill banged a spoon on a pan, sat there and wondered what I could do to cheer Mother, but nothing came to mind. Only my father could really cheer her, and he wasn't about to.

I tried to visualize Father, tried to visualize his coming to New Hampshire, striding tall and strong into the house to make things better, even if he didn't call out "Where's my Marty? Where's my Spring Song?" Even if he only called out: "Where's my April? Where's my new little daughter, Jill?" But I couldn't hear any voice; I couldn't see him. All I could see was Pearlette sitting by the frog stream.

"Here, have another berry," I said to Jill, who tipped her head to one side, listening.

"Berry," she echoed. "Berry." It was her first word.

I gave her another berry before I got out of the rocker to swat a fly for Mother, who hated flies in the house.

Does Father ever swat a fly for anyone? I thought. Does he ever give a berry to Jill?

My thinking didn't make sense, but that didn't stop me from thinking.

Do I really have a father? I thought, and I opened the locket I wore around my neck but I might as well not have bothered, because the picture was no longer a picture. The features were too tiny to make out, the hair could have been either dark or light, and a water spot muddled the mouth.

As I snapped the locket shut, I decided never to open it again. In fact, if I'd had my way, I'd have thrown it in the trash right then and there, because I was suddenly sick of it, sick of trying to learn from it, sick of everything.

I was sick of Mrs. Patterson saying: "That's a man's work, Mrs. Langsmith; you ought to have a man around." I was sick of hearing about Father's war and Father's house and Father's baby. I was sick of the way my father made my mother cry and work and walk the floor, sick of how he made her look, sick of pretending to my friends that I believed in him, in his ever coming home. Maybe he was busy fighting and had to take care of his men, but what was so great about that? It just meant I had to go on doing everything for everyone else, all of which got a whole lot worse before it got better. It got worse even before Mother went into her bad spell, as Pearlette called it.

I mean there was all that business of Joey throwing his Uncle Sam hat in the fire and Aunt Liz staying in the front bedroom for weeks on end, staying there because of what Father did—or, rather, didn't do—again. And after that I didn't even like to answer his letters, though I wrote good letters by then. I only wrote him when Mother reminded me and I couldn't get out of it. And when I wrote I just said Jill was fine and Mother was fine and the house was fine, and the only reason I signed the letters "love" was so as not to hurt Mother's feelings, because she usually read what I'd written. That's why I went on praying for him, too: to please Mother, though of course I never let on. I didn't think my prayers would do any good. I didn't think they'd keep him safe or bring him home, much less give me anything to say to him if he came. For he was no longer a person I knew. He was a drifting, detached shadow shaped by hearsay and conjecture . . . a lost legend of a man and a poor legend, at that. And when Mother went into her bad spell, I was sorry only for her sake, not his, because the bad spell was all his fault.

"Like everything, wouldn't you say?" Pearlette asked, and as I answered "Yes," I curled my fingers into fists.

Because by that time I hated my father.

11

APRIL

The years.

There was a sequence to them once, viewed in short-range retrospect, viewed as time, not space. Seven days made a week, four weeks made a month, and twelve months made the first year, and after that the next and the next. It would have helped if there had been anything to measure the years against, but there wasn't. As women we worked and waited for the men who fought and waited, all of us prisoners with indeterminate sentences who couldn't mark off this or that section on a calendar, saying, We have served a tenth of our term, a third of our term, a half, any more than we could predict how many islands would have to be taken or how many lives lost in the taking as the war went on and on. For though the war was a war we hadn't been prepared for and hadn't started, we had to finish it . . . not for glory, not for prestige, and not for an esteemed or misguided ideology, but for survival. I'm not discussing theories and I'm not discussing choices; I'm discussing how it was, discussing a war that couldn't have been prevented by peace marches unless the peace marches had occurred in Japan. I'm talking twenty-eight years later in a new era where a new generation remembers the mistaken atrocity of Hiroshima and forgets the atrocities of Pearl Harbor and Bataan and the Japanese prison camps, of Mussolini and Ethiopia, of Hitler and the Jews and the death camps. I'm speaking for an accused generation that will never forget the atrocities and never be the same, remembering. And if some of us in the generation have our reticencies toward disarmament—knowing that, like marriage, it has to be a reciprocal affair—we also have our resentments about being held responsible for all the past and present violence in a world that has always been violent, our resentments at being classed with the materialists and the warmongers of that world. Some of us, I suppose, have learned to shrug at the classification, thereby accepting it. And some, having long since been white dust under the white crosses, can neither accept nor refute it. But I for one, who can still rise to my feet when the accusatory finger points at me, refuse to stand up and be counted.

I bore my own grudges toward the generation that preceded mine.

When Liz and the kids and I finished our long trek home from Hawaii, Boston seemed like a haven. At least it did at first. Everything was peaceful and clean and ordered and though I arrived coatless in the middle of a blizzard, Alfred had the car heater going and covered me with the old fur lap robe in his old cherishing manner. Joey and Marty, who had never seen snow before, were surprised and delighted by our drive through the white streets, and my parents met us at the house with a registered nurse for Liz and embraces for everyone. My mother and father were about the same, a little older but not much, and seeing them gave a forgotten continuity to life that was both reassuring and pleasant, just as the house was pleasant and the temporary lack of responsibility pleasant. Fay the maid had aged a good deal and, having gone in for religion in her latter years, was usually reading or misreading the Bible, though in between times she fussed over

Liz and me, saying, "You poor girls. What you've been through would make even Job look sick." Our parents fussed over us, too, until the novelty wore off, which didn't take very long, because—much as they proclaimed to love us—they had their own lives to live and didn't like having the pattern interrupted or altered. They were perfectly willing to buy what was needed—for instance, Liz's nurse—but they weren't about to do any nursing themselves. My mother believed Marty and Joey should have had a nanny, which was a thoughtful enough idea, but it meant fixing one of the servants' rooms where the roof had leaked, which she never quite got around to doing or having done, so the children had to stay inside most of the time. Luckily Liz had a strong constitution and was under the care of a good specialist, so—though she went on being sick and then convalescent for a number of weeks—she eventually got well. I don't recall which month in the spring she recovered or whether that was the spring when I gave up smoking for Lent and she said she didn't think she'd give up anything in particular. "I figure I'll just give up, dear," she said.

Anyhow her old job at *Lovely Lady* happened to be open, so she hired her Boston nurse to take care of Joey and the three of them moved to New York.

"And none too soon, with the way this museum and its keepers are getting on my nerves," she said to me while Alfred was taking out her bags. "I mean, I'm not a child of ten any more, and it's a bit late for me to conform to parental rules." Once she was up and around she insisted on wearing slacks to dinner, which my mother considered ill-bred and slovenly, and her incessant use of profanity horrified my father. "*Must* you swear, Elizabeth?" he'd ask, and she'd glare at him as she answered, "Yes, I must. Especially sometimes." She swore the longest and loudest when Bataan fell, swore and wept as I did for the men we knew in the death march, for the men we didn't know.

Our parents thought the manifestations of our concern ex-

241

cessive. "All of us regret the loss of the Philippines," my father said, "but most of us see no reason to carry on about it." And my mother said, "It isn't as though you girls could help anything. I wonder if I should get a new permanent before I go to Aiken. *If* I go to Aiken." She kept vacillating about taking the usual trip south that year, about abandoning us, but I knew she'd take it, just as I knew she'd gravitate to Bar Harbor in June, however much she demurred ahead of time. When she went to Maine she left Fay with Marty and me, but Fay was always out somewhere, so I don't know how we'd have managed if Rebecca Fineberg hadn't returned to Boston and moved in with us before Jill was born.

"You have no b-business living here alone with Marty," Rebecca said, and I answered: "All this big house, Rebecca. All this big house, and no one to take care of anything in it but me or Marty."

In June Jill was born and that was a happy thing, though sad as well, because Lang wasn't there to see her. He didn't even learn of her arrival until a week later because the cable we sent went to a Captain Langhorn at Shafter by mistake. And until Captain Langhorn, a bachelor, was urged to inquire around, he just assumed some prankster had sent the message: LOVE AND CONGRATULATIONS STOP MOTHER AND BABY DAUGHTER DOING FINE STOP PLEASE GIVE CHILD A NAME SOONEST.

I waited and waited for an answer, but by the time one came I'd already named the baby, which I might have done in the beginning if Lang and I had decided ahead of time what to call a daughter, which we hadn't. Mainly because everyone said the way I carried the baby high meant it was bound to be a boy.

I stayed in the hospital two weeks, and every afternoon and evening I used to lie and listen to the footsteps of husbands in the hall, husbands who hummed as they tiptoed past my door carrying bottles of wine or armloads of flowers.

"Would you mind closing my door?" I'd ask the three-to-eleven nurse, a plain, elderly woman whose name escapes me now, although I remembered it for many years. "I think I'll read a magazine." And the nurse, who used to sit with me occasionally to talk and rest her arthritic joints, would answer: "Certainly, Mrs. Langsmith," knowing that when she returned in twenty minutes or an hour, I probably wouldn't be reading; I'd be crying. "How about some music?" she'd ask, and turn the radio on. But the music was usually either old love songs Lang and I had heard together or new songs we couldn't hear together, so I never listened long. And, once the radio was off, I'd lie and listen to the silence until the silence became unbearable; then ask the nurse to open my door again.

I told her once I was sorry about changing my mind so much, but she said not to apologize.

"Door open. Door shut," she said. "A magazine. No magazine. Music on or off." With an effort she bent to roll up my bed. "Whatever helps," she said.

I remembered her aching joints.

"Is your arthritis bad today?" I asked.

"Who's to say?" She tried not to wince as she tightened my sheets. "Like many problems, I'm sure it's only a small thing in the general scheme of things." She reached one of her swollen hands into a Kleenex box and gave me a tissue to wipe my eyes.

"Which doesn't make it any the less painful," she said.

By July, when Rebecca left me to return to her parents' house, she and I weren't the only women living without husbands. One by one our childhood friends were coming back to Boston to wait out the war, at first viewing the change as little more than a temporary break from routine, a necessary inconvenience, or unplanned vacation as they greeted each other fondly, meeting for luncheon or dinner or bridge to gossip and reminisce. But I could foresee the future, foresee their lightheartedness gradually turning into discontent, the discontent becoming desperation, and their mutual fondness becoming tolerance, then intolerance, and then contempt. I could visualize the ones with no inner resources becoming troublemakers, the light drinkers switching from sherry to double Martinis, the beauties growing restless for male attention and falling into self-recriminatory affairs, as time wore on and they grew more and more bored with each other and themselves, grew more and more apathetic or quarrelsome or despondent.

"And I have no particular desire to stay around and see it happen," I said to Rebecca. "Why don't you and I rent a house somewhere in the country and get the hell out of here while the getting's good?"

Rebecca wanted to leave but she couldn't. Her mother was bedridden, and a spinster aunt who'd been running the household had suddenly died.

"But you could go look at her farmhouse in New Hampshire," Rebecca suggested. "Nobody in our family wants to bother with it, though it could be a nice house with a little work, and it has a brook and forty acres of fields and woods."

I looked at the property and bought it.

"Lang's always wanted a place for the summer," I told my parents, "and renovating the house will keep me busy." Since both reasons were true I didn't go into the third one: that Boston had become claustrophobic and untenable.

I liked New Hampshire and found a therapy in work and in the changing house and seasons, each of them changing slowly and almost imperceptibly until one day a dark room became a bright room, one day the late summer became autumn, the autumn winter, and the winter spring and then summer. The green leaves turned red and yellow and fell from the high elms and maples, and the elms and maples swayed in the cold winds from the north before they grew hushed under the white foliage of snow—waiting, waiting for the time to turn green again. I used to watch the trees, noticing how they adapted to all weathers, holding the snow lightly, letting the spring rains slide over them and off, standing serene in the summer sun, bending with the winds of all seasons so as not to be deformed or broken by the winds. But now and then a tree was felled by lightning, and when I saw it change into three or four cords of prostrate timber I was afraid.

My mother visited me briefly toward the end of the first fall. Walking around in her velveteen suit and hat she should have looked out of place and fussy, but instead she made the newly stripped walls and floors look shabby and bare, made me feel awkward and ill-advised.

"But, April, you're no peasant," she said. "Can't you find someone to help around the place?"

"Only the outside carpenters and painters, and the plasterers," I said. "And Mrs. Patterson from next door, who won't do anything but a little baking and light cleaning. Everything else is man's work, according to her."

"Well, I must say you're a sight." My mother didn't bother to hide her disapproval and neither did Liz when she and Joey came to spend New Year's.

"What's that lumberman's costume you're wearing, dear?" she asked, shucking off her minks. "I thought Halloween was over."

"You got into the driveway, didn't you?" I unlaced my farm boots. "What do you want me to do? Shovel snow in a Schiaparelli dress?"

"No, I guess not." It was quite a concession for her to make, but she was either tired from her trip or had something else on her mind. I suspected the latter. I showed her around the house and she paid it a few absent-minded compliments and admired Jill, whom she'd seen only once before on a short summer weekend in Boston.

"So pretty," she said, "and such a lot of black hair." She watched Marty curl the hair with a baby brush. "I wish I could say the same for mine. I'm getting grayer by the minute, which may come as a shock to Bert."

"Does it matter?" I was sure that wasn't all that troubled her. "Bert would love you if your hair turned white or even pink."

"How do you know?" She followed me down to the kitchen, where I started supper. "It's hard to believe you're desirable with no one telling you you're desirable." She made a Martini and stood looking out at the snowy twilight, though I don't think the view of the hills and sky and trees meant much to her. "What happened to the kids?"

"They're bathing Jill." I was surprised she hadn't heard Marty ask permission. "Don't worry." I poured a glass of sherry and sat down in the green wicker rocker by the stove. "Marty's amazingly responsible for a six-year-old."

"Is that how old she is?" Liz knew Marty's age as well as I did. "She seems a lot older. So sober and helpful. More like a miniature adult than a child."

"She enjoys taking care of Jill and wants Lang to approve of her when he returns." At times Marty's soberness troubled me, but then we were all soberer, and I could tell by the pained expression that came and went on her face whenever her father's name was mentioned that his absence hadn't gotten any easier for her than it had for me.

". . . not that you or I are getting any dreamier or gayer," I heard my sister saying. She stopped looking out the window and sat down. "A year." She stirred her Martini with her thumb. "In less than two weeks it'll be a year since we got on that damn ship. Do you realize?"

I realized.

"I bought another dress for when Bert comes home," she said. "Sort of a pearl-colored dress with a hat to match. And red shoes." She dredged the olive out of her glass and ate it. "The last dress was gold with an ermine collar." She downed her Martini. "Want me to set the table?"

"I'll set it." Marty appeared with Joey and carried Jill to her playpen.

"Let go." She eased Jill's fingers from around the locket she always wore, the one with Lang's picture in it.

"Why don't we get a baby, Mom?" Joey waved a Teddy bear through the bars of the pen.

"We'll discuss babies another time." Liz either didn't want to explain or didn't know how to, so Marty tried.

"You can't have a baby *now*, Joey," she said, taking the bottle I'd warmed. "You have to have a father first, one right around, like Pearlette's father." Pearlette was that funny-looking little girl from across the road. "Not the *other* kind of father." She glanced at me quickly before she turned her attention back to Joey, who was clamoring to feed Jill.

"You can do it if you're careful." She tested the temperature of the milk on the back of her hand. "Here, Joey." She lifted Jill into his lap. "Keep your hand under her head and do it like this," she said.

That night when I heard Marty's prayers, I tried—as usual—not to be distressed by the toneless, stoic way in which she asked God to bring her father home safe and soon. I wanted to tell her I knew how much she missed him; I wanted to tell her to cry if she wanted to. But something—possibly the shut expression on her face—kept me from doing it.

When I rejoined Liz in the kitchen, she wasn't very talkative.

"Well, there's one bright note." I tried to break into her preoccupation. "At least we're not still floating around the Pacific in that overloaded human cattleboat." I began reminiscing about our former shipmates, and when I mentioned Errol Flynn, she spread her fingers over the upper half of her face.

"What is it?" I asked.

"A man." She took down her hand. "And, believe it or not, it has nothing to do with Bert."

I guess I looked shocked.

247

"Well, a year's a year." Her tone was defensive. "And I got so fed up with women, so fed up"—she used Honey's phrase—"with a neuter life."

"You mean you're having an affair?"

"You could call it that. I mean, I've slept with this man once, and I can't make up my mind what to do from here on out." She rubbed the back of her neck. "God knows Bert's the only man I've ever loved. I don't give a damn about this guy as a person, but it's more complicated than that."

New Year's, I thought. And this is how the first year ends.

"It's not just sex," she went on. "It's the God-awful loneliness, and my hair turning gray, and no real guarantee of anything getting better, only worse." She twisted a button on her sweater. "What should I do?" she asked.

"Two things." Even if I'd approved of her actions, which I didn't, I could see she wasn't happy. "First, quit seeing the man. And second, don't tell anyone else what you've told me, and that includes Bert."

"All right." Little by little, Liz relaxed, and as the two of us talked of other things, I tried to tell myself her transgression had been a minor and understandable one.

Still, it took some of the verve out of our New Year's toasts to Bert and Lang and Dora and Sharkbait and the others. And as I read aloud from a recent letter of Honey's, I was embarrassed.

"Faithfulness isn't exactly my dish of scrapple," Honey wrote, "but the 4-F boys have about as much appeal as a plate of worms. All self-satisfaction and paws. Not like the little guy I left behind, which—I might add—seems a hell of a long while ago."

Liz rattled her ice cubes.

"Forever ago. Forever and ever." A couple of tears dripped into her glass. "Oh, April. Do you think they'll ever be back?"

"Yes, they'll be back," I answered, because at the time I believed they would.

•   •

248

The belief died slowly, but it died.

It began to die when Major Workman, ex-Rhodes scholar, moved out of his Guadalcanal foxhole too soon and never made sense again after the doctors put the steel plate in his head. It went on dying when Lopez was killed on New Georgia, where Dora's Jack lost both legs and AnnaLee's husband—unable to wheel and rein circumstances like a polo pony—sat for days with his head in his hands before he was psychoed home.

There was nothing to write to AnnaLee, nothing she would have understood or appreciated or possibly even read, when the last character in the Chekhov play of her life was chosen for needless and ignominious destruction by a wanton destiny. But I wrote to Dora, who'd remained in Honolulu doing defense work, and after a while she wrote back.

"Jack and I have decided to settle here," she wrote. "He's beginning to get around better on his new legs and he's delighted with his insurance job. We miss Raico and Sharon, but they seem to be making a good thing of the gift shop they've opened together in Los Angeles. I wish you could see young Jack. He's beautiful and sings a lot." She and Jack had adopted Raico's baby.

I tried to reach Honey, but her phone had been disconnected. And the only answer I got to any of my letters—if you could call it an answer—was a postcard from Alaska with a picture of a mountain on it, mailed nine or ten months later.

"Keep the faith," the card read, "such as it is. I'm married again and the kid's starting to talk now. What's with you, Boston?" There was no return address.

I wanted to cry but by then I couldn't cry. I wanted to cry for Honey and I wanted to cry for Lopez. I wanted to cry because the Lopezes kept ending while the world kept going. I wanted to cry because as soon as belief dies, hope starts dying, too.

"The luck's running out," Liz said when she came for Thanksgiving. "It isn't fair for a handful of men to go on fighting and fighting forever." It wasn't fair, but she and I both knew it was impossible to raise a big army in a hurry. We both knew that the experienced men—especially the higher-ranking men, the leaders—weren't easy to replace. When they became casualties they were replaced, but not before then.

"Please let's not have turkey," said Liz. "Turkey's for family reunions and Rotary Club luncheons." So, though the children were disappointed, we didn't have turkey; we had ham, and tried to pass a surface afternoon and evening concentrating on trivialities. Or rather I tried, but once Liz and I were alone I can't say I succeeded.

"Nearly two years." Liz was always counting, counting. "I haven't heard a word from Honey since Lopez died, have you?"

"No." I was suddenly full of pain. I felt all right, but I was full of pain.

"Let's not talk about Honey," I said.

We were sitting in the library, which was finished by then. The floors were polished and there was pine-needle wallpaper on the walls. Liz admired the mantel I'd sanded.

"Colonial is colonial, dear," she commented. "And I'll go along with it until you start planting philodendrons in old sunbonnets." She straightened a picture over the couch.

"I gave up the man," she said.

"That's good." I didn't want to know any more.

"Oh, I still go out occasionally," she told me. "Just to have something to do and somewhere to wear the clothes I keep buying. But I may give up the other men, too. I tell my escorts I'm true to the red, white, and blue, but some of the guys are real bastards. 'Look, love,' they say, 'if you think that handsome, sex-starved husband of yours is sitting around twiddling his thumbs between battles in the Pacific, you must be more naïve than I thought.' "

I tried not to hear her. Lang had lost three fingers and

thirty pounds in the Solomons and was currently on a four-month rest leave in New Zealand.

". . . and some even worse bastards than that," Liz went on. "Every so often you run across a real card-carrying sadist who says, 'Come back when you're a widow, sweetie; I can wait.' " She must have seen me shiver because she offered to put more wood on the fire.

"Would you?" I hoped the project would divert her, but it didn't.

"What do *you* do about men?" she asked, centering a birch log.

"I don't do anything." I thought of a widower I'd met at a Grange meeting. Gentleman farmer. Over draft age. Rich. A nice man. I went for dinner on his terrace and there were fireflies in the grass. I wanted him to be my friend. I wanted to touch him, to hold his hand, to kiss him, but I didn't. When his arm brushed mine, I jumped, and when the meal was over, I drank my coffee and went home.

"You mean you never go out at all?" Liz should have known New Hampshire wasn't New York.

"I'm no latter-day Cleopatra," I said. "The jealous suitors aren't exactly battering down my door."

"But how do you get rid of the evenings?"

"I just keep working on the house." Didn't the house show it? Wasn't my work a worthwhile projection of the empty present into the full and fantasied future?

"Well, I guess we all have to keep busy, whether it proves anything or not." Liz, an apartment dweller, couldn't understand my reasons for laboring over a postwar home in the Godforsaken north. "And you can always make an extra dollar if anything happens and you decide to sell it later," she said.

"Why would I want to sell it?" I said the words bravely enough, but as I said them, a sudden shadow slanted across my mind, slanted eastward from where the war was, dispensing with all the restoration I had taken months to achieve;

251

and I could suddenly see the house as someone else's house again, or no one's. I could see the freshly painted woodwork turn dark and blistered, see the gleaming floor change back into dusty, splintery boards, see the wild strawberry wallpaper disappear from the dining room and the pine-needle wallpaper from the library, leaving the walls as I had found them . . . gray and bare, with black cracks threading through the plaster. I could see the starched white curtains fall into rags at windows where the outdoor shutters once more tilted drunkenly on rusty hinges, see the old and patient brambles reclaim the yard below the big maple where another FOR SALE sign was nailed to the trunk.

Nobody owns a house, I thought. Nobody owns a person or an inch of ground or love.

I remembered an arrogant mynah bird sitting on a strand of barbed wire a long long while ago.

Time owns everything, I thought. Time holds all the mortgages. And any hour of any day Time can foreclose.

Five or six weeks after Liz returned to New York, another year began, the third year. January came and so did February. I particularly remember February, because one night in the middle of the month when I'd finished my usual letter to Lang, I started doodling with words on a slip of paper. Outdoors, there was moonlight on the snow, but I found no solace in the moonlight, no solace in the rooms around me. I poured a glass of sherry (my fourth) and looked at what I'd written.

> Go empty the liquor store, Marty.
> Bring Mommy her wine in a van,
> So Mommy, all smiles,
> Can quit counting the isles
> That stretch between here and Japan.

I decided to do a second verse about Liz.

> Go down to the hairdresser's, Joey.
> Buy Mommy a wig that is black,

So we can have fun
Fooling Daddy, my son,
The year that your daddy gets back.

I mailed the verses to my sister, and three evenings later she phoned.

"April?" she said.

"Oh, hi, Liz. I was pretty sure you'd call." I asked how she'd liked my verses. "I'm thinking of running for poet laureate," I said.

"April," said Liz. "Is that you, April?"

"Oh, for heaven's sake, Liz, who else would it be? You know my voice. Do you have a bad connection or what?"

"No. No bad connection." My sister sounded as if she'd just gotten out of bed, though it was 6:00 P.M. on a weekday.

"Are you sick, Liz?" I asked, and she hiccoughed and answered no.

"April . . ." she said again.

"Look, Liz, this is getting tiresome," I said. "If you've been out lapping it up at an office party, hang up and call me back when you're sober."

There was a short silence, and I thought she'd hung up.

"Are you still there?" I asked and she said a word that might have been "Yes" before she added: "Bert's dead," and clicked down the receiver.

I made cab and bus and plane reservations and got Mrs. Patterson to spend the night.

"What's wrong?" Marty came into the room while I was packing.

"It's your Uncle Bert." I couldn't see any point in lying to her. "He's been killed."

"I might have known." It was a peculiar remark for her to make, but Mrs. Patterson was already downstairs, and I didn't have time to ask what the remark meant.

"What about Father?" Marty called after me as I left. "Where was he?"

"In New Zealand," I called back. "Don't worry about your father. He's perfectly safe."

I don't know if there's any truth in the saying that one sick person can kill six well ones; I only know that one person's tragedy is never one person's tragedy. The fatal bullet ricochets, wounding many people.

I brought Liz and Joey back with me, and they lived out the third year with us, though Liz had stopped counting the years by then. She didn't even count the hours as she sat day after day in her bedroom with the shades drawn, wearing an old satin wrapper that even I would have thrown away.

"Bert," she'd say. "Bert." And she'd shuffle her dirty slippers back and forth on the floor as she sat and sat and sat in the pink chintz chair by the darkened window.

"Remember how he looked, April? Remember how good he was?" She'd sit there, sit there, while the soup grew cold beside her and the silver ashtray overflowed onto the hand-rubbed table.

I was nearly out of my mind worrying about her, worrying about when Lang would be going to the Philippines, worrying about Joey's alternating withdrawal and misbehavior, worrying about Marty's worrying over Joey, worrying about Marty's worrying over Lang and Liz and me, worrying about whether Jill would get neglected and lost in the shuffle of worries.

"Did it all happen because of that one man in New York?" Liz kept asking. "That man whose name I can't even remember?"

"No." I'd give the answer for the hundredth time. "It happened because it was going to happen. And you knew it was going to happen from the beginning. You knew it on the ship." I'd smell the beets burning in the kitchen or hear the water overflowing in the basin. "Get up now," I'd tell her, but she wouldn't move.

It was the Grange widower who finally got her moving. He

254

stopped by one evening when the power was off, to see if he could help with anything.

"I wish you could." I was so upset that I told him about Liz, and when I'd finished he asked me to take him upstairs.

"My name is Frank," he said, going over to the pink chair where my sister sat like a ghost in the candlelight. "I understand your name is Liz." He held out his hand.

"How do you do." Liz pulled her soiled wrapper closer around her. She didn't shake hands, but she knew he was there.

"Get up," he ordered quietly, but she only stared at him with her lusterless eyes. And when he said, "Get up," again and she still didn't move, he pulled her up. Gently, but he pulled her up.

"People with one leg walk," he said. "The dying walk," he said. "Only the dead don't walk," he said, "and you're not dead."

By the time Liz married Frank, I was drained emotionally as well as physically, drained of everything except a love that no longer supported me, hard as I tried to change the old deserved and deserving fantasies back into expectations. My belief was gone, my hope was gone, and my strength was gone. Only the loneliness remained, only the weariness, only the cold and constant apprehension. Only the waiting remained, taking me into my fourth year of waiting.

Lang will be back; he'll be back, my mind kept saying. But nothing in me listened.

I used to think: The years will never end; the years will never end. But, of course the years had to end and they ended.

They ended with a telegram from the Secretary of War. They ended on a day in early May when the leaves were barely out. The next time I saw anything, the leaves were fully out, as if summer had been forever. Lang was dead, but the leaves were out. It was somebody else's summer, but it was summer.

I guess I wasn't much good after the telegram came. I

remember seeing a robin fly by the house once, carrying grass for a nest, and I remember counting fifty-one stripes on the wallpaper opposite my bed, and noticing a grease spot shaped like a heart over the kitchen stove. I remember voices coming and going, like voices in a play that didn't interest me.

MY MOTHER: She has no business staying here. She'd better come back to Boston.

MY FATHER: She will in time, my dear. Just give her time.

TIME (the owner of people and love and houses): Remember me, April? I came to foreclose.

MYSELF: Yes, I remember you, Time. I remember you well. You and I are old companions, old enemies.

MY MOTHER: Did you say something, April?

MYSELF: I don't know. Did I?

MARTY: Look. I got three frogs.

MY FATHER: Very nice frogs, Marty. Very nice frogs.

JILL: Very nice fogs, Marty. Very nice fogs.

REBECCA (when did she arrive?): Eat this, April. Drink this, April.

FRANK (Liz's husband): Here, Marty. Let me hold Jill.

JOEY: Why don't we have a baby, Mom?

LIZ: We're going to, Joey.

FAY (why was Fay there?): Don't forget the memorial service, sir.

MY FATHER: I think we'll wait, Fay.

MY MOTHER: Too many bad memories. Is the roast big enough, Fay?

FAY: It'll have to be, ma'am.

LIZ: Any word from Joseph, Rebecca?

REBECCA: Yes, I expect him home on leave this month.

MRS. PATTERSON: The peas are coming up. She'll want to know about the peas.

MR. PATTERSON (what brought him around?): That crab-apple tree of hers fell. The one that was all in bloom. The lightning hit it.

. .

I was upstairs.

"Take all three pills," said Rebecca, and handed me a glass of water.

I didn't go back to Boston with my parents. I stayed in New Hampshire that summer and passed the days as any grieving person passes the days: by getting up each morning and putting one foot in front of the other until night. Fortunately for me, Liz and Frank were always at hand . . . mainly because Liz (whose acceptance of rural living was predicated on the fact that she could whiz off somewhere whenever the atmosphere became too stifling and insular) didn't care to travel during the early stages of her pregnancy. And when she decided to go to Boston on a shopping trip in late October, she talked me into leaving Marty and Jill with her housekeeper and going with her. ("I mean, dear," she said, "don't you think it's about time you bought a few clothes and rejoined the human race?")

The trip would have been just a trip, except that while I was in Boston I met Jason—another visitor from out of town—and three months later I married Jason.

It wasn't as simple as that, of course. I didn't want to go to the cocktail party where I met him. And after I met him I didn't want him to take me home from the party, but he insisted, just as he insisted on spending every weekend in New Hampshire, once I returned to New Hampshire. And when he asked me to marry him a while later, I couldn't think what to answer, much as I was growing to depend on him, much as I enjoyed having him around.

"Do you love me?" he asked, and I told him I wasn't sure.

"Let me know when you decide," he said, and when I decided I didn't let him know, but he knew anyway. He also knew I was troubled about how Marty would react to a marriage that had now become a possibility. I wasn't troubled

257

about Jill; she could hardly wait for Jason's visits and clung to him whenever he appeared, but Marty was less demonstrative.

"It seems to me the two of you had better discuss this soon and openly," Jason said. But when I took Marty aside I couldn't make up my mind where to start. Knowing how she felt about Lang, I was afraid the idea of my remarrying would not only puzzle and upset her; it might even seem so callous and irrevocable a disloyalty that the resultant damage would permanently estrange us. Still, I had myself to consider, and I'd lived alone too long.

"I'm sorry, Marty," I said, "but I want to marry Jason."

"Why be sorry?" She used her Little Old Lady voice. "He's a good man, isn't he?"

"Yes, very good. Different from your father but not too different."

"Will he be for all of us or only for you?"

"For all of us." I tried to present the separate relationships in a way she'd find acceptable. "A husband for me, a father for Jill who's never had a father, and a friend for you."

"Oh." Marty didn't look at me. "You mean he won't be *my* father, then?"

"It's not necessary." I didn't want her to feel Jason was trying to usurp Lang's place. "You certainly don't need two fathers."

"No," said Marty. "Just one. I'd like just one."

"Then we'll leave it at that. Lang for your father and Jason for your friend," I told her, and that's how we left it. And when we returned to the room where Jason was sitting with one arm around Jill, Marty went over and leaned against his other arm, accepting him on approval, perhaps, but accepting him.

Jason tightened his arms around her and Jill.

"These are my girls," he said to me, "and we're going to live in Connecticut. We hope you'll join us."

I thought of Lang. I thought of putting the FOR SALE sign back on the maple. I thought of many things.

The late sun sloped across Jason's forehead, making a triangle of light on one temple. His eyes smiled but his eyes were serious.

"The war is over, Penelope," he said. "Ulysses didn't come back, but the war is over."

"Go run the tub, Marty." I stood up very straight. "You and Jill can take a bath together."

And when the children had gone upstairs, Jason said: "Come here." He said, "Come here," and I went to him.

Seven

THE LION
IN THE LEI SHOP

12

MARTY

I didn't know I hated my father until Uncle Bert was killed. I knew he acted badly enough before that—or anyhow, that's the way it seemed—always worrying Mother and leaving all the work and responsibility to her and me, and never taking care of any of us, like other fathers. But Uncle Bert's death was the last straw. Or the next to the last one.

I remembered the day we boarded the ship in Honolulu. I remembered my father calling to my aunt from the shore.

"I'll take care of him, Liz," he called. "I'll take care of Bert. That's a promise."

And what happened to the promise? Father went off to a place called New Zealand, and that was the end of Uncle Bert.

It was almost the end of Aunt Liz, too, the way she sat and sat and sat in the front bedroom and didn't care whether she lived or not. And Joey was like a stranger, perhaps because the circumstances were strange.

He didn't say much at first. When he arrived at our house wearing his favorite wartime hat—the red, white, and blue Uncle Sam one—Mother asked if he didn't want to toast marshmallows, but he didn't answer. All he did was give her a dirty look as she guided my aunt upstairs.

"That's a good hat," I told him. Actually the hat wasn't very good any more: it was pretty faded, and the little tinfoil stars on the crown were peeling at the edges, but I wanted to say something nice because of Uncle Bert.

I was wasting my time. Joey gave me an even worse look than he'd given Mother, and somehow it wasn't the look of the Joey I was used to, the Joey whose only claim to personality was being an ordinary seven-year-old boy. It wasn't the look of the talk-too-much-about-nothing Joey who was sometimes a passable playmate and sometimes a nuisance, but in either case nobody clever or unusual enough to be interesting.

I don't know what had changed about him, but something had. His eyes reminded me of Uncle Bert's eyes, although they lacked the quiet steadiness, and his jaw was square like Uncle Bert's jaw. Not as strong, maybe, but the same shape.

I guess I shouldn't have mentioned the hat, because when I did he took it off and began whacking it hard against his knee. Precisely and rhythmically. Over and over and over. He was still whacking it when I got back with the marshmallow forks.

"Jesus," he kept saying. "Jesus."

I wondered what kind of kids he'd been playing with in New York.

"Don't say 'Jesus,' Joey," I told him. That was all I told him but the way he carried on you'd have thought I spent all my time giving him orders.

"*Don't tell me what to say!*" he yelled, and he really yelled it. "*I'll say what I want to say.*" He stopped whacking his Uncle Sam hat and stared at it a second. Then for no reason at all—at least no reason I understood at the time—he heaved it into the fireplace, where the shiny brim and crown flared orange and purple before they turned black and fell into the blue ashes, with the little silver stars withering to brown and disappearing last.

"*I've had enough,*" he said, lowering his voice and sort of breathing through his teeth, like a person walking up a high hill.

I wanted to say I'd had enough myself, but I didn't.

Jill was getting too close to the fire.

"Sit on the floor, Jill," I told her, "and I'll fix you a good burned marshmallow as soon as Joey has his turn." I thought if I went on being nice to Joey he might start acting like his old self again.

"I don't want a turn!" Joey batted aside the fork I handed him. "I'm getting out of this place, and you'd better not come looking for me because you won't find me." He grabbed his jacket and slammed out the back door, which surprised me because Joey, for all his threats, was usually too timid or lazy to go anywhere alone.

I carried Jill up to Mother.

"I can't take care of two of them at once," I said.

"No, I suppose not." Mother reached for Jill in a distracted way and asked me to be sure and remind her to order the Thanksgiving turkey.

"Turkey." Aunt Liz spoke as if the word pained her. "Please let's not have turkey." She lay on top of the bedspread, still in her shoes, and dug her muddy heels into the chenille.

I finally found Joey. That is, Pearlette and I found him. He was sitting on a big rock way up back in the meadow whittling on a stick.

"Isn't your head cold?" I asked the question before I thought.

"Yeah, isn't it?" Pearlette had on a stocking cap and mittens.

Joey poked the sharp end of the stick about an inch from my nose.

265

"Mind your own P's and Q's," he told me and swung the stick toward Pearlette.

"Her, too," he said, "with her big mouth."

Joey gave up wearing hats that day. Not completely, of course, but to all intents and purposes. Now and then, when Aunt Liz insisted, he used to put one on for warmth, but he usually took it off as soon as her back was turned. And after he was grown up, he didn't even do that. He's over thirty now and we live in the same town, so I pretty much know his habits. Sometimes, in the rain or sleet or snow, he reverses his coat collar, and once or twice in bitter weather I've seen him in earmuffs. But I've never seen him in a hat.

We didn't have a Thanksgiving turkey, though everyone else did. Pearlette had a turkey. I know because we did the wishbone together.

"I suppose you'll wish for that dumb old father of yours to come home," she said, and that's what I did wish, but only for Mother. And, though I won the wishbone, I might as well have lost, because my father got killed, anyhow.

Pearlette wasn't surprised when she heard the news, and I don't think I was, really. Aside from the damage it did to Mother, I can't honestly say I was upset by my father's death. I mean he was my father and Jill's father, but by then he didn't matter any more to me than he did to Jill.

"Father," she used to say when she first learned the word. "Father," she'd say, following any man anywhere. "Is that my father?"

It was embarrassing.

Right before Father's death, I tried to tell her about him, hoping she'd hush up.

"He's this man like Pearlette's father," I said, which he might have been for all I knew by then, except that Pearlette's father had kind of tannish hair and it seemed to me my father's hair was black.

266

"He's this man," I said, "this soldier who's married to Mother." I wondered how to tell her what a soldier was. "This man," I said, "who keeps going on and on across the sea, which worries Mother because people shoot at him all the time. That's why she has those lines in her face, and her arms and legs are so skinny and she stays up half the night.

"She didn't always look like that," I said. "She used to be pretty once." I couldn't remember how she looked when she was pretty; all I could remember was the fact itself. "A pretty, pretty mommy," I said, and Jill repeated "Pretty mommy" as though the fact were still true, because she was little and didn't know any better. If she'd known better she never would have said it.

At least she never would have said it then, while Father was alive, though she might have said it later after Mother got over her bad spell and went back to wearing dresses and looking decent again. That was when she met Jason and he began coming to see her.

"Father," Jill said the first time he came, and I slapped her.

"That's Jason," I said. "He likes Mother."

"He likes me, too," said Jill, with the easy trust of her three and a half years, the trust that didn't change on Jason's next visit or his next. Or ever, for that matter.

"I think he might *get* to be my father," she said one day. "That would be nice."

"Why?" I enjoyed Jason as much as she did, but I was more cautious about trust.

"It's those songs he sings to me in bed," she answered. "And those gumdrops he always brings. Who else brings gumdrops?"

I couldn't think of anyone.

"Or has those arms that swing you so you laugh? I never got swung like that before he came," she said, and I realized she hadn't. Not even by Uncle Frank, who married Aunt Liz. Uncle Frank was friendly enough, but he didn't swing people.

"And he isn't a soldier." Jill, a listener, never forgot anything. "He isn't always away somewhere like that father you used to have."

"*My* father!" I said. "He was *your* father, too."

"Not mine. I never saw him." Jill's logic wasn't adult logic, or even my logic, but it had a reasonableness to it.

"I like someone who stays around," she said, as if I didn't feel the same way, as if the simplicity of her personal requirements guaranteed their fulfillment.

Her innocence irritated me almost as much as her possessiveness.

"The reason Jason never went anywhere," I said, using the past tense because the war was over by then, "wasn't on account of something he decided. He couldn't go to war on account of his leg."

"Good." She acted as though my explanation proved rather than disproved some point of hers. "What leg?" she asked.

"The one he got from polio when he was little. The short one."

"Short one?" It wasn't really a question. "I never saw any short one." She took a squashed gumdrop out of her pocket.

"Both of his legs seem tall to me," she said.

Pearlette didn't see Jason the first four or five times he came around, because she was sick with chicken pox and then measles and had to stay home. But I told her quite a bit about him over the phone.

I also told Jason about Pearlette, about her questions and way of looking at things, and one day in October, when she finally got out of quarantine, the two of them met. Pearlette was carrying one of her cats, a gray one with a white streak under its chin.

"Do you like cats?" She looked Jason over.

"Yes, I like cats." Jason looked back. "What's your name?" He knew her name.

"Pearlette."

"Where do you live?" Jason knew that, too.

"Across the road."

"In the gray house?"

"Mostly gray. All except for . . ."

"The red blinds?" asked Jason, and Pearlette nodded.

"Do you ever use that pump in the yard?" he asked.

"Not any more. Why?" Pearlette said the "why" fast, but Jason ignored it. He didn't care about her pump.

"I'm about to take Marty away," he said. "You won't mind too much, will you?"

"Yes, I will." She narrowed her little goldy eyes into slits, and I had a feeling she was going to ask, "Who are *you* to take Marty away?" but she didn't get a chance.

"We're all going to live in Connecticut," said Jason. "I'm sure Marty's going to like it there." He took out his watch.

"Five o'clock," he said. "Hadn't you better get along home now, Pearlette? Your dinner must be ready." He didn't say it in a mean way—he even put his arm around her shoulder as he said it—and when Pearlette looked up at him and answered, "Yes," she didn't do it in a mean way, either—just disappointed that I was going, and she'd probably never have another friend like me to listen to her questions.

Jill and I stayed with Joey and Aunt Liz and Uncle Frank and their new baby while Jason and Mother went on their honeymoon.

"Is a honeymoon where you get honey?" Jill asked Jason.

"I'll let you know when I get back," he answered, and when he came back he brought two jars of honey, one for me and one for Jill.

After Jill ate hers, she used to carry the empty jar around with her, even when we moved to Connecticut.

"Father's honey," she'd say, and I'd tell her, "No; Jason's honey," because hearing her call Jason "Father" was getting on my nerves.

It got on my nerves the most the spring day I left her alone in the bird's nest.

269

There was a crab apple tree in our yard, right near the swimming pool, and Jill was always climbing up onto the lower branches, pretending she was a baby bird, so I finally made her a nest out of an old inner tube and stuffed it with grass to make it look real. Sometimes, to please her, I'd get into the nest with her and sit there while she flapped her elbows and said "cheep, cheep," the way a baby bird does.

I got pretty tired of it, hearing her say "cheep, cheep," hour after hour, especially that one afternoon when she kept calling Jason "Father" every two minutes along with everything else. So when Jason came home from his law office I jumped down and ran to meet him, forgetting all about Jill, and she climbed out of her nest and fell into the swimming pool. She didn't drown—just got a little wet—because Jason heard the splash and rescued her almost as soon as she fell. But Mother had a fit.

"My God, Marty." Mother was shaking. "How could you have been so negligent? How could you have been so careless with Jill?"

I'd had enough of Jill.

"She's *your* child, not mine!" I said. "*She's* the one who always wants to be a baby bird. *I* don't." I was shaking, too.

"She's the one who has a father," I said. "*I* don't." I was pretty mad.

Jason handed Jill to Mother.

"Marty and I are going for a walk," he said. "We'll be back." And we walked in some nearby little woods that seemed big then. We didn't talk much, though once or twice Jason pointed out things in or under trees.

"I'm meant to be a big girl," I said.

"You're a little girl," he answered. "Jill's littler, but you're a little girl."

"Am I?" Suddenly I was young as my friends were young, free as my friends were free.

"Yes, you're a little girl," said Jason, "and it's all right."

"I've been trying to figure out that remark you made about not having a father." Mother waited a few weeks before she brought the subject up. "You know you have a father. He may be dead, but he's still your father."

We were sitting by the swimming pool in the spring sunset and everything about the evening had been relaxed and pleasant until then.

"You're getting to look like him," she said. "Your hair is turning dark and so are your eyes." She watched me splashing my feet in the pool.

"You sit like him, too," she added.

"I don't want to hear about my father!" I said. "I don't want to hear about him! *I DON'T WANT TO HEAR ABOUT HIM!*"

The shouting surprised both of us.

Mother stubbed out her cigarette in the ashtray on her chair arm. She twisted it round and round and round, long after the red coal blackened and fell apart.

"What's wrong with you, Marty?" She was shocked, but she was also puzzled. "What's come over you all of a sudden? Why don't you want to hear about your father?" Her fingers were soiled from the cigarette ash and she wiped them on the grass.

"Shut up about my father!" I said. I knew I was being heartless as well as rude, but I said it anyhow. "I hate my father! I'll always hate him!"

My mother killed a mosquito on her knee.

"It isn't your father you'll always hate," she told me as she brushed the mosquito away. "It's the war."

"It's my father." It troubled me to see I was hurting her, so I became defensive. "I guess I ought to know," I said.

Mother gazed at the sun slipping like a shined penny into a slot between the mountains.

"Try to be fair," she said to me or the sun. "Think back.

Can't you remember your father when you were a little girl? Can't you remember about his Spring Song? Can't you remember how he used to build you castles in the sand?"

"No, I can't remember," I said.

The sun was gone, so Mother stopped looking at the sky. She lowered her gaze to watch a robin moving across the lawn; Hop, hop, hop; stop. Hop, hop, hop; stop. She had no great interest in birds, but she concentrated on the robin.

"I didn't think you'd ever forget," she said and her old sorrow began making its wall between us.

"Never mind," I said, because I'd had enough of the sorrow, and I'd had enough of walls.

Mother opened her mouth to say something else.

"Never mind!" I repeated.

I must have been nine years old then. Or ten. I don't know. All I know is I dreamed about the lion again that night. I dreamed about him off and on for another year or two.

The next to the last time was when I'd gotten a prize at school for an essay on war, and though I should have been happy about the prize, that night I dreamed and screamed again. Once more I was on the deck of a ship, a railed and rocking platform that seemed higher than smokestacks, higher than planes or birds, yet still on a level with the flat and blue and endless ocean. I was dressed in my same yellow pinafore, the one with the white forget-me-nots and the cigarette burn on the hem of the skirt and, as usual, I was crying. Far below the deck, at the bottom of some steps that slanted downward and outward from where I was standing, a man was smiling up at me, and I knew he was my father—the way you do in dreams—although I couldn't see his face.

—"Father," said Jill. "Is that my father?"

My mother was waving and calling and Aunt Liz and all the other women were waving and calling, too.

—"Bert," Aunt Liz called. "Take care of yourself, Bert."

In the thicket of calling, waving women, I was as dwarfed as a lantana flower under the mango trees, existing hardy but hidden below their branchlike arms, unable to see either over or out. Yet I saw my father and I saw the steps. And the steps were moving away.

—"Oh, you mean the gangplank," said Mother. "Those aren't steps."

As she spoke, the dream changed, and I found myself running, running, running, toward a blue emptiness that might have been ocean and might have been sky. As I ran, the deck swayed under me, and I stopped and reached for the handrail. But when I tried to steady myself, the rail turned into a strand of barbed wire, and I clamped my lips together so I wouldn't scream. Because I knew where I was. Even before I looked, I knew where I was. I was outside the little locked house where the lion lived.

—"He likes little girls," said Willard. "Girls with curly red hair. Like yours."

—"*Green!*" said Pearlette. "I'm glad you finally told me something *real*. Doesn't it seem to you like the door is moving?"

"No, no!" I cried in the dream. "No-no-no-no-no!" and I was still crying the word aloud when I woke up sobbing.

My mother wasn't standing by my bed. Jason was.

"Hush, Marty." He sat down beside me and held my hands. He held them a long time. Then he said: "Why all these nightmares?" and I told him about the bombs and the barbed wire and the trenches and the ship.

"But the war's over," said Jason. "The ship is just an ordinary ship again, and the trenches are gone and so is the barbed wire."

"But the lion hasn't gone!" For the first time I grew reckless. "The lion won't ever go! He's still waiting in the lei shop. He'll always be waiting in the lei shop, waiting there with his eye to the crack in the wall, waiting to spring out and catch anyone who happens by."

"What lion?" Jason asked, and I answered. "The same lion. The green one."

Jason was silent a while. Then he said: "Suppose you tell me about the lion. Suppose you tell me about everything."

"But it's a secret. Even the part about my father is a secret." I don't know why I thought of that.

"Sometimes a secret can be too much for one person to handle." Jason turned my pillow over. "You can trust me," he said.

So I did what he asked. I told him everything. I told him although it took me until dawn to do it. And when I got through I knew he hadn't missed a word.

"I think we'd better discuss these things one at a time," he decided and smoothed my blanket.

"First," he said, "*there isn't any lion*. There never was a lion."

"But Willard said . . ."

"And who was Willard?" Jason did his best to be fair. "An unloved child with no heart and too much imagination, who confused a helpless little girl by putting an improbable animal into an empty harmless building meant for selling flowers."

"And what about my father? Why, when I hate him so much, does he always have to be in the dreams?"

"I was coming to that." Jason went on to tell me what a fine man my father had been, how many people he had cared for, how many medals he'd won because of the caring.

"But he didn't care for us or Uncle Bert, and Mother put the medals away in a drawer." I'd seen her do it.

"That's because she didn't need the medals to know what kind of man your father was." He explained why my father was in New Zealand when Uncle Bert died, how he wanted to help everyone but couldn't.

"Including you," said Jason, "which—in the long run—he did, though he realized he had to cut you off from unreality in order to do it. I don't mean he foresaw your hating him— that was the last thing in the world he wanted—but perhaps if he had foreseen and weighed the possibility, he would have accepted even that. Because it may have taken your hate to make you overcome the things you couldn't have overcome through love. It may have taken your hate to make you move away from the past and leave him in it."

The darkness was turning into semidarkness and, outside, the birds were starting to murmur together.

"For you see," said Jason, "your father knew that to live in a wish dream is often to die in a wish dream, with no one able to get at you, no one able to bring you out of the dream. No one," he said, "able to keep you from expecting your father one day to stride through the door; no one able to teach you the difference between what's true and what isn't true." He pointed a forefinger into the air and curved it down around my chin.

"Do you understand what I'm saying, Marty?" he asked.

"Not entirely," I answered, "but I believe you, Father."

"Good." When he tiptoed out of the room in the growing light, the birds weren't just murmuring; they were wide awake and singing in the trees. . . . And seeing the light and hearing the birds, I could suddenly remember how it all was in the beginning, how it all was when the skies were wide and untroubled over the white beach at Wianae. I could remember how my mother used to lie curled like a kitten on her straw mat while Sharkbait—who was killed on Leyte—swam beyond the other swimmers out to sea. I could remember how my father and I rode the blue breakers together and afterward built castles in the sand, with lots of little moats around them to let the water in. I could even remember the lei shop the way it was before the air raid, and—with the new day—the little locked building became a flower shop again, and the two big happy Hawaiian women went back to their wooden benches in front of the open door and began stringing blossoms into necklaces once more in the morning sun.

I'm not positive when I had the last dream about the lion. It may have been a week later. It may have been a month. I dreamed the lion was stretched out on the lawn near our

275

swimming pool, where my new father and Jill were swimming, that he was lying there with his green paws on the green grass and his green eyes half-closed. And when I walked up to him and said, "You don't exist," he opened his green mouth and yawned.

My first father was standing beside the lion, and I recognized his face.

"Do you mind about my new father?" I asked him.

"No, I don't mind. That's the way things ought to be." He leaned over and scratched the lion's head. "You're very lucky to have a father like that. How's school?"

"Fine." I told him about the prize I'd gotten for my essay.

"I'm not surprised." He watched Jill swimming. "That's a nice little sister you have. I wish I'd known her."

"Yes, she's okay now that she's not a baby bird any more. I got sick of her when she was a baby bird all the time."

"Baby bird," my father said and laughed. "Baby bird," he said and vanished. I say he vanished. Actually he only vanished for a minute, then came back.

"I forgot the lion," he said, and the lion got up and nuzzled his leg.

And my father put a rope around the lion's neck, although I don't believe he needed to, and the two of them went off together, with my father striding his usual unstriding stride into the gray distance, while the lion ambled along beside him gracefully, politely, docilely . . . growing smaller and smaller and smaller until he wasn't even the size of one of Pearlette's cats.